Melinda West and the Gremlin Queen

Praise for *Melinda West and the Gremlin Queen*

"Melinda West is back, a little weary and battle-worn, but ready to answer the call when a terrifying flock of gremlins threatens all of human civilization…KC Grifant ups the action and the stakes in this twisty, thrilling sequel."
  –Christina Henry, author of *Alice* and *The House That Horror Built*

"Exciting action, compelling characters AND monsters make *Melinda West and the Gremlin Queen* a tale not to be missed. It's such a treat to revisit this rich world."
  –Kate Jonez, *Omnium Gatherum*

"If you're looking for a fun, fast-paced, dusty, western-magic-horror mashup, look no further. Melinda West is a phenomenal character, this world and landscape is perfectly balanced between being accessible and absolutely terrifying."
  –Steve Stred, award-winning author of *Mastodon, Father of Lies &* *Churn the Soil*

"It's a rip-roarin', bronco-buckin' ride through demon hordes, dust storms, and deception before it cranks up another dark notch into the explosive ending. Every buck of that horse is worth the ride."
  –Ef Deal, author of *The Twins of Bellesfées* series

"KC Grifant has artfully drawn a reluctant heroine grappling with a tortured past and tasked her with a seemingly impossible mission. The journey forward is as arduous as the terrain it covers, and as kinetic and fast-paced as a galloping horse."
  –Caroline Dipping, author of *Baker's Dozen*

"Badass! That's how I felt about the first book in this series and that continues in this one. A take-no-prisoners horror western with monsters galore and fantastic characters."
  –*Horror Reads*

Praise for Book 1
Melinda West: Monster Gunslinger

"Great fun. Briskly written and full of surprises. KC Grifant has it cooking."
  —Joe Lansdale, author of the *Hap and Leonard* series and *Dead in the West*

"KC Grifant comes out guns blazing with Melinda West: Monster Gunslinger—a devious action-packed adventure set in a very weird version of the Old West. Fast, furious, and a hell of a lot of fun!"
  —Jonathan Maberry, *NY Times* bestselling author of *Son of the Poison Rose* and *Relentless*

"Grifant takes her time building the world and its characters, imbuing all with a complexity that adds depth to this wildly entertaining story. This fun, imaginative, and confident series opener will be a massive crowd pleaser for general audiences."
  —*Library Journal*

"KC Grifant's horror western hits the road at top speed and never takes its foot off the accelerator, making the book a perfect fit for readers who like their horror weird and their action plentiful … [Melinda West] is a delicious amalgamation of Ash Williams in wise-cracking bravado and Ellen Ripley in triumphant fearlessness."
  —*Ginger Nuts of Horror*

"Imagine *Supernatural* combined with the most badass female lead you can imagine, amazing supporting characters, nail-biting suspense, great action, and the grunge and grit you expect in a Western."
  —Tasha Reynolds, horror reviewer and host of *The Ghoulish Gallery*

MELINDA WEST AND THE GREMLIN QUEEN

BY KC GRIFANT

Collection

Shrouded Horror: Tales of the Uncanny
(Dragon's Roost Press, 2024)

Anthologies

Editor, *Women of the Weird West*
(Brigids Gate Press, 2026)

Co-editor, *Dread Coast: SoCal Horror Tales*
(No Bad Books Press, 2025)

Co-editor, *Of Terrors and Tombstones*
(Stars and Sabers, 2027)

Edited by S.D. Vassallo

Formatted by Stephanie Ellis

Cover illustration and design by Luke Spooner
https://carrionhouse.com/

Map illustration by Becky Appleyard

First Edition: May 2025

ISBN (paperback): 978-1-963355-27-7
ISBN (ebook): 978-1-963355-26-0
Library of Congress Control Number: 2025935280

BRIGIDS GATE PRESS
Overland Park, Kansas
www.brigidsgatepress.com
Printed in the United States of America

To everyone who recognizes evil in the world and tries to fight it.

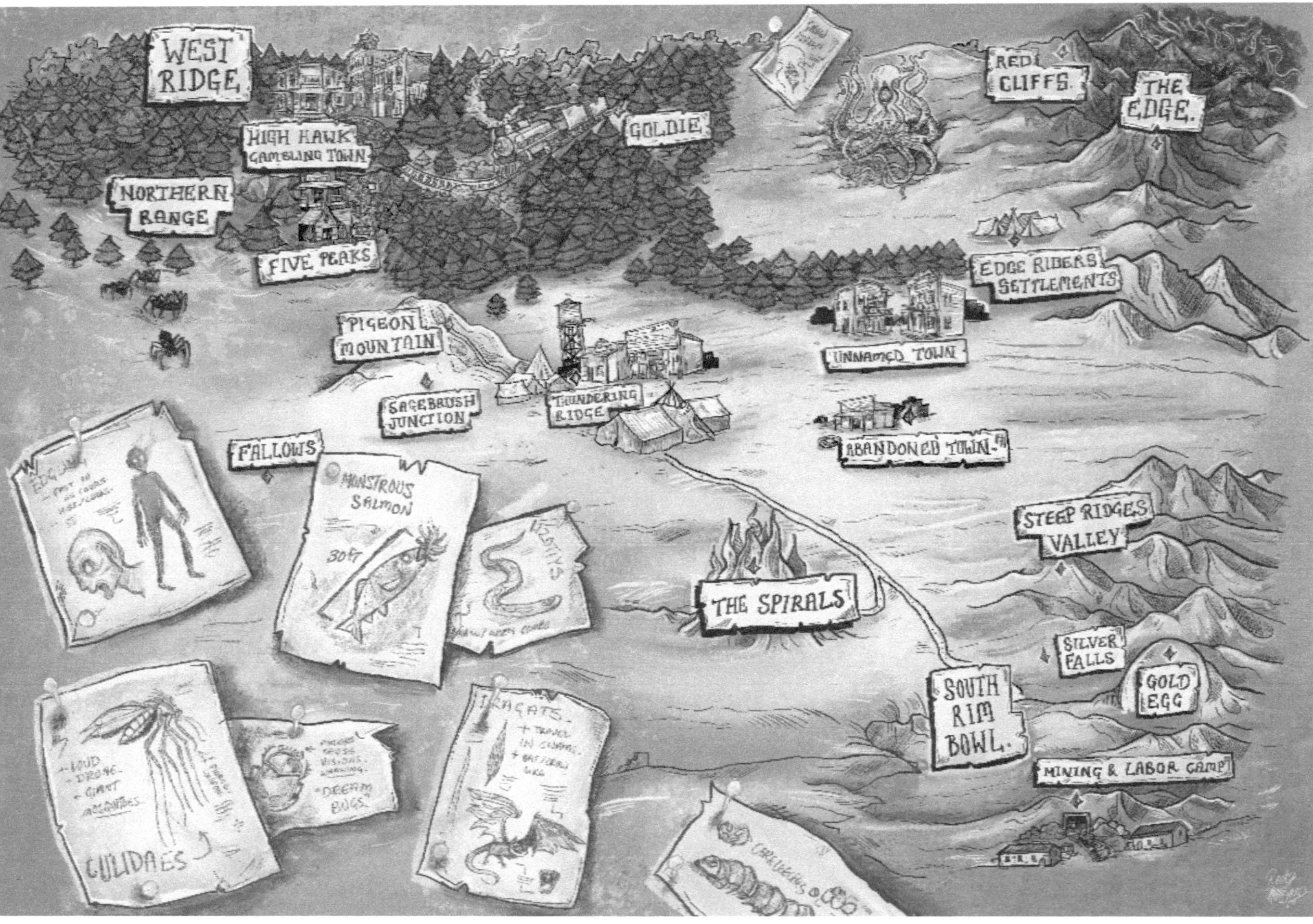

WEST RIDGE.
NORTHERN RANGE
HIGH HAWK GAMBLING TOWN
FIVE PEAKS
GOLDIE.
RED CLIFFS
THE EDGE.
PIGEON MOUNTAIN
SAGEBRUSH JUNCTION
THUNDERING RIDGE
UNNAMED TOWN
EDGE RIDERS SETTLEMENTS
ABANDONED TOWN.
FALLOWS
MONSTROUS SALMON
3047
THE SPIRALS
STEEP RIDGES VALLEY
SILVER FALLS
GOLD EGG
SOUTH RIM BOWL.
MINING & LABOR CAMP
CULIDAES
DREAM BUGS

CHAPTER ONE

Melinda was carrying well water to the trough in the barn and nudging back Cherry, one of the pudgier pigs, when she felt a cold, telltale prickle along the back of her neck.

Everything else seemed normal as pie: the last of the afternoon sun streaking into the barn, the floating motes of dust, the occasional *moo* from the field where Lance was supposedly getting the cattle penned, the distant clanks of the new town hall being repaired.

Despite the run-of-the-mill happenings, something was most definitely not right. Even though she was nearly a year retired from the monster hunting business, the senses she had honed in her 30 years kicked in as she refilled the trough.

Someone—*something*—was watching her.

She made sure not to change the speed of her pouring, using her other hand to push a long strand of her dark hair back under her wide-brimmed hat. She had been through too much not to be within a few feet of a gun, even on their ranch.

She started whistling a tune that she and Lance used to discreetly communicate a problem, and gave Cherry a pat.

"Well girl, settle in now," Melinda murmured and picked up the six-shooter resting a few feet away on their worktable.

She stepped outside, keeping her pace steady as she curled around the barn until the modest-sized field came into view. The pair of heifers were in the corner, and instead of tending to the animals, she spotted Lance's sandy hair and boots peeking out from a hammock under a cluster of oak trees in another corner. That wasn't unusual; what was unusual was that he seemed to be absorbed in a leatherbound book, rubbing the scruff on his chin thoughtfully. He'd never been much for reading, but lately he'd been poring through old texts and histories that he'd never taken an interest in before. Ever since they lost their mentor, Abel, a year ago, he was intent on studying Abel's textbooks, maybe, Melinda figured, as a way to grieve for his friend.

Normally, she'd roll her eyes and list all the things that had to get done before he convinced her to take a break and enjoy the long summer nights.

Instead, she kept whistling the tune and walked casually to the well as her skin tingled, a foreboding feeling looming like a summer thunderstorm. Lance glanced up, blinking out of his concentration to smile at her. She whistled more insistently, and his smile dropped away. His lanky form went upright, boots immediately on the grass.

Too late—a shadow half the size of a human barreled forward, like someone tossed a cup of ink at her. She threw herself out of the way as a rush of air colder than a mountain wind in January swept by.

The shadowy figure scurried like a fleeing child one second, then moved smoothly like a herding dog the next, a disjointed mass of movement that made her eyes hurt. Now it perched on the top of the fence, its blurred gray face cocked but staring straight at her.

An Edgling.

If it was solid, it'd look like it was made of a bundle of sticks come to life and dyed slate and obsidian, but its limbs flowed too freely. This was a big one. But no matter, she'd take care of this shadow creature like she took care of others when she had to venture into the monsters' territory where few humans returned— the Edge, an opening between the human world and monster world nestled in the Northern Ridge Mountain Range.

"Thought I had exterminated you suckers," Melinda muttered. From the corner of her eye, she could see Lance scrambling to get a weapon. The Edglings fed off insecurities and evoked in her mind a vision of her late mother's face, lifeless after a monster infection, along with a memory of Abel's pale expression after a demon had stolen his soul.

Melinda blinked both away and pointed her six-shooter at the Edgling. "Well, say howdy to your siblings."

She went to shoot, but the field and sky darkened as though a shroud had been thrown over her head. Just one of the many tricks the shadow creatures had. Melinda gritted her teeth, hearing the shadow creature's whispers start up:

"Killer. Murderer."

"Melinda!" Lance's voice called to her through the veil.

"I got a clean shot!" She called back, feeling for her revolver's trigger in the gray mist. The Edgling turned, mimicking Melinda's own maneuver a second earlier, even mock adjusting an invisible hat.

"Your fault, your fault," the Edgling whispered. A sudden surge of guilt hit her with everything she had ever felt bad about—the friends they had lost along the way while monster hunting, the missions they failed, her momma's demise. But that was an Edgling's specialty: regret. She bade back the feelings of shame and whirled after the creature as it jumped. A cold rustle rushed past her ears and she shifted her pistol.

She aimed at the Edgling's torso with the familiar satisfaction of eliminating a monster. It was like stomping out a stubborn cockroach nest—one less evil pest in this world.

And she never missed.

"Melinda, stop!" Lance's panicked shout gave her pause.

Instead of the Edgling, Lance's face materialized through the gray mist, alarmed.

And two inches from her revolver.

"Stop," he said again, and she felt his hands push the six-shooter down.

The shroud blocking her vision dropped away just as quickly, the world snapping back into place—the sky streaked with pink and orange, the far-off *moos*.

"The Edgling was right there..." she trailed off. Lance gripped her shoulders, the warmth of his hands bringing her back to herself, and she realized what she had actually seen.

A hallucination.

Another one.

"It was…so real," she muttered. "Worst one yet."

"It's all right," he said simply but that didn't stop the flush of confusion and worse—shame—heating her cheeks.

"It's not," she said. "I almost shot you."

The shadow flitted again at the corner of her vision. Lance gripped her free hand. She focused on the pressure of his fingers and the shadow faded.

"But you didn't." Even though he was easygoing as she was taciturn, he had grown quicker to worry, his eyes a little more guarded after their time monster hunting. "You peachy? It's been a while since you've had a spell like that."

"Dandy." She slumped, tension still in her shoulders and neck, the memories from all the creatures they had fought knotted into her muscles. She willed herself to relax. "Every time I think I'm over it, something happens again."

"We've only been retired for a year. Reckon it'll take longer for us to recover from what we've been through. What you've been through." His face was more laced with worry lines than when she first met him a few years ago in their little town of Five Peaks. In those years they had been through a lifetime together as they roamed the east and north lands, exterminating Edge monsters for substantial fees. Both of them had plenty of scars to show for it. But his real scars, like hers, were deeper than surface level. Ever since part of his soul was sucked out last year along with Abel's, he hadn't been the same. His soul had been restored. Abel's hadn't.

Even so, Lance seemed to get wearier easily, his eyes more haunted. Maybe it was grief or age catching up with them. Hard to say.

He studied her for a second before frowning. "You've been seeing more visions lately. You *need* to tell me when it happens," Lance chided.

"Sometimes, just at night," Melinda said. "That's *exactly* why I don't tell you. Dreams, that's all. Not anything to fret about."

"It *is* something to fret about," Lance said, getting that rare stubborn tilt to his chin. He pulled out some strands of tobacco and placed them into a rolling paper, frowning. "You have to let go of those nightmares, and your obsession with monster killing. We did our part," he said more gently.

"I feel OK now, really I do," Melinda said. "It must've been from insomnia. Do me a favor and don't rat me out to Aunt B. She won't be pleased."

"She's got something else she'll be madder about." Lance said, quickly lighting his cigarette.

"What's that?"

"We're gonna be late for dinner."

Melinda hastily changed, swapping her work pants for cotton trousers and a button-up. Lance traded one plaid shirt for another and his nicer calfskin boots. They donned their hats—Melinda's a newer crisp brown wide-brimmed one and Lance's with a braided leather band—and filled a satchel of lemons from the tree. They rode their horses, Pepper and Mud, at a brisk trot down Second Street in the town they had made home. Those who weren't always welcome elsewhere seemed to find some respite at Five Peaks. The first families who settled there decades ago years ago had claimed it a place where any decent folk would be welcome, no matter what they looked like or where they came from.

It was where she and Lance had found each other. Both fresh off their hurts from losing family members, they had found their way to Five Peaks—her coming to live with Aunt B after losing her momma to the monster infection and Lance, recently orphaned, gone to work for a sympathetic Abel.

They waved at John and Jack—Jack's albino skin nearly glowing in the sunlight—who were working on fixing their front porch. Next door was Miss Patti, who came to Five Peaks years ago so she could live alone in peace. They tipped their hats at the Miller kid, not really a kid anymore, as he worked on one of his metal-and-wood sculptures on the porch.

A hot wind came down to their valley from the rolling mountains to the north, which had grown brown from the long, dry summer. The branches of the oaks overhead swayed as two children darted by them in close pursuit of an energetic chicken. Melinda tried to let the sound of the town and the wind through the branches soothe her, but she couldn't shake the uneasiness in her gut.

Maybe I can't trust my gut anymore.

Her thoughts soured at that. Maybe the monster hunting had been too much, and she'd never recover, maybe she'd always be on the brink of losing her sense of what was what, maybe she'd always be seeing things that weren't there—

Don't think that way. Everything's aces, she reminded herself, channeling a little of Lance. She breathed in the smell of sawdust, livestock, and dried grass and tried to shake off her jitters.

Aunt B's place sat amidst a dozen or so log homes on the other side of Five Peaks, a stone's throw from the birch windmill that marked the town's entrance. They approached the wooden structure, where overgrown flowers and bursting vegetables led from the house to a modest stream. Outside, an unfamiliar horse stood in a sheen of sweat and Melinda's uneasiness intensified. She rubbed her cheeks, trying to snap out of it so she wouldn't worry her aunt.

They paused, as they always did, at the memorial in the corner of the yard. Though there had been no body, a wooden sign carefully calligraphed with "Abel Yao, beloved friend" was always adorned with fresh flowers. He, along with Aunt B, had taught Lance and Melinda practically everything they knew about monster hunting.

Wish I could've saved you, Melinda thought, as she always did, when they spotted his name.

"You raised me like my pa couldn't," Lance said quietly to the sign as they neared. "Miss you every day, Abel." He gave a shuddery sigh and Melinda touched his shoulder.

"I just thought I would feel something when he passed," Lance said. "A sign from him. *Something.*"

"I didn't feel anything for a long time when Momma passed," Melinda said. "But once in a while, something catches me unexpected, and I get the feeling she's right there. But the grief keeps on gnawing."

They turned as Aunt B threw open the door.

"Thank goodness you're here!" Roughly twice Melinda's age, Aunt B's bun glinted black and silver against her perpetually sunburnt freckled face.

"Hi Aunt B." Melinda breathed in the scent of beans and beef escaping through the door and handed her the sack of fresh lemons. "Peace offering for being late." Melinda braced for the usual barrage of questions about what they had eaten that day, what they were reading, when they were going to get married.

"Chili's better the longer it sits, isn't that right?" Lance said hopefully.

"I'm glad you're here, and not just for dinner." Aunt B's sage green cotton skirt swept against the steps while she talked in her rapid-fire way. They moved into the sitting room, where doilies hung crooked from furniture piled high with books and bundles of notes tied with twine. Her place, it seemed, had gotten messier since Abel passed. They had been close friends, and Abel had been as neat as Aunt B was messy. That influence wore off quickly, it seemed. But Aunt B's usual chattiness had a more frenzied air than usual.

"You're jumpier than a long-tailed cat under a rocking chair," Melinda said. "What's going on?"

"Town of Fallows," Aunt B said. "They sent word for help. For you."

"For us? We're retired," Melinda said, ignoring the sensation of her heart sinking into her boots.

Aunt B shook her head. "This sounds bad. Several dead from a mysterious attack."

"We've done enough," Melinda protested. "If we keep going anytime someone calls with some monster situation, we'll never be finished. Is that what you want? Us out there, taking care of other towns' problems forever?"

"This is different," Aunt B said as she poured hot water from a kettle into a large teacup.

"It's always different." Melinda shooed away the feeling of sinking in quicksand. Why was Aunt B bringing this up with them? They were done monster hunting, for good. "After everything we went through last year. We lost Abel, nearly lost Lance—" Melinda stopped, her words curdling on her tongue like sour milk.

Lance chewed his lip, looking pained and Aunt B's eyes were bright at the mention of Abel's name. Guilt immediately shot through Melinda. Well, what did Aunt B expect? That they'd drop everything every time someone needed help?

"Maybe someone else can do it," Lance squeezed her hand. "Like Mellie said, we're officially retired, after all."

"They've been trying with no luck," Aunt B said quietly. "According to the rider."

"Rider?"

They turned as a woman who looked to be older than Melinda but younger than Aunt B, maybe 40 or so, strode in from the direction of the outhouse. Her dark face glistened with sweat, and she moved with the stiffness of someone who had ridden for too long. Purple scarves wound around her neck over a linen blouse covered in dust.

"This is Priya Bedi," Aunt B introduced, handing the woman a cup of tea. "Meet Melinda West and Lance Putnam."

Priya smoothed back her tousled, chin-length black hair and her glazed eyes seemed to brighten. "You are the experts on mysterious happenings?"

"We're retir—" Melinda began.

"Please," Priya said hoarsely. Her voice was scratchy as if she had been shouting all day. That, along with a way of pronouncing words uncommon around these parts, took Melinda's ears a second to follow what she was saying. "Please, we need your help."

"Tell them," Aunt B urged.

"People are turning up dead. It is like nothing we have ever seen," Priya paused as if holding herself back from tears. "The town is panicking."

"From what you told me before, it sounds like it could be a sickness associated with the Edge," Aunt B said slowly, glancing down at one of the open books. "Mainly due to the color. Veins that give off a white-blue light. But I can't identify the source."

"How can it be?" Priya wavered on her feet and Aunt B gestured to her cup of tea encouragingly.

"We don't really know how monsters spread infection. Suspect it's like some animals—fleas, rabies, like that." Lance chimed in, rolling a cigarette. "It's rare for them to affect humans."

"We only know of two monster species that confer fatal infections. A centipede type and—" Aunt B shot an apologetic look at Melinda. "A slug species."

Melinda merely nodded, blinking away the memory of the speckled, rotting flesh of her momma before she passed. Melinda had been 17 when they encountered the rare slug. Most of the monster slug infections were mild, clearing up for whatever reason. But her momma had succumbed, getting worse until she died, just a few weeks after the exposure. Melinda had urgently gone from house to house looking for a remedy to see if anyone knew what to do while her mother's body slowly rotted, to no avail.

"You see either of those creatures? Or any Edge bugs?" Melinda said, more brusquely than she meant to. Priya shook her head.

"Could be a plant, potentially," Aunt B murmured. "Flora, fungi."

"Tell us everything," Lance said to Priya.

"We found one body a few weeks ago. It was unusual." Priya's voice cracked before she continued. "He had been perfectly healthy before. But then two deaths last week. Three on Monday, one elderly. Two more this morning. It is getting worse. The doctor doesn't know what to do. The bodies, they fall into themselves. They glow. They have a smell like nothing we have encountered." Priya pressed her eyes shut. By the way Aunt B held herself very still, Melinda knew what she'd say next wouldn't be good. "People are scared. They burned all the food. Bodies. They do not want people going out. I do not know what they may burn next. I am worried… it will get worse." She buried her face in her hands. "Excuse me."

Melinda sucked in a breath as Lance cursed quietly. As Aunt B coaxed Priya to drink more tea, Lance and Melinda stood by the window to talk.

"We don't know for sure if this has anything to do with an Edge monster," Melinda said.

"Don't see how we can't offer our help," Lance murmured.

"What about us? Our plans?" Melinda said and he looked pained. She didn't mean children, but the peace they always talked about, the *settling down* that always seemed to evade them. "Monster hunting isn't supposed to be our lives forever."

"I just don't know how we can live with ourselves if we don't try to help," Lance replied. "People act foolish when they panic.

And it's a straightforward job. Calm people down. Check for any Edge creatures. Kill 'em."

She could feel Aunt B's keen eyes on them. Everything in Melinda screamed *no*, but something deeper, something at her center, knew with resignation she had to.

It's your fate, a small voice seemed to whisper. *You can never escape.*

"That settles it then," Melinda said. Beneath the reluctance an older feeling bubbled up, one she hadn't felt in a while and didn't quite know how to name – a focus, a determination to take care of a messy problem and the grim satisfaction that followed. "We'll figure out what's causing the deaths."

Aunt B looked both relieved and pained. "I already packed bags for you with the best of Abel's arsenal. Have some chili, *quickly*, and we'll get you on your way."

Melinda glanced briskly toward the rider. "Anything else you can tell us before we head out?"

Priya looked out the window toward the setting sun. "You ride fast, and hard, I believe you can make it by sunrise. Who knows how many people have—" she choked up again and stood. "I will go too. I will show you."

"No dear," Aunt B said gently. "You did too much already, you need to rest."

"My friends are there. My brother." Priya wavered and Aunt B touched her shoulder.

"We'll get there fast as a bullet and solve the problem before you know it. By the time you rest up and head home tomorrow, I'm sure we'll have some answers," Lance chimed with the quick confidence he turned on whenever they needed to reassure someone of their work. "Easy as slicing warm butter on a hot day."

"Why do I think it'll be anything but," Melinda muttered as they readied to leave.

"We'll handle it, like we've done plenty of times before," Lance replied.

Lance was right. They'd figure it out, like they always did. Feeling better, Melinda hoisted the sack Aunt B had put together for them. Plenty of explosives, ammo, and Abel's specialty concoctions. Whatever waited for them at Fallows wouldn't have much of a chance.

CHAPTER TWO

As Melinda rode with Lance due south toward Fallows, she couldn't get Priya's distraught face out of her head. She had seen plenty of folks upset before, but Priya's combination of grief and shock made a knot in Melinda's stomach as heavy as a sack of stones. She turned her gaze upwards as they rode under the densely starred sky, but even the occasional flare of a meteorite seemed foreboding.

They stopped twice for brief breaks, dozing for half an hour while the horses rested, and then again at a small stream to hydrate, before continuing. As the beginning rays of sunlight set the dawn aglow, Melinda urged Pepper into a gallop. Pepper obliged grudgingly, reluctant from the weight of Abel's arsenal.

Plenty of bullets, along with a rifle fitted with a long-range scope.

Tacky bombs, that could cling to any surface and exploded when fired on.

Two large sticks of dynamite, nestled safely in cloth wrapping.

And a crossbow that Aunt B had unearthed from Abel's stuff, an experimental weapon rigged with smaller, hooked arrows that splayed out to take down anything within range.

"Sorry girl," Melinda said to her horse. "I want to get back home as much as you."

"See anything?" Lance asked.

Her eyesight was better than his, so she spotted it first even in the slowly growing light: narrow funnels of smoke. Fallows finally came into view through the smoke as the dawn's sunlight spilt its rays over the horizon.

They slowed as they approached the town. Whether a newcomer or oldcomer settlement, you never knew what you might encounter. Some places were hospitable and welcoming to guests, others hostile, and others simply closed off.

Fallows seemed to be a well-kept, newer establishment by the looks of the gleaming wood and cleanly packed roads. They passed an empty school building and modest city hall. The town was chock full of trees, bathing the paths in shadows. They paused at a symmetrical three-foot crater, its bowl full of rocks.

"Explosive?" Lance wondered and she shrugged. They took a left toward the smoke tendrils and a faint cry. The horses shifted uneasily—whether from the noise, smell or something else, she couldn't tell. They dismounted, tying Pepper and Mud to a post outside a stable.

On foot and with Abel's bag of weapons, they turned another corner and the sound of agitated talking increased. So that's where all the town people were—clustered roughly in two groups beneath lofty oak trees.

Each group around a corpse.

"Take it easy, take it easy," a middle-aged, pale man was shouting from beneath an exceptionally broad gray hat. His overgrown sideburns blended into an equally bushy mustache. "Give 'em space now."

"Howdy. One of your residents called for us," Lance said as they neared the speaker. "Heard you have a supernatural problem. That's our expertise."

Normally people were relieved to know that Lance and Melinda were experts at monsters and the like, but not always—they had learned the hard way to make sure places wanted their help first. Just another time-wasting formality that Melinda had no patience for when they had a job to do. That's what Lance was for.

"Who are you?" The man glared at them impatiently, tugging on his mustache. Melinda noticed the magnifying glass and tweezers peeking out of his vest pocket. "You know, never mind, we have a situation here. No time for spectators. Burn it quickly," he said irritably to another resident. "We don't have all day."

"Got it, doc," a no-nonsense woman replied, pushing through the first crowd with a heap of dried twigs. She kept her distance from the body as she scattered the twigs alongside it.

"We're here to help," Lance said, louder. "Your rider sent for us. She said things were pretty dire."

The doctor looked irritated. "Miss Bedi, I imagine. I told her we'd have it under control. We've already tried everything imaginable. Fire is the only way."

"We've dealt with these kinds of things before. Please, let us take a look so we can assist," Lance said. At that, the residents reluctantly shuffled aside and that's when the smell hit Melinda. Like dead meat mixed with month-old milk tinged with something else, something that reminded her of a sickly cow on its last legs.

They both lifted their handkerchiefs to their faces as they neared the first body.

An older man lay on his back with his chest cavity caved in around his stained cotton shirt, his torso looking like it was made of dried paper that had been punched in. Azure dust spread from his open cavity, dark with guts and entrails.

"That dust. Don't touch it," the doctor warned. Someone had dropped a cloth over the dead man's face, under which a few gray curls peeked out. The veins along his pockmarked beige skin lit up white with a tinge of blue.

"We have the benefit of education when it comes to situations like these," the doctor continued. "We know that touch and breath can breed sickness, isn't that right?" The crowd murmured in affirmation.

"Never seen anything like this," Melinda muttered as she stood next to Lance.

"Definitely supernatural," he said and raised his voice. "Did anyone see any strange critters? Any monsters?" The crowd shuffled, agitated.

The doctor gave a snort. "We're hundreds of miles from…that place," he said. Just like others Melinda and Lance had encountered, he clearly didn't want to say the word "Edge." Lots of people held a superstitious fear of accidentally attracting attention from the creatures that poured out of the Edge, a miles-long mountain range that housed the fissure to the monster world.

"Yessir, but you still get the occasional Edge monster that wanders far. That glow on his veins ain't natural. You see anything unusual?" Lanced turned to the crowd. "Any of you?"

Melinda scanned the crowd with a broad gaze, waiting for an erratic movement to catch her eye and alert her that someone might have more to say than they let on.

"Surely someone's seen *something*," Melinda added, drumming her fingers on her holster. A shadow darkened the corner of her eye, starting to take the shape of an Edgling. She spoke louder to distract herself from the vision. "Sooner you tell us, sooner we can stop the dying. So speak up, someone."

"Anything even a little out of ordinary can be a clue," Lance added. "Odd tracks. Odd plant. Odd weather even. We got weapons to handle these kinds of things."

"Your weapons don't mean anything here," the doctor sniffed. "It's a sickness." The others around him nodded and Melinda rolled her eyes at their naivete.

"You got no idea what you're dealing with," Melinda said to him.

"We need to light more fires to ward off the bad smells," the doctor went on as if she hadn't spoken. "Don't want a plague starting after all. Now we have to burn the rest of the bodies."

"No!" A scream erupted.

"Mellie," Lance said. She followed his gaze to the second cluster of people. She could just make out a heap on the ground. As they threaded through the crowd, she spotted a petite woman, visibly pregnant, crouched awkwardly next to the body of a young man.

"I won't let you burn him!" the woman shouted. She looked to be in her early 20s, with a smooth brown face and braids that reached past her shoulders. A larger bald man tried to pry her away, looking just as stricken.

"Brigitta, it doesn't matter now," the large man said. He looked to be a few years older than her, with long lashes and a heavy mustache against a brown face. Stringed charms dangled around his neck and leather bands wound around his wrists.

"Don't touch it! Rafi, don't let her touch the body," someone shrieked. "She'll get sick if she does!" The pregnant woman,

Brigitta, ignored the shouts, staring at the corpse and hugging herself. Rafi rose to his considerable height and gently eased her up.

"We're burning the body immediately before there's further contamination," the doctor said. "And the homes. We simply can't risk a widespread infection that may wipe out our town. Rafi, please tend to Ms. Brigitta's hysterics."

"That's a terrific bedside manner you got, doc," Melinda said.

The doctor turned, sizing her up for the first time it seemed, even though she was a good foot taller. "It is of the utmost urgency that we address this potential catastrophe before it worsens."

"I won't let you burn our home," Brigitta said, trying to shake off Rafi's arm. "He just finished building the crib."

"We must take precautions, just in case," Rafi scratched the back of his bald head in agitation. "I don't want to either, but Samuel would have understood."

"He's gone," Melinda said bluntly. Sometimes stating the obvious helped a person snap out of their daze. "Sorry but it's true."

Brigitta dusted herself off and stood, her mauve dress stained at the bottom. "That's my…*was*…my husband." Her voice was flat. "We were going to…." She stopped, eyes wide, unable to comprehend her new reality. Melinda felt for the woman, given her state. What probably should've been a happy occasion now was marked with tragedy, and it made her heart hurt. Melinda knew what it was to forever be haunted by the things that might've been, even now, years after her mother's death.

"Very sorry for your loss, Miss," Lance said and tipped his hat to Brigitta, who stared blankly past him.

They watched solemnly as Rafi pulled a blanket over the deceased. Even though the man's body was about to burn, the gesture seemed like one last act of kindness that maybe could help usher the spirit away in peace.

"Well, out-of-towners, any helpful wisdom you'd deign to bestow upon us? Or can we continue with our efforts now?" The doc asked and Melinda ignored his tone. People acted funny in the face of fear and the unusual. It irked her, but she'd learned to not take it personally. Besides, people changed their tune real quick once their problem was solved.

A few people brought larger branches and placed them around the body. A woman moved forward with a large torch. Something flicked, barely visible, but this time it wasn't one of her visions.

"Wait," Melinda said.

With a heavy dread as though she was in one of her nightmares, she pulled her handkerchief up and used a booted toe to nudge the side of the body. Brigitta made a noise—something between anguish and rage—but Melinda ignored it when her suspicion was confirmed.

The blanket over the dead man's chest moved.

"Mellie?" Lance followed her gaze, squinting for a second. His hand shot to his hip.

He had seen it too.

"Stand back. Now!" Melinda said to the town's residents. They glanced at her, confused.

"What are you going on about? We don't have time for this," the doc barked. "We've already waited too long and risk more contamination."

Lance stepped forward as she turned in unison so they were cattycorner. They had worked together long enough to move as a single unit, their subtle shifts speaking as loud as any words. She lifted her pistol—a clear shot—as he grabbed the corner of the blanket.

"What are you doing?" Brigitta shrieked.

"That is no way to treat our recently departed," Rafi chimed.

"Sometimes people come back that aren't meant to," Lance said.

"The undead?" someone yelped and the crowd took an instinctive step back. The woman with the burning torch looked ready to throw it.

"Good news is we've encountered undead before," Lance announced. "They tend to be immortal, but shots to the back of the neck, or severing the head, usually does the trick."

"Evil magic, I'd wager," one muttered.

"We need to burn it," the doc snapped, and looked toward the torch bearer, who gulped and took a tiny step forward. "Destruction by fire is the only sure way."

Lance glanced at Melinda, and she nodded. If the pistols didn't do it, they had plenty of other weapons to draw on. He snatched off the blanket.

Everyone held their breaths. But the body didn't sit up. It was still as any corpse.

Except for its gut.

Melinda took a step closer, steeling herself against the growing stench that was coaxing her stomach up through her throat. In between entrails something moved, just barely visible in the dark space of the man's gut. What looked like a white worm stretched out, half the size of her pinky and ending in a sharp tip. Another small white worm joined it, bloodstained.

The worms moved and she realized they were small fingers, attached to a hand. One that could fit within her own palm.

A hand with claws.

"La—" she started when the owner of the hand popped up.

The bluish white face was the size of a piglet's, squashed like a stomped-on rat. Its forehead looked more ape-like, with heavy furrows as it squirmed upwards out of the man. Red-rimmed white eyes with dotted pupils blinked as a piece of entrail dropped off its cheek.

Whatever it was, they had never seen a creature like this.

"Devil! Gremlin!" the doc hollered and the woman next to him lurched forward with the torch.

The creature snarled with a catlike hiss, displaying a row of tiny dagger teeth that matched its claws. It reminded Melinda of a cross between a rat and ape.

"Stay calm now, we don't want the little grem to scamper off," Lance urged them.

"Kill it!" Brigitta screamed amidst the commotion. She scooped up one of the bigger branches from the dirt and rushed forward. "Bastard!"

"No!" Melinda yelled. The grem looked at the raised branch and leapt clear out of the man's chest. Quick as if it were on a spring, it stretched its claws toward Brigitta's face as it jumped.

Faster than Melinda could shoot.

Brigitta swung hard, her braids whipping forward as the branch smacked the grem. She shook from the impact, making Melinda suspect the creature was denser and stronger than it looked. But the grem dropped, and Rafi's shot from a dingy-looking pocket pistol rang out. The small creature lay in a heap, a blue-and-white mass with brown blood pooling out from under it.

Melinda steadied her gun, waiting, even as the others relaxed.

"Fine shot," the doc said.

"You got it!" someone cheered, patting Rafi on the back. "Hey, they killed it!"

"We're not clear yet. Sometimes they come back up," Melinda said, not taking her eyes off the critter's still body.

"Mellie," Lance said in a way that made her tense, even though she wasn't seeing any movement. Then she heard the noise.

Above her.

A hissing worse than a rattler's shot a blade of ice between her shoulder blades. She dove and ducked, knowing whatever it was, Lance would have it in his sights.

She turned to see another of those creatures—another *grem*—perched in a tree above them.

With tufts of barely glowing blue fur sprouting from its chin and ears and along its back, it was half the height of a human and clearly an older version of the first grem they had seen.

Lance fired once, twice, but the grem moved faster than any living thing she had seen. It appeared on a second branch even higher, hissing over the crowd's screams and commotion. Others' gunshots rang out and Melinda cursed. Too much chaos and gunfire was never a good thing. Lance shot again but the creature twisted nimbly midair, its eyes narrowed in an all-too-human emotion: rage. And it had its sights on Brigitta, who had frozen, the stick still in her hands.

"Duck!" Lance yelled. Melinda aimed above Brigitta's head as the creature tensed.

Melinda never missed, not even if it was a faster-than-natural grem.

But the creature didn't jump on Brigitta. Instead, it soared a few feet overhead and made a sound like a cat expelling a particularly vile hairball. As it did, a dust that made Melinda think of pulverized robin eggs swirled from its mouth.

The blast of cerulean dust rained down onto Brigitta's head and shoulders in a fine powder.

"No!" Rafi yanked Brigitta back by the hand. Meanwhile, the monster moved in a ghostly blur up over the roof of the school and vanished into woods that led up to a steep mountain.

"We can't let it get away," Lance said. "Quick now."

"Leave it," the doctor countered. "Burn the bodies immediately in case there are others. But we don't need to expend resources to pursue the creature. It's not our problem anymore."

"For some other town to deal with?" Lance shot him a hard gaze.

"We can't go up into Pigeon Mountain anyway," someone chimed. "It's oldcomer territory."

Melinda used her handkerchief to brush the glittering blue dust off Brigitta, careful not to touch her just in case, and threw the handkerchief next to the corpse. The dust dissipated within seconds, winking out of existence. Brigitta rubbed her arms agitatedly, scrubbing away any invisible motes. Everyone had fallen silent, watching her.

"What do we do?" Rafi stared at Brigitta in dismay. "What do we *do*?"

"Whatever it is, she's infected now, under the evil vapors. Contagious." The doctor took a purposeful step back. "My educated guess: it won't be but a few hours before she falls sickly like the others."

"Wait a minute, we don't know she's infected. We don't know how it's spread," Lance protested.

"You touch her then, if you're so sure," the doc said and crossed his arms.

"Some things are transmitted through blood. Breathing. Or another way," Lance said to the doctor. "Truth is, you have no idea how that grem sickness works."

"It got all over her!" someone shouted. "We all saw it!"

"She's got to get away from us!"

"No need to panic," Melinda said to them.

Brigitta had fallen silent, nearly unresponsive. Melinda scrutinized her. She didn't seem sick, not yet, but more like someone in shock. Her hands rested on her swollen belly, and she hadn't stopped trembling even in the dappled morning sun that reached them beneath the leaves. Rafi seemed to notice at the same time, shrugging off his threadbare brown summer jacket and throwing it around her, the large material nearly swallowing her up.

"Normally I'd suggest we'd bleed her and purge her." The doc rubbed his mustache in agitation. "But I've seen enough in my profession to warrant extreme caution here. We have learned much from plagues of the past, but this is not natural. This is supernatural, you see." He nodded once, as if he had decided, and a bit of pity fell over his face, supplanting his scowl. "We can't risk it. It's like cutting off a diseased limb. We must spare the whole of the town at the expense of a few."

"Doc's right. You have to go," an elderly woman said.

Rafi glared into the crowd. "What do you mean?"

"Sorry Rafi," one of the men said. "Can't risk it. Better get."

Rafi straightened, a good head taller than most in the crowd and well aware of it. He hovered over the nearest man, menacing. "She is with child. We are not going anywhere."

The crowd chimed in. "How do we know the rest of you ain't sick?" "—Exposed, what if they infect other towns—" "Another one will burst out of her too!" "You may be big, Rafi, but that doesn't mean you can do what you want!"

Melinda felt that shift in the air, something she had experienced before when a crowd turned. The faces around them—tired, angry, but mostly afraid—had stepped back, leaving the four of them and the body in a wide circle. In the heavy shade beneath the trees, two of the townspeople lifted the torches, casting wild shadows. Melinda and Lance instinctively placed themselves in front of Brigitta and Rafi.

"You leave her alone," Melinda said to the nearest one. "Shame on you, harassing your neighbors."

"Get out of here!" Another person shouted, waving his torch.

"You don't intend to burn an innocent person," Lance said bluntly.

"Of course not," the doctor said hastily, though Melinda wondered if that's exactly what he had meant. "But she can't stay.

None of you can, not a second longer. Leave immediately, if you please, or we will be forced to take more drastic action, for our own protection."

Next to the doctor, a stern woman in overalls raised the torch, pointing it at them.

"And where are we going to go?" Rafi shot back and balled both of his fists, as if he were ready to attack. "Brigitta is a new widow. You would cast her out?"

"Hold your horses," Lance said. "No sense in fighting when time's a ticking. We're going. But we need a healer or alchemist, someone nearby who devises antidotes. You got anyone close who can help? Please." He lifted his hands, palms up, the voice of reason.

"The next town over," the doc said reluctantly. "Their doctor's completely incompetent, but there's a witchy woman who knows what she's doing. Take your troubles there. Now, go!"

Slowly they backed up, Rafi holding Brigitta's shoulders over his jacket to guide her, though she moved slower than molasses.

"Come on Brigitta, we must get you help." Rafi was breathing angrily, reminding Melinda of a bull. "Since our neighbors have forsaken us. We must find someone…do something…*promptly*."

She didn't respond and worry sliced through Melinda. Poor woman was pregnant, just lost her husband and might be infected. An image of Melinda's momma's sick face flashed to her, and she shoved it away. She wouldn't let it happen again, not to Brigitta.

"Brig, what is wrong?" Rafi's voice nearly boomed as he pleaded with her. "Please, speak."

Brigitta didn't respond, for all the world looking like her attention had turned inwards, her breathing shallow and quick.

"She's not hearing us," Lance said, leading them swiftly toward the horses. "From shock or the sickness."

"That *abomination*." Rafi's hands were shaking and he quickly clasped them to steady himself. "What did it want? Why was it attacking us?"

"How long till the infections took hold in the others?" Melinda asked.

Rafi slumped. "I do not know. Samuel seemed dandy yesterday." His gaze turned misty at the mention of his friend. "Just dandy."

"So it likely hits people fast." Lance untied Pepper and Mud. "You got horses?"

Rafi nodded, running toward the stable.

"We got to hurry," Lance said to Melinda. "Find her help, then we come back and hunt the grem."

Melinda turned to Brigitta. "Did your husband have any signs before then? Encounter that powder?"

Brigitta stared off, not acknowledging her.

A few tense moments later, Rafi hurried toward them, now with a wide-brimmed brown hat over his bare head. He guided a giant chestnut mustang fit for his size along with a smaller golden Palomino.

"Samuel's," Rafi said of the Palomino and gently placed a smaller gray hat on Brigitta's braids. "But Brig shouldn't be riding in her condition."

"We don't have a choice," Melinda reminded him as Lance and Rafi gingerly helped Brigitta up, both of them careful not to touch her bare skin.

"The doc mentioned a woman who could help. You know where she is?" Lance asked Rafi. "Or any other nearby healers? We might have a chance for a remedy if we find help soon."

"That one's not too far. She brews concoctions. Samuel would get his mixtures from her store, ease his stomach," Rafi hesitated as he mounted the mustang. "She is a witch though."

"Nothing wrong with that," Lance said. "Most of the time people sling that word around like a weapon, when they're really referring to herbalists or worshippers of the moon. None of which is cause for concern. How far?"

"East along the mountain base to Sagebrush Junction. Hour or so ride," Rafi responded. Sweat poured down his forehead. Melinda felt bad for him—seeing his friend dead, his community casting him out—it was a lot for anyone to handle.

"Let's get a move on before your friends decide it's safer to burn us too," Melinda said. Every second they spent debating was a second Brigitta was more at risk. They set off under the blazing morning sun, leaving the smell of burning bodies behind.

CHAPTER THREE

They rode in silence along the base of Pigeon Mountain due east. Melinda stayed vigilant, keeping her attention toward the trees at the base of the mountain on their left in case the grem should appear again. The only movement she spotted was a brown coyote darting along the brush and a vulture wheeling overhead, catching the wind in graceful arcs.

Brigitta's horse walked eagerly beside Pepper, while Brigitta sat upright and held the reins on her own out of habit it seemed. Rafi's bulky figure led the way and Lance pulled up the rear. They took a break at a sturdy bridge by a small stream to refill canteens and let the horses sip so they wouldn't bake.

Sagebrush Junction showed itself a few hours later, as the sun kept climbing and the relentless heat slowed the horses.

"It's a trading town," Rafi said as they approached. "We come here whenever we need anything."

Half a dozen intersecting streets were packed with small buildings made up of storefronts on the first floor and sleeping quarters up top. Fresh flowers grew on windowpanes and the sounds of children shouting rose amidst the bleating of farm animals. They paid to board their horses at the livery stable before Rafi led them to an especially busy shop. Outside the store, two shopkeepers loaded a wagon full of bottles and furs.

"This is her spot," Rafi said cautiously. "I have never been inside. You cannot trust witchcraft with your soul." He looked worriedly at Brigitta, who had shrugged off the jacket and stood in her stained purple dress, silent and sullen. "But we have no other options."

Inside, a dozen or so people crammed into the neat but crowded shop. A stooped older man in a wrinkled linen shirt looked up as they entered, stepping away from two women in cowskins, both sporting pairs of long braids and vertically lined tattoos down their chins.

"Help you find something," the man grunted.

"We're looking for the witch," Melinda said.

"Nox. She's behind you," he said.

Melinda turned to see a woman nearly as tall as her, but angular and willowy, maybe in her mid-30s. A sleeveless green dress gathered at the waist with a coil of rope revealed her light brown shoulders.

"Much appreciated, Mary," Nox said, her voice nasally but pleased as she took a paper-wrapped bag from a courier in a black hat. "Rare ingredient," Nox added by way of explanation and absently touched her dark braided bun. "Can I help you with something?"

"You are the witch that brews the concoctions, yes?" Rafi asked. "We—"

"Witch. Potion master. I've been called lots of things," Nox said. Her face was about as sharp as her gaze, with lips thin as fingerbones. "I *prefer* alchemist. Or scientist."

"Miss Nox?" someone asked, lifting a crate of slim glass vials full of an opaque substance. Nox directed them to a wooden shelf as another attendant hurried by to place a crate onto the wagon outside.

Nox smiled in a way that reminded Melinda of a smug cat. "Gearing up for the festival of the season over in Thundering Ridge," she explained. "The demand for potions and elixirs never wanes. It's quite an event. Newcomers and oldcomers alike, all bartering, shopping, talking goods."

"And Nox brews the best," the older man called. "So you can see she's busy!"

"Thanks, Uncle," Nox replied.

"Pleased to meet you, miss. I'm Lance and this is Melinda," Lance introduced hastily. "And Miss Brigitta and Mr. Rafi—"

"This lady here is Samuel's wife," Rafi interjected. "One of your customers. She—"

"Ah yes, I always remember a dreadfully handsome face like his," Nox said. Melinda immediately disliked her but couldn't put her finger on it. Maybe it was the showy display, or the careless attitude. Lance always told her she was too fast to dismiss others, so she tried to ignore her snap judgement. Besides, they needed help and fast.

"Samuel is recently deceased," Rafi said.

"I'm mighty sorry for your loss." Nox made a motion with her fingers, like a kiss to the sky. She sounded genuine. "I offer my wish that he passes peacefully onwards."

"Hoping we could talk to you about something," Lance continued. "Important."

"Regrettably, I'm a bit busy right now," Nox waved an arm heavy with copper bangles. "I'm sure one of my attendants can assist."

Her uncle stepped forward to guide them out of the store. Melinda drew to her full height and shot him a look, giving him pause.

"It's important, like the man said," Melinda said.

"Lives are in danger." Lance lowered his voice in the busy shop and glanced meaningfully at Brigitta. "She needs your help."

"Hmm, I have an excellent pregnancy balm that can ease childbirth or coax it when you're ready." Nox swept up a jar from a small table and placed it into Brigitta's limp hand. Brigitta stared at it.

"Here. Free of charge," Nox said kindly. "Given your tragic loss." She glanced at Rafi. "And for you, I can mix something to relieve grief. Nothing really can help mourning, but sometimes a quieting of the mind can facilitate peace." She turned her sights to Melinda next with a slightly puzzled brow. "Hmm."

"No thanks," Melinda cut. "We came to—"

"Let me guess, nightmares? Those are trickier, more complex. Crushed moonstone mixed with dried catnip, lavender, chamomile may help. This is my own proprietary blend. For your pillow." She picked up a small knapsack and pressed it into Melinda's palm and then glanced at Lance. "And for you. Something for grief as well."

"She's been exposed, infected." Lance gestured. "People have died."

"I feel fine," Brigitta said flatly, and the others glanced at her in surprise. Some focus had come back into her eyes, and she glanced defiantly back at them. "Aside from my life being turned into a bag of rusty nails."

"That powder from the grem touched you," Rafi said urgently. "We must get you an antidote. Miss Nox, we require your immediate assistance. We will pay, of course."

"It's a mysterious illness. Deadly," Lance added. "And word is, you're the best alchemist on this side of the range." They hadn't heard that necessarily, but Melinda knew Lance's way of buttering people up like freshly baked bread. That's why he did the talking.

"Hmm." Nox feigned disinterest, but Melinda could see she was intrigued. The flattery had worked. "Uncle, keep an eye on things, would you?"

Nox marched toward the back room of the store, leading the others to a cluttered space where glass vials and tubes, stone statues and books crammed onto tables and shelves over a hearth. For a second, the sight of the workspace sent a pang through Melinda, reminding her of Abel when he was tinkering with his latest invention.

"Symptoms?" Nox asked while she cleared off part of a table, moving aside melted candles and a speckled stone mortar as big as her head.

"None," Brigitta said.

Nox unearthed a magnifying glass. "You mentioned people have died."

"There's a monster unlike any we've seen. It's got this dust on it," Lance said. "The victims' veins turned the same blue as the dust."

"So, this dust touched you but didn't affect you." Nox used the magnifier to peer at Brigitta's face and neck. "Why?"

A beat of silence.

"Could be a function of pregnancy," Nox mused, answering herself. She used tweezers to remove a strand of hair from one of

Brigitta's fraying braids. "Pregnancy does unusual things to a body. It can make your smell more powerful, can make you feel things you've never felt before. And—can make you sicker or less sick, depending."

"The dust will not harm her baby, will it?" Rafi hovered next to Brigitta, carefully watching every one of Nox's actions.

Nox shrugged. "Hard to say. Let's hope not."

The rest of them shifted uneasily.

"What were the symptoms of the others?" Nox asked.

"We believe they fell dead in a few hours," Rafi said. "No symptoms beforehand. But after, they had collapsed chests. Glowing veins. And…" He swallowed as though he was fighting back the urge to retch. "He was my friend…"

"And we found a critter inside one of the deceased," Melinda finished. "Do you have something that can help or not? We don't got time to keep yapping."

Nox used a metal scalpel to scrape a bit of skin from Brigitta's cheek and back of her hand, then placed the skin and hair into a jar with dozens of tiny green flies the size of freckles. Herald flies, Melinda recognized. Rare, hard to find. Aunt B had had a stash once. The insects interacted with toxins and produced antidotes. They were exactly what Brigitta needed.

Melinda nearly sagged in relief, until Nox frowned and lowered the magnifier.

"There's no trace of unusual dust. Not on the clothes or on the skin," Nox said.

"I told you I was fine," Brigitta said sullenly. "Doomed anyway, I suppose."

"We all saw the monster's dust touch her." Lance looked at Nox. "You can't do anything?"

"Could be you have to breathe it in or have it go into the blood for infection." Nox pointed to the flies. "They change color when they produce an antidote. They got nothing either, perhaps because the sample is not potent enough. I'd surmise gathering the dust directly from a specimen would prompt a better response. Really *any* response."

"Give her something, *now*." Rafi pounded the table.

Nox glanced at him. "Are you the father?"

"No." Rafi glared. "But her husband was my friend. So she is now my charge. I will *not* see her die as well."

"How far along are you, dear?" Nox asked.

"Soon." Brigitta touched her swollen stomach before falling into a moody silence.

Nox shook her head. "I could give her a mix of miscellaneous treatments targeting symptoms, but it's risky. And, far as I can tell, you don't even *have* symptoms at the moment. I would like to see this dust—"

"Look, there's still a grem running around up in Pigeon Mountain," Lance said. "We'll find it, bring it back so you can figure something out."

"Yes, that would work," Nox said thoughtfully.

"How will we find it in time?" Rafi asked and paced, pausing to look absently at various glass chemistry setups. "What if she falls ill like the others?"

"It's your only choice, as far as I can tell." Nox grabbed a sack off a nearby hook and set a few items inside, including the glass jar of flies, after she carefully wrapped it in a linen.

"What are you doing?" Melinda asked with a sinking feeling.

"Coming with you of course," Nox said. "To collect a live sample."

"We work alone. You'll get in the way." Melinda folded her arms.

"You don't have time to wait," Nox said matter-of-factly. "And no telling what the creature will do in captivity. Could initiate its own death. Could stop producing the dust. I'd rather be there."

"We'll do it. Give us the jar of flies, we'll make sure the dust goes in," Lance said.

"Absolutely not." Nox gave a short laugh. "Herald flies are rare and hard to breed. As such, I'll keep them in my sights at all times. Besides." She smirked again, a look Melinda was beginning to immensely dislike. "You won't get far up Pigeon Mountain without my help."

At the quizzical silence, Nox continued. "Warring tribes live on either side of the river up there. They like outsiders even less. But they like me all right. We trade. And learning the languages helps."

"Don't you have the festival to get ready for?" Lance asked. A clumsy last attempt, Melinda saw, to convince her but it wasn't going to work. She briefly considered if she needed to resort to brute force to take the flies. But it probably couldn't hurt to have Nox there, as inconvenient as it might be, in case Brigitta's situation deteriorated.

Nox waved him off. "Knowing the folks on Pigeon, it will be a quick trip. I wouldn't be surprised if they caught your grem already. Uncle and the staff can take care of the festival prep. This is much more fun."

"It's not fun," Melinda snapped, seeing Brigitta stiffen. "People died."

Nox raised her hands, ringed fingers flashing, and gave a wry grin. "I know. Apologies. I'd be the first to tell you my tact is sometimes lacking. One of my very few faults."

Lance gave a small shrug toward Melinda. If they wanted the help, they'd have to take Nox along. Every second they waited, they risked Brigitta falling dead like the others.

"Let's go." Melinda paused when she saw Brigitta wavering on her feet. "The last time you ate?" Melinda asked her briskly.

Before Brigitta could answer, a shout rang through the shop.

"What's the hellabaloo?" Nox called as they hurried back into the main area of the shop. Everyone was gone, save for Nox's uncle, who stood frozen at the front door.

"The grem," Lance guessed, but when Melinda and Lance pushed their way past the uncle to get outside, the buzzing overhead made them duck instinctively.

What looked like two dozen brown mosquitos the size of her forearm circled overhead. Three pairs of hanging, hairy striped legs swung from each of the insect's bodies, while their inscrutable bulbous eyes fixed on the people running down the street.

"Culidaes!" Lance said over the noise. The monstrous bugs droned louder than a field of locusts as their ashy purple wings, easily 14 inches long, beat together rapidly. Their striated wings might've been reminiscent of sick butterflies.

"What are those?" Rafi gaped from the doorway.

"Edge creatures that bred with mosquitos." Melinda grimaced. "Don't let one land on you."

"Why?" Rafi asked and ushered Brigitta back into the store.

"You don't want to know. Stay inside!" Out of the corner of Melinda's eye, she saw a shadowy shape flit by, taking the shape of an Edgling ready to taunt her. *Not now*, she thought.

"Mellie," Lance said with a pause in his voice that wasn't good. "These ain't acting right. They don't normally swarm. Or attack."

"Oh, they're attacking," she said. The creatures' legs swung as they flew, clawed pincers grasped the air like they were looking for something. The culidaes were positively angry as they dove toward running townsfolk, tents and wagons. What's more, their mouths were extended from below their cluster of eyes, ready to pierce and draw blood. The last time they'd encountered culidaes, a couple had employed them to get rid of a swarm that had taken up residence in their barn. The bugs had been docile and kept their mouths retracted unless provoked.

"Don't let them latch onto you!" Melinda said.

"What do they do?" Nox called from the doorway, watching.

"You had a mosquito bite before?" Lance said. "Usually, you can walk away from those. These not so much."

Two of the culidaes turned midair, and another pair followed. They beelined toward Melinda and Lance. One dove toward Nox in the doorframe, its mouth like a glass tube extending farther.

"Close the door!" Melinda ordered and ducked away from the giant insect. "Stay inside. We'll take care of them."

"They're in quite the frenzy," Lance observed as they dodged another pair of wings.

"We could use blood as bait, draw them into something," Melinda said.

Lance snapped his fingers. "Like we did in Lilly Brooks with the rat vamps."

Melinda's gaze rested on a pair of covered wagons near the store. "Knife?" She asked and Lance rummaged in their bag before unsheathing a decent sized hunting blade. They unfastened part of the white canvas from the top of one wagon.

While Melinda sliced the fabric, Lance shot at one, then another culidae, sending them wheeling back into the sky.

"You got any blood in there from any of your spells?" Melinda hollered at the store.

"No!" Nox's voice floated from inside, barely audible above the droning. "And they're not spells, they're mixtures. Butcher is around the corner."

"You need blood to get rid of these things? I'll get it," Nox's uncle said and darted out of the building. He glanced at them slicing the piece of canvas. "Owner gonna be mad."

"They'll be madder if they get a culidae bite. Dead in fact," Melinda said. Before she could caution him to be careful, the man disappeared around the corner.

"Wonder why they're erratic as a rabid racoon," Melinda said as she and Lance finished getting the tarp off. They darted to a second wagon that looked just about large enough to hold the two dozen swarming bugs. Lance paused to shoot at a culidae targeting a man holding a kid against his chest as he ran, his hat flying off behind him.

"Maybe the grem's been by and it set them off," Lance said. "One type of predator spooking another."

"Maybe," she said doubtfully. She shot two in rapid succession, aiming at the centers of their eyes and causing them to drop. "Too many to shoot them all!"

"You're in luck, here." Nox's uncle appeared, sweating and heaving a slopping bucket, barely sealed. "Steer blood."

The culidaes already sensed it and started diving at them faster.

"Quick, in the wagon!" Melinda shouted. She and Lance propped the piece of heavy canvas over the intact prairie wagon, ready to drop it over the back opening once the bugs were in. "Now!"

Nox's uncle grunted as he splashed the blood into the wagon bed, small drops spattering onto his linen shirt. He stepped back as the swarm of culidaes gathered and flew swiftly into the wagon. Melinda and Lance waited until the last one swept in before dropping the canvas cover over the back. Wings flapped against the fabric briefly, then stopped as the creatures feasted on the blood within.

"Will that hold em?" The uncle said.

"Indeed. Once they're done feasting, they go into a stupor," Lance said.

"What'd we do with them?" The uncle asked.

"Someone can take this wagon out into the woods, let them go," Lance said.

"Better yet, burn them," Melinda added absently and exchanged a look with Lance. "They shouldn't be so aggressive. Wonder if…"

Before she could, finish Lance turned more fully and her heart dropped.

A culidae clung to his back, its foot-long violet wings folded. Its stick-like mouth pushed above the fabric of his duster, right into his neck.

CHAPTER FOUR

"I got one on me, don't I?" Lance said, holding still.

Melinda nodded and turned the pistol in her hand in preparation to whack the monstrous insect off Lance's back. She paused as tidbits she had memorized about the creature came back to her. Interrupting a culidae's bite was the worst thing someone could do. A culidae's mouth—made of six thin, needle-like parts longer than her finger—would automatically extend a hundred tiny spikes along its length if disturbed and cause mass bleeding.

But she had to do something, and fast. When they bit, they injected a numbing agent into their host, just like a regular mosquito. But this numbing saliva could stop a man's heart, if the bug didn't drain him of all his blood first.

"Scat!" Melinda yelled, swinging her gun close to try to scare the culidae away. It didn't flinch.

"Don't bother," Lance said, trying to sound light but she could hear the worry creeping into his voice. He was already looking pale. "It won't come off."

"Regular culidaes won't come off," she corrected, stemming her rising panic. The insect's brown thorax was growing darker as it sucked Lance's blood. "There's something wrong with these. They're *angry*. C'mon," she taunted as she poked the side of the insect with her gun barrel. Normally once they latched pretty much nothing could sway them, and the host was good as gone. But this culidae buzzed again, lifting its dusty purple wings and giving an irritated flap. Maybe she could use its anger to distract it away from Lance.

"Whatever you're doing, do it faster," Lance muttered, sounding fainter by the second.

"Hold your horses. I'll get you out of this." The insect wasn't budging though, and in fact seemed to drink faster. She stepped back, wiping the sweat from her forehead.

Nox's uncle watched them a second and hurried back to the store. Probably the sight of the gorging culidae was too much for him, Melinda figured.

She contemplated cutting its head if she could find shears or an axe. But even that would probably release too much of the numbing agent into Lance. Her mind ran through the circumstances that usually deterred a creature—freezing, burning, loud noises, blunt force—while Lance wavered, about to pass out. They were almost out of time.

"Here!" Nox's uncle emerged from the store with a vial of amber-colored liquid.

"Put it on the bug!" Nox said from the doorway.

Melinda didn't have time to ask what it was or why. She stepped back as Nox's uncle shook a few drops onto the culidae's back. The culidae's wings lifted.

"Heady pheromone," Nox called. "Doesn't have much effect on people but seems to work well on animals."

The monster's mouth retracted, splashing drops of Lance's blood along his duster. The giant insect stayed perched on Lance for an instant before slowly flying up and hovering a foot above them.

Melinda grabbed Lance, steadying him.

"Another second there and I…" He shook his head.

"You've been through worse," Melinda said lightly, pressing her spare handkerchief to the bleeding spot behind his neck. "You'll brush it off." She turned to Nox's uncle. "He needs something to drink and eat."

The uncle nodded and headed back inside. The culidae flapped unsteadily overhead, as though it had drunk a barrel of whiskey. As it hovered, something glimmered under its leg.

A bright white-blue vein, thinner than a hair, gleamed in the afternoon sun.

"Did they all have those?" Melinda asked and Lance shook his head uncertainly.

"Same color as the body's veins back in Fallows," Lance said. "Same color as the grem."

"What does it mean?"

"Grem infected the bugs somehow." Lance looked troubled and took the handkerchief, pressing it into his neck and sitting on a nearby tree stump.

"That was quite a show," Nox said appreciatively as people gradually emerged from buildings, muttering in hushed tones. "Ready for our next adventure?"

"We need to get up that mountain now, talk to your friends to find the grem," Lance said, gratefully taking the strips of beef jerky and canteen that Nox handed him. A little color came back into his cheeks after he took a long swig.

Rafi and Brigitta joined them, chewing bread and hard cheese from a cloth embroidered in the yellow colors of Nox's shop.

"Let's hope the grem is still up in Pigeon Mountain," Lance said. "So we go up there, use the vantage points to see any traces."

"The path is very narrow through the trees, so on foot is best," Nox said, taking the bag her uncle handed her. "Quickly now."

"I'm sure we'll make good time," Melinda said dryly and glanced at Brigitta. Though she was an infected pregnant woman, she seemed nimble enough despite her girth. Her balance was off, that much was clear, but her feet were sure. The cheese and bread must've helped, but there was something else, a different kind of energy infusing Brigitta's steps.

She nudged Lance and he followed her gaze, his forehead creasing in worry. Rafi caught their look and turned to Brigitta.

"What're you all staring at me for?" Brigitta asked as they followed Nox toward the trees, leaving her uncle scratching his head over the wagon full of giant mosquito monsters.

"You seem spryer, Brig," Rafi said. "Feeling better, I presume?"

"Like I said," Brigitta replied, her voice stronger and a bit defiant. She smoothed her braids back, replacing her gray hat on her head. "I don't feel sick. And I'm going to make sure that monster pays for what it did."

"*We'll* make sure," Melinda corrected. "We don't need you acting all rash again and getting us in trouble."

Brigitta turned a full glare onto Melinda. Melinda had been on the other side of plenty of frowning looks but Brigitta's fury almost made her take a step back.

"No thanks to you," Brigitta snapped. "I'm not about to let that grem get away. Especially since you were too slow to shoot it."

Melinda's jaw nearly dropped. She'd been called plenty of things, but slow was never one of them. "Listen, you don't have—"

"We won't let it escape," Lance interjected. "But first we've got to let Nox look at it so she can help you, if need be."

Nox led them up the steep path. Melinda hurried to catch up with her and avoid Brigitta for the moment. Ungratefulness she could deal with, but ungrateful *and* rash?

She's grieving, Melinda reminded herself and fell into step next to Nox as they maneuvered between thick tree trunks, the dappled leaves providing some relief from the heat.

"Now that we have a moment, tell me more," Nox said. "What exactly did this creature act like?"

"Like it was straight outta hell," Melinda said. "Popped out of the caved-in body of her husband. About yay big." As she talked, she continually scanned the dirt and plants around them, looking for any telltale sign of azure dust or broken brush.

"Goodness." Nox shook her head and gathered the green skirt of her dress in one hand, gripping the drawstring bag in the other as the path grew steeper. Her steady sandaled feet led them through the narrowing path beneath pines, cedars and oaks.

They fell silent for a few minutes and Melinda stifled a shudder, remembering the grem's small white hand, the sharp claws. She tried not to think of what might happen to Brigitta if they didn't figure out a cure for her. "What's in the bag?"

"Food, bribes," Nox said. The sun beat down on them between the leaves and the air heavy with birds chirping and insects buzzing. "Equipment. My sample pouch. And of course, our little flies."

"So, the folks that live up here," Lance called over to them. "Anything we need to know?"

Nox continued past thickening brush as the path all but disappeared. "The two groups have qualms over the river and water use, a sacred place as far as they're both concerned. Something about a protective entity essential to an annual ceremonial ritual. People of the Downstream River are more artistic—they collect driftwood and make striking wood carvings. They're also a little more volatile, I've found." She shooed away a pair of bees and made her way over gnarling roots. "We'll start with the People of the Riverside Trails, whose hunting and weaving skills are unmatched. Terrible translation of their names, but you get the gist. They weave fish nets stronger than any you've ever seen. They're oldcomers, here long before the rest of us made our way."

Melinda nodded. She knew general history. Most towns, tribes and settlements were roughly grouped as "oldcomer" or "newcomer," with newcomers traveling from various isles to make new homes, while oldcomers lived in settlements that had been around for hundreds of years. When the Edge formed a century ago and unleashed monsters on the land, the influx of newcomers slowed, scared by tales of unnatural creatures overrunning humans.

"Are the oldcomers friendly?" Lance asked as they passed a cluster of pecking gray pigeons sporting iridescent green bands of feathers on the back of their necks. The birds for which the mountain was named, Melinda figured.

"Not really," Nox said. "They have what they need and prefer to be left alone. Though they find some of my mixtures unique and beneficial. I trade with both. Discreetly of course."

"What's that?" Rafi pointed. Melinda pushed forward with Lance to examine the mangled brush. The ground was kicked up and what looked like a claw mark was pressed into the rich dirt.

"About the size of the grem hand," Melinda said. "Can't be sure it's the grem though."

"That's it," Lance turned to look up at the mountain's pinnacle. They had been walking for an hour or so and were about halfway there, as near as Melinda could tell. "I'd wager a pint the grem came this way."

Afternoon sunlight flitted down, and they wiped off sweat as they picked up the pace, invigorated by the discovery. They hadn't gone more than ten minutes when Melinda heard a snap and commotion behind her, followed by Brigitta's shriek and Rafi's grunt.

Melinda spun, her gun already unholstered, to see Brigitta backing up as Rafi struggled, caught in a rope net. Rafi's legs were bound by two loops lifting him a foot off the ground, with more ropes draped around his torso. He was trapped.

CHAPTER FIVE

Lance started to rush forward to help Rafi but Melinda grabbed his arm.

"Where there's one trap there might be more," she warned.

Nox rapidly shouted something—words in an oldcomer language—and Rafi's rope slowly went slack, lowering him to the ground. He threw it off and stepped away from the rope lattice.

"I didn't even see it," Rafi grunted. "That was quite the trap."

"No one up here without creating trouble," a voice said in words Melinda could understand. A broad-shouldered young man emerged, maybe 17, in a lightweight linen and deerskin that she had seen others in Sagebrush Junction wear. Two dark, long braids hung down either shoulder alongside a stern face and quick eyes. "Not to be here, Nox. No place for outsiders. You've brought enough noise already to disturb the mountain."

"From People of the Riverside Trails group, this is Lo'qua'cho, Watcher of the Trail," Nox introduced. "Nothing gets by him."

"We're tracking a monster," Lance said, and pointed to Brigitta. "To save her. And possibly others. We think it went up this mountain."

"No pass," Lo'qua'cho said firmly. Melinda could tell by his relaxed but alert stance that he was probably a decent fighter, and she glimpsed a white knife handle tied to a braided belt alongside small brown satchels.

"You're in danger too, as long as this monster is running free," Melinda said.

"She needs help!" Rafi all but shouted. "It is urgent."

"And we need peace on this mountain," Lo'qua'cho said, kindly but firmly. "Outsiders like you do not understand. Your steps may bring danger. No one crosses without stirring the mountain's veins. No passing."

"They're annoyingly strict about visitors here as you can see," Nox said, using a small cloth to dab at her neck and forehead, where small strands of dark hair escaped her braided bun. "Anything we can do or trade to change your mind, Lo'qua'cho?"

At his lack of a reaction, Lance chimed in. "Is there someone else we can talk to? A leader in your group who might want to hear about this?"

Lo'qua'cho looked closely at his face for a second. Melinda had seen that look before, when someone noticed the curve of Lance's cheekbones or something subtle in the shape of his eyes. "Oldcomer?"

"My pa's side," Lance said, easily enough. "He was from the Northern People of the Horizon. Don't know much about them though. Ma was a newcomer from one of the Grand Isles. Pa's group didn't take too kindly to her."

"Still no pass," Lo'qua'cho said, a little gentler this time.

"Let us ask your wisest council," Nox demanded.

He strode off suddenly and Melinda realized they were supposed to follow. A few minutes later, the smell of lemon and cooked fish made her stomach rumble. The oldcomer settlement that came into view was made up of small cedar planked houses sprawling under the trees between partially underground wooden structures.

"Those are beautiful," Brigitta said, pointing to baskets full of greens and berries that clustered in front of some of the houses.

Lo'qua'cho smiled. "We spent a long time learning the best ways to weave baskets. More than art and craft. It's how we catch our food, how we carry what the trees and the river offer."

From one of the homes in the center emerged a figure not distinctly male or female, with more layers of deerskin than Lo'qua'cho wore, and a skirt made of tree bark. Their gaze settled on Brigitta's stomach with a gentle murmur—a well wish or blessing, Melinda guessed—before pursing their lips.

Lo'qua'cho clinked the stones on his wristband together, rapidly relaying information. The leader frowned and shifted their broad shoulders at an angle away from them. They glanced at Lo'qua'cho, murmuring something low in their own tongue—maybe a reminder of the last time newcomers had crossed sacred boundaries.

"No pass," Lo'qua'cho said and waved his hand behind them, toward the mountain's pinnacle. "What do you call it? *Sacred*. No pass."

Melinda's hope flew away faster than a startled jaybird. There would be no convincing them, then.

"Isn't there any way around the protected land?" Lance asked. "We have reason to think the monster went up the summit. We can stop it before it attacks someone else, or your home here."

Lo'qua'cho hesitated but the leader shook their head.

"We are not worried about attacks," Lo'qua'cho replied.

Melinda bit her tongue. Plenty of towns and groups, newcomers and oldcomers, thought they could take on Edge creatures themselves. And most realized too late that they had underestimated the monsters.

"You have experience fighting supernatural threats?" Lance asked.

Lo'qua'cho shook his head but looked unconcerned. "We've never been attacked. We have a guardian. It keeps away all dangers."

"Well, you don't want your luck to run out," Lance said. "We can help. Let us."

"Please," Rafi growled.

"What about some sort of trade, would you consider?" Nox asked, lifting her bag, but the leader looked away.

"No interest," Lo'qua'cho said. He shifted from foot to foot, the beaded stones around his wrists gently clinking. He fidgeted more than a judge late to an appointment, Melinda thought, but couldn't place why. "There is no trade equal to passage. Outsiders disrupt. We guard."

"Any other day we'd say fine, but these creatures are not like anything you've seen," Melinda retorted and pointed at Brigitta. "We have to save her. And keep you all safe." She heard the tension growing in her voice like a taut string and Lance shifted slightly next to her, a silent cue to stay diplomatic. She ground the inside of her lip between her teeth. They were wasting valuable time.

Lo'qua'cho glanced at the leader and exchanged a silent message.

"You leave," he said to the group, not unkindly. He hurried off and Nox spoke a little longer, but the leader was not swayed.

Melinda stepped away, stifling a groan of frustration. Lance joined her, rolling loose tobacco in a torn piece of paper he pulled from his pocket.

"We can't pass through sacred land without permission," Lance said. "Morally and practically."

At Melinda's silence, he shot her a look. "Any paths through the sacred land may be guarded by other residents up here and traps," he continued. "And no telling if sacred land has curses or creatures attached to it that we best not disturb."

Nox joined them, rolling her eyes in exasperation. "A lot of times I can sway people with a bribe. Not this group."

"I'm not leaving." Brigitta, who had been perching on a rock to rest while she waited, stood. "Without the monster. Dead."

"We're not going anywhere," Melinda agreed.

"That rage will eat the both of you alive," Nox said mildly. "We have to leave. Try to understand: they will take us prisoner if they have to. And if we really ignore them? Well, they'll be speaking the language of pain next. They take their duties very seriously."

"Fair enough. For now, let's keep moving, " Lance said, glancing at the leader and two new figures who had come out to stare at them.

They backtracked on the path they had come from, picking their way around wide tree trunks, a roar of a river just barely audible in the distance.

"Now what?" Brigitta asked, slowing to catch her breath.

"We could go back down, head around the other side and up the mountain that way," Lance suggested.

Rafi groaned. "That will take far too long."

"There's got to be other paths. Other ways we can get through undetected?" Melinda asked Nox, who shook her head.

"They are watchful over this entire south side," Nox said. "Lance is right; you'd need to try re-entering from another vantage point. The far east of the mountain is steep and rocky. It'd be fairly treacherous to climb that side."

Brigitta leaned against a tree abruptly.

"You all right?" Melinda asked. Last thing they needed was her giving birth now.

"She should rest," Nox said. Rafi nodded in agreement, offering Brigitta his canteen.

"How many times do I have to tell you all I feel fine?" Brigitta said, ignoring the canteen and gathering her braids off her neck to wipe away sweat. "I just need some privacy to relieve myself."

"I'll go with you. It'd be just your luck to have the grem attack." Melinda followed her past fluttering oak and fir trees and stood vigilant while Brigitta disappeared behind an overgrown sagebrush.

"You would not believe how many times I have to relieve myself in this state," Brigitta grumbled. "It will take me a minute or two."

While Melinda waited, she studied the terrain. Two hummingbirds zipped by, and one of the mountain pigeons pecking a few feet away startled suddenly. Melinda scanned the bushes, but no trace of the grem.

A sound caught her ears beyond Brigitta's rustling. Melinda strained to make out the clicking noise. A bird, she thought at first, but it was more like small objects clanking together.

Like beaded stones.

"You hear that?" Melinda asked as Brigitta re-emerged from the bush, wiping her hands on her dress. Brigitta shook her head.

Melinda pushed through more brush on her left toward the sound. The brush cleared and she caught a darker shade of brown behind a tree trunk. It was Lo'qua'cho sitting on the ground, his back to them.

"Hey! " Melinda barked, resting her hand on her six-shooter.

Lo'qua'cho turned in surprise and jumped up. He looked sheepish, some of the intensity in his face drained away.

"Spying on us?" Melinda said. "Guess I'm not surprised. You don't have to worry. We're leaving your mountain. For now, at least. Though if you see that grem, you'd have wished we stayed."

"Not spying," Lo'qua'cho said as Nox, Lance and Rafi wandered over at the noise.

That was when Melinda noticed the young woman next to him, obscured by a particularly wide fir tree. The woman stepped forward, her long black hair sleek in the dappled light. She wore a deerskin dress with a grass overlay. A dozen intricate tattoos curled up her chin, fine as hair. For some reason, both the woman and Lo'qua'cho seemed flustered.

"Ah," A look of dawning fell over Nox. Her eyes lit up as if she had found a pile of gold as she studied the woman's tattoos and smooth stone ornament earrings. "People of the Downstream River, yes?"

The woman nodded stiffly. "Chenawa."

Nox smiled, but it wasn't a kind smile. Something about it would've given Melinda warning bells if it was directed at her.

"I imagine your Elders wouldn't approve of crossing the river—especially for something as fleeting as love." Nox pointed at the pair. "You'll help us. Or I'll tell." The pair looked at each other.

"Warring groups from either side of the river," Nox explained smugly to the others. "Star-crossed lovers, that sort of thing. They would be in a lot of trouble if they were found to be canoodling."

"So, you're blackmailing them," Melinda said dryly.

"You want to save your friend or not?" Nox asked.

"We will help with your problem," Lo'qua'cho said reluctantly, squeezing Chenawa's hand after murmuring something to her. "In exchange for your solemn silence."

"You'll let us through the sacred land?" Lance asked, wiping his brow with a handkerchief.

"There is another path through the mountain over the river, between the impassable and our place, that we don't talk about," Lo'qua'cho said. "They worry too many people will hear, too many people will come. We can take that way and not touch the sacred area. Only if you swear to not speak of it after."

"Yes of course," Melinda said impatiently as the others nodded.

"But we have to climb." Lo'qua'cho pointed up where, past the towering trees, a bit of rope was just visible. "We have to go high."

Nox craned her head up. "Color me impressed. Why so high?"

"We built them to avoid dangers, predators. And newcomers," Lo'qua'cho said pointedly.

Lance glanced at Melinda, and she shook her head dismissively. More recently, heights had been giving her a sense of vertigo. Just another new trait along with the visions she was contending with, but no matter; that wouldn't stop her.

"At least we'll be able to see better," Melinda said. "Good vantage point to spot the monster."

"Let's go," Brigitta said.

"No way you can climb those," Melinda said sternly and Brigitta scowled at her. "Stay here. We'll take a peek and find that grem."

"I'll stay too," Rafi said. "It will be a rest for you, Brig."

"Me too," Nox said. "Heights don't agree with me. We'll wait right here for you while you find the critter."

Melinda and Lance followed Lo'qua'cho around several trees to a rope ladder swinging from a giant oak branch. Lance had always been a better climber than her, easily keeping up with Lo'qua'cho and Chenawa as they moved speedily up the rope ladder.

Once they started, Melinda got the hang of the rope and made sure not to look down. The ladder led them to a makeshift bridge that connected one tree to another, just wide enough for an adult to pass. Now that she was up here, she glimpsed bits of wood swinging through the thick oak leaves, a whole system of bridgework and complicated paths made of crisscrossing rope, reminiscent of the baskets she had seen earlier. The network was all invisible from the ground, an entire system of transportation that was a testament to generations of craftsmanship and planning.

Melinda went slow to make sure her boot heels didn't get stuck in the gaps between the coiled ropes, as the roar of a river rose. Ahead of them, Lo'qua'cho's village sprawled with its cedar roofs. East of those, the sliver of a river snaked ahead. What she assumed was Chenawa's home—brown tents across the river—was just barely visible.

Suddenly the roar of the water dropped away. The sky darkened and the sweat that collected at her forehead turned cold. Melinda looked up, dreading what she knew she would see.

CHAPTER SIX

Not now, Melinda thought, trying with all her might to will away the hallucination. But the vision of the Edgling remained, perching on one of the ropes a few feet away. Watching her.

The Edgling had a blurred face, contrasting its sharp elbows and longer fingers. A memory came back to her of when countless Edglings swarmed right before Abel was killed by the demon Melinda had inadvertently led to him.

You didn't know. It wasn't your fault, she reminded herself, but she had a hard time getting forgiveness to break through the blanket of guilt that descended. She tried not to look at the Edgling and focused instead on watching her boots against the entwined ropes.

The darkness tunneling into her vision was making it hard to see her next steps. The rope bridge swung slightly and she leaned into it. There was nothing to hold onto, just the tightly knit bridge beneath her feet. It shook as she wavered, trying to keep her balance.

Hard to balance if you can't see, she thought in panic as the dim light and leaves around her seemed to reel.

"You peachy back there?" Lance called from ahead.

His voice. She focused on Lance's words and took the slightest step forward again. Then another, ignoring the sensation of the shadow creature watching her.

"Just dandy," she called back and bit down hard on her lip, the bit of pain distracting her and forcing away the darkness. She ignored the layers of sweat coating her neck and back as she caught up to him.

Lance's gaze searched her. Not with doubt, exactly, just a question.

"I'm fine," she muttered. The daylight grew brighter and the shadows faded. "I swear."

"You got that look," he said in concern.

She blinked, catching sight of Lo'qua'cho and Chenawa climbing onto the next bridge. Below spread the vast forest of green and brown. A family of deer moved to the east, grazing. Quails and the banded pigeons plucked along the ground, and the trees rustled in the breeze.

"What if we don't find the grem?" Melinda said to change the subject. No need to talk about the Edgling vision again, or how she had almost plummeted to her doom. The breeze, cooled by the water, swirled by them, a welcome relief from the stifling heat. "Brigitta's time might be running out. Your time might be running out too if that bug bite was infected."

"I don't *feel* infected," Lance replied. "And we have to hope she's not sick either. But we won't stop till we find that grem."

They followed the pair up higher and toward the river. The sound of rushing water swelled, and the streaming water came into sight as they started across the next bridge. The river looked like a living, vibrant thing, easily 60 feet across, with white rapids sloshing between wet gleaming boulders. Fish flashed below and two brown otters floated along. On the far side of the river, a trail of disturbed leaves and trees cut a distinct line, as if a hurried animal had trampled through. The grem, maybe.

"We have to get closer," Melinda said to Lance and pointed to the disturbance. They caught up to the middle of the rope bridge directly over the water where Lo'qua'cho paused next to Chenawa. Chenawa's bright eyes watched the stream intensely.

"What is she doing?" Melinda said.

"Remembering this sight, the sunlight on the ripples," Lo'qua'cho said. "She is an artist who carves. One of the very best." His voice held a hint of pride.

Melinda was about to remind them they didn't have time to admire the view when something in the water caught her eye. Far below them, the river churned.

Not the grem—something bigger.

"What's that?" Lance asked.

A shine of pink broke through the water—the back of a fish. It had to be 8 feet wide and 20 feet long at least. Melinda stared, taking in the enormity of the creature.

Lance gave a low whistle. "That's some fish."

"Monstrous but not monster," Lo'qua'cho said as he and Chenawa gazed reverently at the creature. "At least, unless you get close. The great fish has been known to snatch deer from the riverbank. Even a small black bear once, according to stories. It protects us and gives us bountiful fish each year."

The gigantic fish flailed in the river, creating a splash that sprayed them with water even from here, some 40 feet up. Salmon glittered in the dappled sunlight before falling back down. As the giant fish turned slightly out of the water they could see hundreds of smaller fish clinging to its underside like barnacles.

Melinda shook off the river drops from her sleeve and peered back down. Now she could see the fish's giant mouth, downturned in a perpetual lipless frown, with a cluster of pink tentacles emanating from it. The tentacles were flicking against a boulder on the riverbank.

Chenawa screamed. Not a scream of terror but one of solidarity, Melinda realized. She watched in shock as Chenawa dove off the bridge with a grace and strength Melinda had to admire.

"What's she doing?" Lance yelled.

"It needs help," Lo'qua'cho said. "It is not acting normal. In pain."

Melinda followed the trajectory of his pointing to see more of the fish creature's tentacles whipping against the boulder. Around the boulder looked to be a freshly fallen pile of stones and branches.

"Something about that debris is bothering it," Melinda observed.

Chenawa emerged a few feet from the head of the fish and was carried swiftly along by the current before she managed to climb onto the riverbank. She ran back toward the debris pile.

"What happens if people get too close?" Lance asked, and judging by Lo'qua'cho's worried face, Melinda could guess.

"It's a protector, but can be hurt," Lo'qua'cho responded. "Disturb or threaten it, it will protect itself first."

"You know this creature better than us," Melinda said, resisting the urge to reach for her gun. She glanced at Lance. They could move on, but they wouldn't get too far without Lo'qua'cho and Chenawa. They needed to find that damn grem. "How can we help?"

"Do you swim?" Lo'qua'cho asked, never pulling his eyes from Chenawa as he spoke. Below, she was throwing herself against the rock with little success, trying to budge it. "My group is never permitted to touch the water when sighting the great fish, for risk of angering her. It will take us too long to climb back down." He tensed, readying to dive but hesitated, torn.

"Water's one thing I don't do," Melinda said and glanced at Lance. "You up for it?"

"A refreshing dip sounds nice about now. How can I help?" Lance asked, shrugging off his duster and unbuckling his holster.

"There's something under the rock that's upsetting it. Together you and Chenawa move it." Lo'qua'cho pointed. Lance dove into the water, more of a cannonball than Chenawa's smooth swan dive.

Melinda waited, the urge to draw her gun even stronger. "We got reason to worry?" she said to Lo'qua'cho. "Tell me the truth."

A small muscle flicked in his jaw. "The great fish normally does not attack people. But it is not acting normal."

Lance's sandy hair emerged from the froth a second later, carried quickly along the stream. He climbed out onto the riverbank and made his way over to Chenawa, who ducked the flicking tentacles in between heaving off smaller rocks from beneath the boulder.

Lance looked up at Melinda, his mouth moving.

They were too far away to hear. "Can we get down there? We gotta help." Melinda said.

"Normally no footsteps are allowed on this side of the river. But the great fish needs help. We can go down. I will take responsibility." Lo'qua'cho made the decision quickly and then retraced their path along the bridges, twice as fast as before. Melinda hastened to keep up as they climbed down the rope lattices. It felt like forever before leaves parted and the ground came into view.

Never so happy to see dirt, Melinda thought. They ran to the riverbank, where the smell of fish and wet dirt intensified amidst the watercress. From down here she could clearly see what had happened: a rupture had torn open the ground next to the river. It looked as though a meteor had hit it in reverse, with the pile of rocks and a nearby tree freshly felled. The boulder too had been displaced, teetering on the edge of the riverbank.

"There." Lo'qua'cho pointed. What looked like a tentacle flicked from beneath the boulder. The fish thrashed again, sending streams of water over them. "It is stuck. In pain."

Meanwhile, Chenawa and Lance had removed plenty of the fallen rocks, but the boulder hadn't budged. They had taken to shoving themselves against it but with no success.

"Wait." Melinda set down Lance's things and rummaged in their bag, carefully pulling out one of their dynamites and unwrapping it from its cloth cushioning. "We wedge it here in the ground, maybe it gives enough of a rumble. It's a small one."

Lo'qua'cho nodded. "Don't hurt it."

"I don't think a boom stick can slow down that fish," Lance said.

"Stand back!" Melinda called over the roar of the water and held up a fist before spraying out her fingers. *Boom.* The others backed up as she set off the fuse.

It went off with a sharp *pop!* and the rock rumbled and shifted. The tentacle slid out, squashed and bleeding. The boulder continued its trajectory, teetering for a moment before falling into the water.

They all ducked as the giant salmon creature squirmed, its tentacles flicking wildly, slapping at the tall grass around them. With one last great heave, the monster slipped beneath the waves.

"It will be OK," Lo'qua'cho said in relief.

Lance grinned, shaking off the water from his head and about to say something when his face fell. Melinda spun to look behind her, half-expecting another monster.

"The hole," Lance said. She peered into the hollowed-out ground and mess of rocks freshly revealed by the boulder's absence. Just barely visible, a trail of azure motes coated the rocks.

"It's the same blue dust we saw earlier," Lance said.

"What does it mean?" Lo'qua'cho asked, looking troubled. "Disturbed earth like this risks unbalancing the mountain and all who live here."

Chenawa responded in a clipped tone, glaring at them.

"She thinks you brought this danger here to us," Lo'qua'cho said. "Is that true? This is why no outsiders. They bring noise, sickness. Danger and destruction. Now our protector suffers." He looked more agitated by the second. "Our great fish might have died had we not come across it."

"*We* didn't bring any danger here," Melinda said impatiently. "This is what we're trying to stop. What we warned you about."

"We don't know what it means yet, but it's not good," Lance said. "Let's get to Brigitta and the others."

"Not with us," Lo'qua'cho said coldly. He and Chenawa climbed swiftly back up the ropes onto one of the bridges through the green and were gone. Melinda and Lance watched for a second, the roaring river the only sound.

"Thanks anyway," Melinda said to the empty trees. She crouched next to the disturbed ground. "Doesn't look like something hit it."

"Or came out of it," Lance agreed.

Melinda glanced behind them to the west, where the branches were broken and ragged, where down the mountain rested the town of Fallows. "The grem came through there and *burrowed*… into this ground."

"And covered its tracks," Lance continued. "That's a smart monster."

"And damned strong," Melinda said, as they stared at the ground, stunned. The grem was even more powerful than they had initially guessed, if it was able to move the boulder aside that four of them had barely been able to budge.

"Why would it go underground here after running up the mountain?" Lance mused then answered his own question. "To avoid crossing the river, maybe?"

"Or to take a shortcut somewhere." Rocks blocked any view of a tunnel. "Another explosive could open it up so we can follow its trail."

"If the grem is covering its tracks as it digs, any path is good as gone." Lance leaned back on his heels.

"You do not have to look too far," a familiar voice called from overhead. Lo'qua'cho returned alone, lofty above them. He pointed northeast, back across the river.

"You're back," Lance said. "Why?"

"Come to see." Lo'qua'cho gestured. The way he said it—short, affectless—filled Melinda with dread. They climbed up the nearest rope ladder again and made their way across the river, but this time took a sharp left, heading northeast. They hurried for a few minutes in silence along the interconnected bridges. She breathed in the fresh air, the smell of fish still lingering. The hot breeze brought up another smell, one that sent her stomach into a warning lurch.

Blood.

She didn't want to see what would be at the top as they emerged out of the trees. A steep overlook revealed a panoramic view of miles upon miles of dry fields stretching to the northeast.

Lance sucked in a sharp breath. Melinda peered over the drop. It took her a minute to understand what she was seeing. Movement flitted across the field. At first she thought it was a herd of small albino horses or large pigs, but they were moving all wrong, racing along the ground with purpose.

"It's not just one grem," Lance gasped. "It's a whole army."

CHAPTER SEVEN

Down the sharp incline of Pigeon Mountain, at least fifty of the grems flashed hues of blue as they scurried across the field. They barreled forward, their claws slicing through the dirt and sending up plumes of dust. A single farmhouse lay devastated in the southwest corner of the field where the grems had passed. Its wooden rails sat destroyed and half a dozen cows sprawled dead and gutted.

"I have never seen animals move like this," Lo'qua'cho said. "Even monsters. These are something else." His face creased in worry. "Their movement is not good. They risk bringing danger to the sacred sites. Disrupting hunting. Many problems."

"Where on earth are they going?" Melinda's gaze shot east, where a steep gorge began at an opposing peak and Pigeon Mountain. "What's on the other side of that gorge?"

"Towns." Lo'qua'cho stood behind them. "I care not for them, but they leave us alone. They should not be hurt. They call the first one Thundering Ridge."

"How long you reckon we have to get to Thundering Ridge and warn them?" Lance asked.

"Fastest." Lo'qua'cho pointed. "You go down the way you came. Then you ride on a good horse and can get to Thundering when the sun starts its descent."

Melinda glanced at the sky, then Lance. "So, what, 3 or 4 hours to ride? But look at how fast the grems are going."

Lance studied the creatures. "They'll have to funnel through the gorge. We can beat them there. Got to get back to Sagebrush Junction first to get the horses."

Lo'qua'cho paused. "Before you go, I want to say, thank you for help at the river. We were too fast to anger. Chenawa does not like visitors."

"Thank *you* for the help," Lance replied. "Knowing where those grems are heading is gonna let us save lives."

They followed Lo'qua'cho rapidly down an intricate path of ropes that had Melinda turned around. As they descended, she felt a stab of worry for Brigitta and her infection. But focusing on the grem hoard was their best chance to find an antidote, and to stop many more from dying.

When their boots landed on the ground, there was no sign of the others.

"This is where they were," Lo'qua'cho said, and Melinda recognized the boulder Brigitta had been sitting on.

"Damn," Melinda swore. "Where did they go? We don't have time for this."

"I will find them, tell them to meet you in Thundering Ridge." Lo'qua'cho pointed past them, east. "Fastest way to Sagebrush for your horses. Go, now."

Melinda and Lance headed down the steep rocky path, half running until they got back to Sagebrush Junction. No sign of the others, and most of the stores were closed, but they didn't have time to waste. Rafi and Brigitta's horses were still in the livery stable, getting groomed.

They saddled up Pepper and Mud and pushed them hard toward Thundering Ridge. On the outskirts of town, they had to slow as wagons and other riders clogged up the road. The horses eased to a walk as crumbling dirt gave way to a packed path full of carriages, horses and pedestrians.

"Must be preparations for the festival Nox mentioned," Lance said. The horses took the opportunity to snatch eager mouthfuls of purple radish flowers growing along the shaded path. "We got to warn the mayor and get everyone to evacuate. Then we set a trap for the grems."

"There's too many people," Melinda said in frustration. "With the roads this crammed it'd be a mess to get everyone out." She resisted the urge to shout at them all to leave. It wouldn't work—they needed to enlist the aid of the local lawmakers to lend them authority. Otherwise, they'd be deemed troublemakers and ignored.

"Let us through," Melinda grunted and finally nudged Pepper away from the flowers up on the grassy bank, passing the wagons and other riders, despite a few dirty looks.

"We're all waiting here," someone grumbled. "Why should you go ahead?"

"This is an emergency," Lance said. "Folks, coming through please."

Thundering Ridge was a large town, nearly twice as big as Five Peaks by the looks of it, with four parallel main streets crisscrossed by nearly a dozen smaller ones, featuring a heavy concentration of blacksmiths, tanneries, butchers and several taverns. Tops of large tents flapped to the south of the town, where the festival was being erected. To the north, one could just see the mountain ridges that marked the end of the gorge, maybe a mile or so from town.

They found their way to an especially grand building, with lace-like ironworking and gold touches at the corners of its windows and a towering, steel-studded wooden door.

"Guessing this would be where we can find the lawmakers of Thundering Ridge," Lance said. "Let's hope they're reasonable."

They secured the horses on a hitching post and hurried in, waving off a protesting administrator and passing through another set of doors into the mayor's office.

Inside, a slim black man sat at a massive oak desk, halfway through an early dinner of roasted potatoes and shoots of asparagus, the sight of which made Melinda's mouth water. Around him, a handful of people argued over the placement of a particular tent or vendor. One barrel-shaped man rushed past them with a stack of notes he barely managed to keep from dropping.

"*Sir and ma'am,*" a middle-aged woman said with a note of exasperation as she followed Melinda and Lance into the office. Her high-collared cotton shirt was immaculate under wavy hair set back with a pin. "You simply cannot burst in here like that. Especially without an appointment." She pursed heart-shaped lips at the mud they had tracked onto the polished floor. "If you're looking for a watering hole, I'd suggest trying the one on Second Street," the woman continued. "Or better yet, the bath houses on Fourth."

"Sorry ma'am, this is an emergency," Lance said.

The mayor looked up, serene amidst the chatter and chaos. "It's all right, Ginny, we have a lot going on today. I'm happy to help, but our festival organizers can probably assist you better than I." He gestured to the pair next to him whose voices rose as their argument over a tent placement grew more heated. "If you don't mind, gentleman, taking this outside. I would suggest you see if the proprietaries would like to pair up to solve this particular dilemma."

The pair hustled out without missing a beat. "Double booked a vendor," the mayor explained. "Once they sort it out, I'm sure they can help you with your questions."

"It's not about the festival," Lance said. "It's a—"

"First, a proper introduction." The mayor wiped his hands and stood, gesturing to himself and then the woman with the wavy hair. "Allen Fields, at your service. Mrs. Ginny Quan, there, my right-hand woman. And there in the chair, our newspaper man, Mr. Abrams Miranda."

Abrams, a medium-sized man in a dapper vest, reclined in a wooden rocker. His round darkened spectacles disguised his expression, and his neat mustache stretched cheek-to-cheek. He handled a fountain pen and a small notebook, slowly writing without looking.

"Covering the festival here," Abrams said. "Pleased to make your acquaintance."

"Melinda West and Lance Putnam," Lance introduced. "You've got a problem here."

"A big one," Melinda interjected. "You need to get people out."

"A monster herd is coming your way down the gorge," Lance said. "They killed a few people in a town called Fallows, not too far off."

Melinda watched for the mayor's reaction to see how he'd handle the news. A lot of folks clammed up at the mention of monsters, all but sticking their fingers in their ears to ignore a coming disaster.

When she first started monster exterminating with Lance, she'd assume—wrongly— that people would appreciate their help. But plenty of towns thought they were swindling or lying. Some flat out wouldn't listen. It was one of the things that haunted her still, the occasional town or group of people they'd come across in their work that, for one reason or another, wouldn't accept the danger of the Edge monsters. Sometimes people thought they could tame them or live harmoniously with them. Those folks wouldn't help, worse yet, would stop Melinda and Lance from doing their jobs— usually ending in disaster. When the stubbornness of people stopped them from saving lives, well, she'd just about quit for good.

"You don't say," Mayor Fields replied, and Ginny crossed her arms.

Abrams cocked his head, expressionless behind his spectacles, though his hand started penning rapidly across his paper. "Don't mind my asking, but you got any proof of this?" Abrams asked.

"*Proof?*" Melinda scowled. So, he thought they were lying or exaggerating. Figured.

"There's a woman infected and a hoard of grems on the way," Lance said.

Mayor Fields nodded slowly. "I understand that you are concerned. But this is the expo of the year, starting tomorrow. We had new canvas tents made. We got sellers coming from as far as South Ridge. Everyone expects it to be a hog-killin' good time. My mother and father started it years ago. Grew it and put our name on the map. It's no simple matter to cancel and evacuate."

"Do you hear what we're saying?" Melinda snapped. "People will die."

Mayor Fields smiled patiently. Not condescendingly, she saw, which would've really made her jaw grind.

"I'll be frank," the mayor said. "One thing you'd find if you ran a town like mine is a lot of people come 'round offering help. Services for this or that. Put up a nice show, convincing. Come to find out afterwards, those services are heavy on the pockets."

Lance opened his mouth, but the mayor held up a hand as he continued. "I'm sure you are honest folks but nonetheless, I have a responsibility to this town to be discerning and not exhaust our collective funds with every passerby that comes through, take my meaning?"

"I've heard of these two," Abrams piped up suddenly, smoothing his brown hair. "Monster hunters. Cleaned up Edge infestations in the northern territory."

"That's right." Lance perked. "So, you know we're above board."

"I believe you can trust them at their word," Abrams said.

"We're not interested in payment anyhow," Melinda said between clenched teeth. "We are trying to save lives. Your town. Cancel the festival at least. Get these people out of here."

"We're the most prosperous settlement on this side of the mountain ridge," Ginny said. "Word gets out that we cancel this year's festival due to a rumor of some animals and well, that's not good for our reputation."

"Some things are more important than a reputation," Melinda said to which Ginny raised an eyebrow.

"I would argue that few things are more important than a reputation," Ginny replied.

"You say they're coming through the gorge," the mayor mused. "And you're going to take care of them. So, take care of them there. No need to disrupt the festival's activities."

"That's the plan, but things get unpredictable when it comes to monsters," Lance said. "No guarantee we catch them all."

"Tell you what." The mayor stood. "We do appreciate your vigilance here. We see landslides at the gorge occasionally. I suggest setting one off and that should kill 'em, right? I'll send my best shooter along to help, seeing as how you're doing this free of charge." He nodded at Ginny, who sighed.

"All right." Ginny went over to a glass case behind him to select a shotgun. "I'll meet you there shortly."

Lance bid the mayor thanks and farewell, before they saddled up and rode the mile out of town, north toward the gorge.

"Damn people," Melinda grumbled as they rode. "We try to help and it's like pulling teeth."

"They don't know what they don't know," Lance said mildly. "Least we got some help for this one. Here we go." They stopped on a small dirt mound a quarter mile from the mouth of the gorge.

A glinting cloud the hue of crushed turquoise hung over the gorge. It wasn't like any color she'd ever seen at sunrise or sunset.

"The grems, heralding their approach," Melinda said. "Gives us time to set the trap."

"A well-timed rockslide should take out even the strongest little mutts," Lance said.

Melinda turned at a horse's trot behind them to see Abrams on a spritely chestnut horse. He dismounted carefully.

"Well, that's unusual." Abrams' head turned, his glasses reflecting the glowing gorge. "What kind of creatures are we dealing with here?"

"We don't need any spectators," Melinda said. Lance cleared his throat at that, and she could practically hear him telling her to not be so blunt. But she didn't care; any tact she had was long gone; all that mattered was stopping those grems and making sure no one else got hurt.

"I heard a bit about your work, maybe two years ago." Abrams settled on a nearby rock and took out a notebook while his horse grazed. "The accounts have always been oddly vague."

"Most people won't talk too much about their monsters, for superstitious fear that it'll bring them back or make the monsters stronger," Lance replied.

"I'm curious to see your work in action," Abrams said. "May I interview you both, time permitting, after this extermination?"

"We keep a low profile nowadays," Lance said. "Mr. Miranda, we appreciate your wanting to record happenings and what not. But this could go sideways real quick and I just wouldn't feel right with you in the line of danger."

"Call me Abrams, please," he said, but didn't budge. "It's my duty and honor to observe and report. No need to worry about me."

Ginny rode up on a small black Mustang and handed Melinda two satchels of food. "Mayor thought you looked starving back there," she said. She stayed on her horse, who stomped testily, and laid her shotgun across her knees.

Lance removed the four sticky traps from their bag and Melinda took out her rifle. Through the specialty magnifying scope, she'd be able to watch Lance and keep any unexpected attacks at bay as he placed the traps.

"Quick now," Melinda said. He nodded, lifted his handkerchief across his mouth and rode Mud toward the gorge.

"So how does this all work?" Abrams asked.

"Abrams here has been looking for his big scoop," Ginny said dryly. "Maybe this'll be it. Get your name on the map so you can move to a big city, isn't that right?"

"Writing about town festivals just don't cut it," Abrams said amicably. "So, Ms. West, what is the plan here?"

"He places the bombs, I shoot," Melinda said shortly. The bread from Ginny's bag was probably moist and delectable but felt dry as sand in her mouth. As she ate, she kept watch on Lance through her scope. The sight of the unnatural blue cloud made her stomach churn.

"Hmm." Ginny watched with interest as Lance tossed up the contraptions as high as he could along the rocky walls, two on either side. "Those bombs attach onto the rock?"

Melinda nodded curtly, ignoring a small pang. Abel had invented the sticky traps years ago when Melinda and Lance first started hunting monsters. Armed with compressed gunpowder cake and a potion he had devised years ago, the tacky bombs explode with a single bullet. She held her breath until Lance and Mud cantered back to them.

"All set." Lance removed the custom crossbow next from the bag. "Been looking forward to trying this out," he said, hoisting it up.

"Did you create that specifically for hunting monsters?" Abrams asked. His pen hadn't stopped moving across the page since he sat.

"Not me, but a brilliant man named Abel Yao." Lance turned it proudly in his hands. "See here, it's equipped with smaller, hooked arrows alongside of the bigger ones. That lets it shoot several projectiles with a single shot." He offered Melinda the weapons bag. "You want the last boom stick?"

"Not yet," Melinda said. "I'll save the dynamite for when things really get going."

The rest of the sky glowed pinker than swollen gums as the sun made its descent. Time ticked on, the minutes dragging slowly. Abrams asked Lance a barrage of questions, which he obliged, telling stories of their previous monster hunting adventures. Ginny and Melinda sat silent and watchful.

Now that the trap was set, the waiting was worse than ever. They all fell quiet as the sun hit the horizon and the sapphire cloud darkened.

Abrams shivered. "There's surely something in the air that doesn't feel right."

Melinda knew what he meant. The slight breeze felt like a thunderstorm was gathering overhead, though there wasn't a cloud in the sky. Just that damned glow.

"What do you think they want?" Melinda said out loud. If she wasn't on Pepper, she'd be pacing. Instead, she fought to keep her boot tips from tapping against the horse. Usually, her eyesight was nearly sharp as a hawk's, but a shadow flitted in the corners of her vision. The dark shape elongated to four impossibly long fingers as an Edgling started to take form.

Not now. She wiped the sweat off her forehead and focused on Lance's words to force the vision away.

"Most monsters we've seen act more or less like regular animals," Lance was saying to Ginny and Abrams as he rolled shreds of tobacco in a bit of torn paper from his pocket. "They're looking for food, shelter or defending themselves. But these grems, we're not so sure."

"Y'all!" Abrams exclaimed. "There's something…" His forehead was creased, puzzled, as he held out his hands face down on the rock he perched on. "Rumble in the ground. But it's not coming from the gorge. Feel that?"

Melinda did now that he mentioned it, a little tremor beneath Pepper's uneasy feet. Like an earthquake.

"Landslide already?" Ginny mused.

"There they are!" Lance shouted.

Something emerged out of the gorge. Melinda looked through the rifle's scope to see the grem better.

It was a hunched-up mass the texture of a maggot and coated in patches of blue fur. The grem looked to be about as high as her waist. It reminded her of a dog that might've had its face flattened, with a mouth that stretched the entire width of its blocky head. A double layer of angled pewter teeth sparking beneath its red-rimmed white eyes.

But it was only one grem. The rest of the herd was nowhere in sight.

CHAPTER EIGHT

As the single grem emerged from the gorge, Melinda trained her sights back on the first tacky bomb, waiting.

"Oh my." Ginny squinted and strained to keep her mustang in place.

"What does it look like?" Abraham asked, adjusting his spectacles and standing.

"Like something that crawled out of the outhouse," Ginny said.

"Wait for the swarm," Lance said to Melinda, "before we set it off."

"The rest of them aren't there," Melinda said through gritted teeth. The horses shifted uneasily.

Ginny glanced around her at that, raising her shotgun.

The single grem barreled toward them, fifty feet away now. Motes of cobalt trailed behind it like crushed crystals.

"Got to take this one out before it gets too close," Melinda said. Mud reared up, his eyes showing white with panic, and Lance fought to keep him in check. Pepper tried to do the same and Melinda tsked her to stay steady.

"Horses never reacted to Edge monsters like this before," Lance said. Pepper and Mud had been in proximity to plenty of monsters and usually kept their cool, but not this time.

The grem stopped 20-some feet away. It titled its head up and hacked, sending blue dust into a smaller cloud above it. Then it looked at them with eyes that had a cluster of pupils in its center, like a pile of black beans, encircled with red.

And… smiled.

Melinda lowered the rifle. "It's a trick," she said.

That's when she heard the very faint but unmistakable rapid fire of bullets, carried on the sudden breeze that picked up. The sound sent her stomach dropping down through her boots.

"The town!" Ginny shouted and tore her horse around.

"It's the grems," Lance said. "Has to be. Hurry!"

Melinda's heart thundered as fast as the horses' hooves as they galloped south. The gorge was about a mile from the town, and she hoped they'd get there in time. She urged Pepper faster along the dirt road, rising in the stirrups. Lance rode close behind with Ginny in the lead. They passed the neatly painted town sign and a wagon with a single horse making its way toward the festival.

"Turn around!" Ginny ordered the driver as they sped by.

The screams and gunshots grew louder as they bolted through the town, dodging frightened pedestrians who had stopped in confusion.

"The ruckus is coming from the festival!" Abrams hollered from behind them.

"Take cover, get out of here!" Ginny instructed the people, before urging her mustang down main street. The south field came into sight a few moments later, along with the flapping of torn tents. People scattered in a way Melinda recognized: terrified and trying to survive.

The horses slowed at the destroyed ground that met them at the edge of the street. They picked their way past steep mounds and fresh ditches while a handful of people ran by them with shrieks. Melinda spotted a few figures limp on the ground.

Three grems popped out of the dirt amidst a spray of rocks.

"Cover your mouths, your skin! We got reason to think their dust makes you sick. Try not to touch it," Melinda shouted, feeling Pepper tense as if to bolt. The four of them dismounted, letting the horses trot back to a safe distance.

Lance and Melinda came to one felled body and raised their handkerchiefs over their noses. The figure—nearly unidentifiable as human—was torn to pieces, with a chest open like a crater, but rather than a hole in the dirt this was a hole in flesh. And in that flesh…

A grem had climbed in, writhing and bathing in the guts.

She heard someone—Ginny or Abrams—heave behind her.

"Kill as many of the grems as you can!" Lance commanded. "They're fast and strong but not immune to bullets!"

A grem burrowed up from the packed dirt next to them, clawing its way out of the ground with a snarl. Melinda waited until its head, the size of her fist, had fully emerged before she shot it.

The whitish head lolled back, brown blood spilling from the hole in its cheek.

Other grems were already upon the bodies. One the size of a tomcat in front of them hissed, its mouth full of more teeth than any creature on this earth needed. It leapt onto a man who lay unconscious. Before they could shoot it, it tore into his torso as if it were no more than parchment paper. It wiggled half its body inside as the man's chest began to cave in.

They shot and shot again, until the grem inside stopped moving. Lance fell in line next to her, and they fired in unison, strategically separating and drawing closer together as they picked off the grems one by one. In her periphery, Ginny, Abrams and others fired off shots in between helping people up and ushering them away from the massacre.

Melinda turned to see a smaller grem the size of a prairie dog wiggling in a freshly bleeding corpse. She reeled but her senses snapped together, everything getting slow and sharp as she moved with purpose: shooting one grem here, another there. The bullets blasted through the stiff monster bodies, sending them staggering just as they burst from the ground. With each shot, she felt lighter, the rush of the fight keeping her focused. She never missed her mark.

This is what she was good at. What she was born to do.

But something nagged at Melinda: the sight of those blue-white veins of the Fallows corpses. She didn't see any glowing veins here. The handful of people that fell or died were torn open, with no time for infection. The infection didn't kill them, at least not yet. What killed them, Melinda thought, were the grems themselves. *But why?*

She approached yet another grem sitting in an elderly man's body, coating itself in blood. As she shot it dead, she wracked her mind until an image of the first, small grem they had seen in Fallows came up. She nudged the corpse of the man, shoving the limp body of the grem away with her boot. Then she spotted it; a pair of smooth glistening orbs nestled deep in the guts. One was vibrating.

Cracking.

Eggs.

"They're using the bodies to reproduce!" she shouted. Just saying it aloud nearly made Melinda wretch. The doctor at Fallows had been right but for the wrong reason: they needed to burn the bodies—not to stop infection but to stop the monsters from breeding. "We gotta burn them!"

Lance called back to Ginny who had stayed close behind them. "You all start burning the dead, fast as you can." He pointed. "Looks to be half a dozen at least. Get to it."

"We can't." Ginny spoke with an uncharacteristic stammer, and her wide eyes were on the verge of shock. "We haven't taken stock of who they were. We have to do proper burials—"

"We don't have a choice," Lance replied. "We have to contain the grems. This is our best chance."

Melinda continued to shoot the monsters, reload, shoot. More grems started moving with purpose, now ignoring the bodies.

"Eyes up," Melinda said, and Lance stiffened next to her, undoubtedly noticing the same thing.

They were making a circle around Lance and Melinda. Acting *intelligently* and moving simultaneously. They had figured out their biggest threat—Lance and Melinda—and were going to do something about it.

The pair backed up as more grems emerged from the dirt.

"There's too many. We're outnumbered." Lance grabbed her arm. "Mellie—"

His gaze bore into her, the same worried look he gave each night when she woke up half-screaming from her dreams.

She shook her head. "We can't leave. And we got to make sure every single one is dead, so they can't keep breeding."

Part of monster hunting was knowing when to cut their losses and surrender, at least temporarily. It was how they survived for so long. But as the screams continued amidst the torn and flapping tents, she saw the grim agreement in his face despite their odds.

They weren't going anywhere.

"We need a plan," he said as they kept backing up from nearly a dozen blood-stained grems. The smell of smoke pricked her nose as Ginny and Abrams went to work burning the bodies. "Almost out of bullets. We got the crossbow and dynamite, then we're out."

"Slim arsenal," she said. "We gotta figure out their pattern. They're using the bodies to lay eggs like reptiles, but they look like mammals and move like…"

"They were moving in a swarm," Lance said. "Hive-like. Like an ant colony. Which means…"

"There may be a leader," Melinda said. "Queen bee. We got to find it."

"We get it, maybe the swarm disperses," he said, wiping his brow.

She fired off two shots as the grems kept pressing them backwards against one of the few intact giant tents. "You draw them away, and I'll get into the center of the swarm and attack. Like we did on Daracors Riverbends." That job had featured small but strong weasel-type creatures with a fear of sun and a taste for blood. Once they got rid of the largest one, the leader, the rest had scattered and become easier to pick off.

"Take this," Lance gave her the stick of dynamite and matchbook from his bag. "It should do a number."

He lifted the crossbow, drew the string and hit the trigger. Dozens of barbed arrows flew out with his shot, hitting at least six grems. In between his shots, Melinda ran, dodging claws as she neared the highest concentration of grems ahead of them.

The grems snarled around her, a sound like hissing between chattering teeth as more clawed out of the ground. A gaping mouth nearly took off a chunk of her arm before Lance's arrows hit a new batch of grems, clearing the way for her. Someone else's—Ginny's or Abrams'—steady gunshots picked off the grems on either side of her that lunged out. One miss, and she'd be done.

The bullets and arrows were slowing them down but not nearly as fast as she hoped. She kept moving, dodging two grems that attacked in a coordinated effort—much more sophisticated than she was used to from monsters.

I have never seen animals move like this, Lo'qua'cho had said, and Melinda had to agree. The grems were adapting their fighting to Melinda's attacks and closing in. She managed to fend off a pair, whacking one with the butt of her gun and landing a square kick on another.

"Look!" The single, hollered word from Lance shot a spike of dread through her as she turned. Something large loomed behind the snarling grems and growing smoke.

There it was. The bigger grem.

Their leader.

Melinda gasped at its size. The grem leader sat, twice as large as the others—nearly as tall as an average human—with much darker cobalt fur and bands of white around its limbs. Folded-up ears framed a squashed face and nose, and its open mouth showed rows of crooked gray teeth. The creature squatted on a wagon about 50 yards away, watching the scene before it. The sight sent a primal fear through Melinda that she thought she had mastered long ago, only to come back full force now: the urge to flee. She thought she might actually do it, but mustered every ounce of resolve to keep her feet rooted.

"We've killed most of your swarm," Melinda said to it. "You're dead meat."

Part of a torn canvas tent had wrapped around the large grem, nearly giving it the illusion of a cape. It stared coldly at Melinda, teeth clicking.

"Cocky, aren't ya?" Melinda moved closer to it, firing at a handful of grems with her gun but never letting the leader out of her sight. Once she was in throwing distance, she holstered her gun and took out the stick of dynamite.

A trio of grems jumped in front of Melinda and more moved in systematically. As if they knew. They were blocking her. Protecting their leader.

"Mellie! There's too many!" Lance hollered from somewhere outside the swarm.

They were outnumbered, and her odds of success were dropping by the second. But the leader was there—a mark she couldn't pass up—so she pressed deeper into the hoard. She wouldn't let the leader get away and take the swarm to another town, kill how many more people.

A smaller grem snarled close to her, a cross between a dog's growl and the wild chittering of a rabid racoon. The chitters, she saw, came from its gray teeth snapping together, like a cat with its sights on a bird.

She thought of Brigitta, crouched over her husband's body as Rafi tried to pull her away.

"Almost got it!" she shouted to Lance. She looked back to glimpse him reloading the crossbow before firing as fast as he could. Grems fell around her as the arrows hit them, but more were rushing at her.

"Get out of there!" Lance yelled and she understood that he couldn't protect her anymore. "We'll find another way!"

But she couldn't stop now. The grem leader smirked at her from its perch on the overturned wagon, a smile that seemed to drink in the pain around them. Rage boiled under Melinda's skin. She might not have been able to save the people they'd lost but she could stop the grems, here and now.

"Smile all you want," Melinda said to the leader, striking a match to light the dynamite. "We've wiped out plenty of other monsters. You're no different."

She tossed the dynamite stick toward the leader. Five seconds to detonation, and then she'd watch the monsters' guts splatter the sky like painted fireworks.

Until a hand reached out, catching the dynamite.

A grem hand.

Three seconds.

She knew what was coming. She turned to run before seeing the grem hurl the dynamite back toward her.

Two seconds.

She leapt.

CHAPTER NINE

As Melinda dove backwards, she covered her head and braced.

One second.

The dynamite went off as she slammed into the ground. Her ears rang and grem body parts rained down. Pain streaked into her left shoulder and hip from the fall. Dust stung her eyes, and noises warbled like she was underwater.

Weapon gone, her hands were bare save for spots of blood bright from under the dirt. The specks of blood were the only color in the gray dust, oddly soothing, like catching a glimpse of a wildflower in a field of green, or a flash of cardinal wings.

Focus, she told her body, trying to coax it out of its shock and prompt her senses, her mind, back to normal. *Breath*. In, out, in, out. Lance's muted shouts drifted to her.

She pulled her fallen handkerchief up around her mouth again as the acrid smell of burning flesh made her nearly gag. That, and the smell of the blasted grem bodies hit like a mix between week-old pig intestines and something rancid that her body immediately wanted to expel out.

Patches of her exposed skin—wrists, forehead—burned slightly where brown grem blood landed. She wiped it off as she sat up. Her ears still rang from the explosion, but she breathed in a sigh, taking in the twitching limbs around her. The grem's throw had been too slow.

She might be covered in stinky grem guts, but at least they were dead.

"Woo-ee! Mellie!" Lance's face floated in front of her, blue eyes bright above his dust-covered handkerchief. He gripped her by the shoulders. "You got em, you got em good! You alright?"

Lance's face wavered and then stuck in place, like a pin on a paper backdrop. She blinked and her lungs moved again, as reality snapped back.

"Peachy as pie," she said, and meant it as she spotted the larger grem's body, nearly unrecognizable from the blast. The relief at seeing the grems' corpses amidst the torn tents was empty compared to the human bodies near them. A handful of survivors helped each other up. The dozen or so corpses around them burned in the twilight. In one, a little grem the size of a rabbit howled and screamed amidst the flames. She watched it for a minute to distract herself from the mutilated human bodies, a gruesome sight that made her want to curl up and never open her eyes again.

But they had done it.

"How many dead?" she asked and spotted her fallen hat a few feet away, somehow still intact. She wiped it off, standing next to the body of a young man in what was once a pinstriped vest, probably around the age of Lance when she had first met him. The man's guts had been torn out, just visible through the licking fire. But what got her was his face, which the fire hadn't reached yet. It still had a look of surprise, innocence almost, the hazel eyes gazing upwards as if he had just seen a meteorite.

It broke her heart.

"Too many," Lance said, quieter. "At least we were able to stop them. Thought you were a goner there for a minute, charging in like that."

"Had to," she started to tell him when someone shouted behind them.

They turned to see Nox, Rafi and Brigitta silhouetted in the dusk on their horses. Nox scurried off the saddle of her white-and-black speckled Appaloosa and rushed to one of the twitching grem bodies, crouching with her bag.

"Lo'qua'cho told us where to find you. But we had to travel slowly due to her condition," Rafi said, nodding at Brigitta on the horse. He looked especially grim and a permanent scowl seemed to have settled over Brigitta, who held a shotgun.

"Gross little creatures, huh?" Nox called from where she was kneeling and began scraping off the monster's skin. "We're going to need a lot of samples. You, can you help me with this?" She called over to Abrams, who obliged, kneeling and holding her bag and a glass bottle she extracted.

"The antidote," Rafi urged her.

"No, look," Melinda said, pointing to the caved-in chest of the nearest corpse, one that had been an elderly woman. Beneath the shreds of her bloodied apron, the veins along her arms and legs had turned a faint blue. "It wasn't a sickness. The grems attack through the chest to lay eggs. The deaths were caused by the grem attacking, not an illness."

"So she's not infected?" Rafi asked. They all looked at Brigitta.

"Told you all I was fine," Brigitta said.

"Can't hurt to test an antidote, just in case. Surely this blue dust does *something*," Nox said as she quickly scooped up grem guts. Too quickly. Something was going on, but Melinda couldn't place it.

"Mercy to the stars," Rafi said. His tone sounded too bleak—he didn't seem as happy as Melinda thought he ought to be.

Nox rapidly wrapped up one of the severed grem arms and a crushed egg. Ginny, done with her gruesome job of setting the bodies on fire, joined them, covered in grem guts and ash. She started to say something before struggling with a coughing fit.

"We got them, Rafi," Lance said. "And Brigitta is OK. You don't have to worry anymore."

But Rafi's grimace made Melinda go on alert.

"There's more. A lot more," Rafi said.

"What?" Melinda asked. His words didn't make sense. Maybe she was still recovering from the after-effects of the fight.

"You did not kill them all," Rafi said bluntly. "There's another swarm. Larger than the last. Lo'qua'cho got word after you left."

"That's impossible," Melinda said, colder than she intended. "We killed them. And their leader."

Brigitta piped up angrily, stroking her shotgun. "They're attacking other towns. Multiplying."

Melinda stepped back and exchanged a stricken glance with Lance. Her head swam as she pictured a field of gutted humans. She could see the realization hit Lance hard too; he blanched and was quiet. With most colony-based creatures, the queen was the one who reproduced—laid eggs. But these seemed to be an exception, so if even one grem kept laying eggs the swarm would grow exponentially.

"He said part of the swarm broke off, heading this way," Rafi said.

"This way?" Ginny nearly shrieked. "The town…" She trailed off, undoubtedly calculating what she needed to do to minimize death and damage.

"We need more gunfire, what other weapons you got?" Melinda said.

"Mellie, we got to go," Lance said, his face gaunt, as if the very words pained him. "We're out of firepower. Out of everything. Last time we did something impossible, we lost Abel. And nearly lost you. We can't help here anymore. We have to regroup. Figure out what to do."

"The town!" Ginny said. "You're just going to abandon us? Not help us defend ourselves?"

"Suggest you evacuate everyone fast as you can." Lance looked helpless. Small, which he never did. "Your town is lost. We can't stop them. Not now."

The distinct rotten stench floated through the air, cutting beneath the smoke and guts. The ground gave a warning rumble, as if to announce more grems were on the way.

Melinda spotted the rage and desperation in Ginny's eyes. A look Melinda was used to fixing. But this, they couldn't fix.

"Suggest we get going," Rafi urged Nox.

Nox scooped some goop into another small glass vial, and reluctantly stood. "All right," she said. "Got plenty of samples."

"Go," Abrams urged Ginny. "Get the doctor. Tell everyone else to leave." He turned to look at Melinda and Lance. "I want to help you, best I can. I can send out word, bulletins to other towns to take cover and tell them you're trying to stop the grems."

"Good man," Lance said. "We have to leave, now."

Melinda nodded numbly. They stumbled back to the outskirts of the festival. Her eyes burned from the billowing smoke as they saddled up and did the one thing they never did before.

They fled.

CHAPTER TEN

The horses, all too eager, ran.

They fled across the terrain, leaving the smoke and stench of burning flesh behind them. The landscape grew more desert-like every minute, shrubs shrinking in the distance as sand and rocks stretched endlessly ahead. Behind them, the ground rumbled while the faintest screeches of the grems echoed in the velvety night.

Nox took the lead on her Appaloosa, shouting something about an abandoned town that would be safe. Rafi and Brigitta rode behind her, Brigitta grimacing and standing in the stirrups best she could as her horse cantered. Melinda's body and mind screamed for sleep, but they kept pressing across the rolling fields of dried grass peppered with scraggly succulents lit only by moonlight.

At some point, hours later, a few shadowy buildings rose ahead. No noise or distinct smells greeted them, just the decaying smell of overgrown, drying stalks of various vegetation determined to take over. A crooked wooden sign, barely legible with its faded ink and multiple cracks, read "Town of" with the name scratched out.

"Defunct mining camp," Nox said as they slowed to the town's single street. "A promise of copper was based on a grifter who spread the rumor. They say he got nearly 20 families to pay him, move here and start up a mining operation. When they got wise, he started a fire to cover his escape." Decrepit buildings slumped on either side of them in the one-horse town, some hastily boarded up, others with the doors busted or missing. "I stop here sometimes when I make the long trip south. Rumors of ghosts, so most people steer clear."

Nox led them to a building in the center of the street that looked like it had been the start of a restaurant. The few other structures that lined the street stood haphazardly. Melinda shuddered at the eerie silence. It wasn't her first time passing through an abandoned mining camp, but settlements that had disappeared all but overnight once the promise of wealth dissolved always felt tragic. Her eyes fell to a piece of dirty cloth half-wedged in the dirt, the skirt of a child's doll.

Lance set about to getting the horses settled near a tiny well, while the others approached the building. Melinda hung up her duster, thick with grem funk, on a rickety nail outside the half-busted door.

"Welcome," Nox said, swinging open what remained of the door and plopping down her bag that held a grem arm, egg remnants and who knew what else.

Inside the building, one counter lined the length of the left wall. Wooden planks barely covered the packed dirt to make up a floor, while a few splits in the beams overhead let the moonlight in. In the back corner, a small table stood with half-melted candles. Linens, bottles of preserves, and few books lovingly piled on a shelf to the side.

"This is quite the set-up," Rafi observed.

Nox shooed away an inquisitive mouse and plopped into a pile of furs in the corner with a deep sigh. "I store a few items here for when I stop." She pointed. "Preserved food under the boards there. Some linens, not enough but it's hot still so they'll do. You take them, Brigitta."

"What's this?" Melinda lifted a sheet hanging from one of the broken windows, dingy but bundled in a way to make it look like a figure.

"The ghosts of course," Nox smirked. "Otherwise, how would I keep this pitstop to myself?"

"So you're the source of the ghost rumors." Brigitta gave a mirthless laugh and winced, rubbing her side.

Melinda glanced at her. "You better not be giving birth now."

"Contractions, huh?" Nox nodded. "Common at this point. They're false usually. Practice contractions from your body."

"They're awful," Brigitta responded. "You have kids?"

Nox shook her head with a laugh. "Goodness no. Never, I hope. But human anatomy is one of my interests."

"We need to get her to a town. A safe one," Rafi said. "Somewhere the grems aren't going."

"What we need to get is weapons," Melinda said, turning as Lance came in with two rickety buckets of well water. Rafi gratefully dipped his handkerchief in one of the buckets and set about to wiping his face. "Lots of weapons. You got any stashed away here with the linens?"

Nox shook her head and jumped up to unwrap the small severed grem arm from her bag. The others drew back instinctively at the sight of the curled clawed hands, and that putrid, mud-mixed-with-sick-dung smell.

"What are you doing?" Rafi asked, covering his nose.

"Finally got my sample," Nox said. "You saw the grems' mark on those giant mosquitos, is that right? I'm guessing this dust has an effect, but to what end is unclear. I'm curious if we can devise an antidote for whatever it does."

"Can't hurt," Melinda said.

Nox set out the small glass jar of flies and used her tweezers to pull off a bit of the mottled white skin coated in azure.

She dropped it in the jar.

They waited. Melinda had seen bugs work instantly in the past when Abel and Aunt B had experimented with various Edge monsters' venoms. When faced with a sample of material, the bugs would ingest and turn a different color as they produced an antidote.

Then, it was a matter of consuming the bugs or mashing them into a topical paste to counter any toxins.

This time, the bugs turned cobalt.

"Never seen that before," Lance said.

"Is that the antidote?" Rafi asked before the bugs did something unusual. They all landed on the glass wall nearest to Melinda and Brigitta. Still. Watching.

Like they're listening, Melinda thought, even though that was absurd.

Nox stared. "That's curious."

"Kill them," Melinda said. "Kill them now."

"What?" Lance stared at her in confusion and Rafi looked on in alarm.

"Now," Melinda said, and lit a match. Lance began nodding, following her train of thought.

"Your reason?" Nox asked.

"If the grem dust can effect a control over other critters and make them act odd, no telling what it'd do to the bugs," Lance chimed in. "Last thing we need is unstable herald flies."

"They're useless now anyways. Such a waste," Nox sighed and unscrewed the jar to let Melinda drop the match in before recapping it. They silently watched the fire go out and the smoke billow in the jar. The flies dropped dead.

"Now, we got to find a proper town for weapons," Lance said. "Hoping Abrams got word out to the towns in the swarm's path."

"And we need medical supplies," Rafi added, casting a worried look at Brigitta.

"I'm not a child," Brigitta snapped back, and Rafi recoiled in surprise. "Tired of you fussing over me. I can handle myself just fine."

"I know that," Rafi said stiffly. "But I'm seeing you through until you're safe, whether you like it or not. It's what Samuel would have wished."

Brigitta nodded curtly, chewing on her lip.

"So what's our nearest bet?" Lance said, quickly changing the subject and unfolding a map from his pocket. "Looks like the Spirals aren't too far from here, if I'm reading this right."

Nox shuddered as she pulled down jars of preserves. "Far South is better. Plenty of towns and resources in that region if we can evade the grems."

"Too far." Lance shook his head. "The Spirals are much closer, aren't they?"

Nox made a sour face as she handed Brigitta one of the plates with a preserved potato, beets and a pickle. "I nearly got hung as a witch last time I was there. It's a sordid town. Nothing but drifters, lowlifes and scoundrels."

"But it is the place where you can get whatever you need, for a price." Lance said, settling onto a creaking bar stool. "That's what they say, isn't it? Information. Hired hands. And…" His gaze met Melinda's. "Firepower."

"How far?" Melinda asked, accepting the jar of food Nox handed her. She jammed some figs into her mouth. The sugar flooded her tongue, but she couldn't savor it.

We have to go go go, something in her screamed and she set down the jar.

"Forty miles, give or take." Nox offered Rafi a preserved pear. Brigitta had already cleared her plate and laid down on the thickest fur Nox had put out for her.

"All right, let's get," Melinda said. Everyone looked up at her but didn't move.

"We best stay here for the night, love," Lance said. "Set out first thing."

"How many more people are gonna be torn up by the grems while we get our beauty sleep?" Melinda replied.

"I know," Lance said. "But the horses need a rest. And we're no good to anyone if we can't fire straight."

"Just a few hours," Rafi agreed around a mouthful of pear. She could see they were distracted by the food and the chance to sit. She knew rest was important, even when hunting monsters, but the grems weren't ordinary monsters. They didn't have time for even the slightest of luxuries. She gestured Lance over to a corner to talk privately as the others finished eating.

"It's not right to stay," Melinda said. "We got to saddle up. They can wait here."

"Listen." Lance gripped her elbows, his gaze drilling into her with those stormy blue eyes that had seen countless monsters alongside her, that had grown a little dimmer once Abel was lost.

"People are dying," Melinda cut in before he could continue. "Every minute we wait here we risk more grems. More deaths."

"We're no good exhausted, with or without them. And we have never faced anything like this. We need our wits. We need to be sharp. And clear. And that means…" He gently pushed her back on a stout wooden chair covered with a wool blanket that had seen better days. "We rest. We take them to the Spirals and make sure they're safe. Stock up. Figure out our next steps."

"We can't—" Melinda started again, and he shook his head, uncharacteristically firm.

"What if the grems find us here?" she asked.

"I'll keep an eye out. We'll trade off."

The wave of exhaustion was now a tsunami, as though Lance's words had cast a spell over her. Her body was rebelling wakefulness, making her eyes heavier than soggy quilts. She curled up best she could on the chair. "Just for a bit," she mumbled. She was asleep before she knew it.

Sometime during the night, Melinda woke to hear Brigitta choking back sobs, just audible beneath Nox's snores. Two candles Nox had lit burned low; between those and the sinking moonlight sneaking in through the cracks in the wood, she spotted Rafi holding Brigitta as her body shook with silent cries. The sobs subsided after a minute. Melinda's heart swelled for her. It was no good to hold in all her emotions like that. She wasn't one for bawling much herself but knew that crying had a place. Crying could help Brigitta heal.

Melinda dozed off again and when she fully woke up, it felt like no time at all had passed. The first of dawn's light slipped through the edges of the curtain-ghost. Most of her muscles ached—her entire left side seemed to be on fire—from yesterday's fall and the fighting. She sat upright, the fog of sleep disappearing from her mind, replaced by memories of the grem leader sneering at her, rows of silver teeth like nails gleaming, white arching claws.

We have to go.

The others were still sleeping. In the corner, Lance hunched over on a small stool, a torn piece of paper on his knee, scribbling a makeshift map in his journal.

Melinda grabbed the remaining preserved figs and sat next to him, chewing and massaging her left shoulder. "Plan?"

"As far as we know, the grem swarm was heading east." He showed her the map. "Once they hit the mountain ridge, they could veer down toward South Bowl or up toward more towns. If they cross the ridge, there's a whole slew of more settlements in danger."

"Too bad Aunt B is so far," Melinda said over her mouthful of fig. Her aunt would've expertly assessed the situation with her intuitive intellect and decades of experience. And more importantly, she'd have plenty of ideas for how they could combat this newest threat.

"What kinds of questions would she have for us right now?" Lance asked. It was an exercise they did sometimes when they had been on the road offering their monster exterminating services and encountered a particularly puzzling or vexing Edge monster. Aunt B and Abel had taught them to think strategically, scientifically.

"What they want," Melinda said. "Why they wanna lay eggs in human guts."

Lance nodded, ticking off the points on his fingers. "If they roam or plan to settle somewhere. What terrain they prefer. What they eat. What they don't like. We know they can climb and dig and run. How do they communicate? How long do they live?"

"We don't have time for the full naturalist approach." Melinda wiped her hands on a small square of dingy linen. "We just need two answers: What they want, and how to kill them. How to kill them being the number one question."

"Fire," Lance mused. He stared at his map and Melinda nodded slowly. Fire worked nearly against every monster they had encountered, with a few exceptions.

"We know they burn," Melinda said, trying not to think about the human corpses. "But they also burrow."

"It's summer. Fire season. We risk wildfires spreading to towns."

"That's better than monsters spreading." Melinda tapped the map. "We send word to the towns they're most likely to get to. Have them set up a fire wall."

Lance rubbed the scruff on his chin. "We come up behind them. Set more fires if they retreat. Wait for them to pop out of the ground. Get boom sticks ready and drop them into the holes. We'll need a lot of help and fire power to coordinate."

Melinda nodded. It was something at least–the beginnings of a plan. "First we get weapons."

He folded the map and tucked it into his pocket before shooting her a tired smile. "We'll figure it out. We always do." He stood, gently hugging her. She let herself sink into his embrace for a second, the warmth of his arms and the bristled chin against her cheek making her want to give up and rush home.

But that wasn't happening, not today. The others stirred and the growing blue of dawn hung heavy, promising another hot day.

"We leave in ten, stock up and saddle up," Melinda said loudly. Brigitta hurried off to look for an outhouse. Lance and Rafi went to ready the horses while Nox packed up sacks of food.

Melinda stepped outside to clean her duster as best she could, using an old rag and well water to wipe off the guts. The air was still, save for a hawk wheeling overhead and the shuffling of the horses nearby. It'd almost be peaceful if not for their circumstances.

Melinda washed her face and hands and chewed on one of Nox's cubes of tree gum mixed with spearmint leaves. As she turned back to the house, she spotted Brigitta sitting on a stump next to a patch of cacti a few feet away. She had a hunch to her shoulders—a universal sign Melinda recognized. Defeat.

"I'm hanging up my hat," Brigitta said. Melinda handed her a wet linen and Brigitta slowly wiped her face as she kept talking. "Honest as the sky is blue, you can just leave me here. Don't try to convince me otherwise."

Melinda looked around for someone else, Lance or anyone, to deal with these theatrics and give Brigitta a rousing talk, but the others were out of earshot. Only them and the prickly pear cacti. Melinda stifled a sigh.

"I know," Melinda said brusquely. "Nothing to do but to keep on going."

Brigitta remained silent and Melinda started to roll her eyes before she remembered Brigitta's stifled sobs from the night. Brigitta had gone through plenty, surely Melinda could extend her some grace.

"We're gonna do everything we can to stop the swarm and avenge your husband," Melinda said firmly. Brigitta's head tilted a minuscule amount at that. "I swear it."

"It's impossible," Brigitta said, still not looking at her, instead picking at her dirty dress. Melinda made a mental note to get her a new frock once they got to the Spirals. Last thing anyone needed was to be wearing their spouse's dried blood and grem guts.

"Just look at the facts," Brigitta went on, tugging at one of her long braids. "Those monsters pop faster than bunnies. They control other monsters. We don't stand a chance. So what's the point?"

"The point is we aren't giving up," Melinda said. "That's it. Once we get to the Spirals, we'll get cleaned up. Real food. It'll make a difference." Melinda paused. The words weren't hers, they were Abel's.

Let's get you both cleaned up. A real meal. That'll make a world of difference, he would say the same when they had returned from an especially grueling monster extermination that didn't go the way they planned.

"You look like how I feel." Brigitta glanced at her. "You lost someone too, huh?"

"Grief is a funny thing," Melinda said stiffly and willed away the sadness. "Comes and goes, likes to sneak up when you don't expect it." Lance waved at them and Melinda straightened in relief. "Time to go. You'll be OK riding a little longer?"

"It's mighty uncomfortable, but I'll manage." Brigitta struggled to stand from the stump. She nearly toppled but righted herself as Melinda grasped her arm.

"This is a bad idea," Nox cautioned as they approached to mount their horses.

"No other choice for now," Lance said. "We need help, and the Spirals is the closest option."

They started off. Melinda swore she could hear rumblings beneath the ground or catch the sour smell of the grems on the wind, but nothing appeared except for endless desert, hardy succulents, patches of cacti and rocks as they rode. At least, in all the commotion, the shadowy visions had gone away for now. *Small consolation,* she thought wryly.

It felt like only a few inches separated her from the blazing sun, scorching the side of her neck despite her upturn collar and hat. The horses glistened with sweat and eventually slowed as honey-combed towers came into view. A sickly yellow and easily 100 feet tall, the leaning structures looked like an unnatural growth. A central cluster of them grew more prominent as they neared.

The Spirals.

CHAPTER ELEVEN

"Is that them?" Brigitta gaped at the pockmarked yellow towers puncturing the deep blue of the late afternoon sky. Clusters and solo Spirals stretched in front of them, marking the unnatural oasis beyond dunes, acacia trees and shrubs. Melinda stared too. She had never seen the Spirals in person, only in drawings.

"Welcome to the Spirals," Nox said dryly, patting the sweat off her forehead with a handkerchief. "Outpost of outlaws and refugees. If we don't get swindled, pickpocketed or murdered, it'll be a miracle."

"Who made these?" Rafi asked, craning his neck.

"Massive monsters long before our time," Lance said. "Behemoths. Ow!" He shook a tiny red fleck off his hand. At Rafi's quizzical look, he explained. "Mikrabs from the Edge. Mostly harmless, more of a nuisance than anything, sort of like our regular sand crabs. They give you a little sting and numbing. Settled in around these deserts."

"Funny place," Brigitta murmured, gazing up at the towers.

Melinda silently agreed, facts stirring in her memory. The Spirals—the material that looked like caved-in honeycomb and stung to the touch—were often near reservoirs of water that used to lie under the desert. Once the monsters that created the Spirals left, people had settled into the cluster, making it a crossroads. Anyone traveling—merchants and drifters alike—found it to be a central hub in the desert, a wayward oasis for those heading to

South Bowl and the ocean, or North toward a scattering of towns that sprang up by the Edge.

They dismounted and tied the horses by the trough at the entrance, which was marked by sagging, interlocking Spirals that made a type of archway overhead. Past the entrance, storefronts squashed beneath the towering hives. Makeshift tents dotted a large central clearing, between an unreasonable number of saloons. The stench of too many outhouses and spilt whiskey wafted up along with meat smoke.

A woman cleaning a rifle on a bench gave them a brief, scrutinizing look that alerted Melinda she was a watch for someone. Probably whoever was the powerhouse in this makeshift town.

"We need weapons and ammo," Lance reiterated.

"Change of clothes too." Melinda gestured to Brigitta. Rafi stood protectively near her as they walked deeper into the town.

"Anything else?" Lance asked. They all looked at Nox, but she had fallen into a gloomy silence.

The Spirals grew denser with people of all hues. A bright red-haired tribe and oldcomer family in beads and braids beckoned to them, waving their wares. While everyone seemed shifty and eager to make a buck—swindlers aplenty—Melinda felt no real threat. It didn't seem like the type of place where shootouts were the norm. There was money to be made.

From water, for one thing.

"Five pieces a gallon," Lance grimaced as he paid to fill up their canteens. "No wonder people here got such big smiles. It's a racket."

A tall, dark fellow wearing a red feather tucked into a broad strap in his fedora sauntered up to them.

"Y'all find whatever you need here," the stranger said. "It's not cheap, but you'll find it. For another piece I can save you some time, direct you to whatever you need." He tipped his hat. "Deo 'Bad Hat' Varman at your service."

"It's not that bad of a hat," Nox said, and Deo beamed at her, tipping it.

"How about you direct us complimentary this time?" Lance said, friendly as could be. "Seeing as how there's a bloodthirsty cannibalistic swarm of some of the ugliest, most brutal monsters we've seen that need some stopping."

Deo chuckled but then glanced at Lance's face. "Oh, you mean it?" He paled, his eyes sliding over them and their filthy clothes. "Nearby?"

"Could be," Rafi said. "They're fast and travel underground."

"What kind of weapons do people sell around here?" Melinda asked, shaking a small trail of ruby mikrabs off her boot that marched along like miniscule fire ants.

"Ah," Deo said with a pause. "That's the one thing that don't flow freely. Keeps violence at a minimum."

"We need all manner of firepower to stop the grems," Melinda snapped. "So they best flow free for us."

"You want weapons, you make friendly with Lone-Gun Jolene," Deo said with a shrug. "She runs Spirals now. You wanna buy anything that has real power, you gotta talk to her."

"And how do we do that?" Lance asked and Deo pointed to one of the buildings.

"We'll take care of it," Lance said to the others.

Rafi nodded. "We will find supplies, clothes." He, Nox and Brigitta continued to the next storefront while Melinda and Lance headed to the building Deo had pointed to.

In front of the wide structure stood a guard. At first Melinda assumed it was a gangly man in loose linens, but the figure turned to reveal a woman who stood even taller than Melinda. That was a first.

"Women's club, ladies only," the guard said to Lance. Her sandy hair was slung in a braid over a shoulder. "You want to talk with Jolene, that's the rules."

Lance stepped back to murmur to Melinda. "Just be straightforward with them but friendly enough, all right? I'll scope out the surrounding streets, see what other resources there are."

Melinda stifled a groan. Buttering up people for favors was more Lance's cup of tea.

"Most people are decent and good and want to help," Lance told her. "Tell them the truth, *politely*, and they'll see."

Melinda disagreed but stepped forward regardless.

"What's your business?" The guard asked, scanning Melinda up and down, unimpressed.

"Monster hunters. Need firepower to handle an invasion." She waited to see if the guard would clam up like most at the mention of monsters, but she could see the guard was considering.

"Invasion coming here?"

"Dunno." Melinda wasn't a great liar in general so didn't bother. "But near enough that people will get hurt. Maybe not *your* people, but people. We need to buy supplies. I'll be faster than a fly."

Now the guard looked amused. "That would be a first. Jolene likes her games."

"What do you mean?"

"You'll see." The guard stepped back. "Upstairs in the back."

Melinda entered the club, dominated by a large oak-paneled room scarred with knife knicks and carvings. A dozen or so people filled the room, the smell of alcohol and tobacco heavy in the air. Two women with babies sat along the windows, one laughing about something. A painter sat in the corner with a half-done canvas, coiled tubes of near empty-paint on a chair next to her. Most wore dresses but a few wore mining clothes or worker's pants, putting Melinda a little more at ease. It didn't seem like a place where she'd get shunned for wearing pants and a beat-up hat like some spots. A large rectangular bar rested in the middle of the room, crowded with women, mostly older than Melinda. A few shot looks her way—not friendly but not unfriendly—before returning to their conversations.

Maybe this won't be so bad, she thought as she climbed the steep wooden steps in the back.

At the top of the stairs, the door attendant—a freckled, silent woman with a holstered revolver—opened double doors leading to an expansive room with three round tables covered in red cloth. A group of people played cards around the largest table in the center, but Melinda's eyes drifted to the wall on the right.

Weapons. A *lot* of them. Guns from single-shot pocket pistols to gleaming shotguns rested in a glass case. A case of what she'd guess held ammo or dynamite. There were even a few close-quarter weapons ranging from a spiked mace to a coiled leather whip hanging in the case. It was an impressive arsenal.

And just what they needed.

Melinda followed the attendant to the large table. Seated in the center was who she could only assume was Jolene, a woman with a dark bun, linen shirt and hard smile. Next to her stood a woman with a shock of orange-red hair in an embroidered black dress, leaning on Jolene's shoulder, whispering something. On the other side of Jolene, a woman with two braids and a sizable pistol holstered under a rabbit skin cloak stood with folded arms, stared Melinda down.

"Miss Melinda West," the attendant announced. "She has a request." The attendant gestured to the woman with the bun and the two figures flanking her as she introduced them. "Lone-Gun Jolene Xue-Min, Karla Colter, and Bright Sun Dyani Sharp."

Jolene didn't respond but instead flipped over a card, showing it to the player sitting across from her. Faro, Melinda guessed. A common game that she enjoyed, under more relaxing circumstances.

"You owe me now. Vamoose," Jolene said to the player, a curly-haired woman in a purple dress. The player pressed her fingerless gloves together and seemed to fight back tears before she rushed out.

Melinda faced the remaining trio as they took in her dirty duster and the smell of blood and battle she doubted she had fully scrubbed out.

"Where did you crawl out from under?" Jolene snorted. "Don't matter much—most are welcome here. What can we do you for?" Something in the way she sat, superficially at ease, but with her elbow cocked so her right hand was within reach of the embossed holster hanging from the wooden chair next to her, reminded Melinda of all the other outlaws she had encountered. Ready to turn in a second when the wind blew the wrong way.

Couldn't trust her one whiff.

"Word is you can help us get some firepower." Melinda nodded her head toward the wall. Their faces didn't move, and she wished Lance was here to use his easy charm to get this deal done.

Karla, paler than candlewax, with a shock of frizzy orange-red hair falling to her shoulders amidst a cloud of cigarette smoke, folded her arms under her considerable bosom. She spoke in a rapid stream, pronouncing words in a way that took Melinda's ear a second to decipher. "Sit. Play. We'll see if ye winna request."

"I don't have time to gamble," Melinda said. She opened her mouth to explain about the grems, but Jolene held up a silencing hand.

"If you want something, or want to tell me something, you best make the time," Jolene said. "How someone conducts themselves in cards is how I decide if I want to do business with them."

Melinda sighed through her nose. She could almost hear Lance: *five minutes of effort can save fifty minutes of pain.* Catching flies with honey and all that. At least faro was quick.

She sat as Jolene dealt the faceup cards. The others scrutinized her; Dyani with quick, almost hateful, glances and Karla more demurely as she passed Melinda copper betting tokens. Cigarette smoke hung in the air like an acrid cloud, making Melinda's nose prickle and giving the room a dreamy haze.

"You hear anything about a pair of horse thieves," Dyani asked, watching her closely.

"Nothing about that," Melinda said, setting her bet down. Behind Jolene, a thump sounded along the back wall from behind a nondescript door.

"I gotta say it really boils my blood when people steal my stuff," Jolene said louder, ignoring the thump.

"I ain't seen no horses but my own," Melinda said steadily.

"Where ye coming from?" Karla asked, fiddling with the black strap of her dress.

"West." Melinda stifled a curse as Jolene turned over the next card. Losing hand.

Jolene watched her closely, half-grinning. "You've gotta play better than that if you want to do a deal."

Something banged against the back door again and Melinda cocked her head. "You got someone tied up back there?"

"You may've heard I used to be an outlaw. But I'm reformed." Jolene waved an arm and Karla nodded, a protective hand on her shoulder. "I built this place here, turned the Spirals into what it is today. Some people look to religion to help them. Others look to all matters of intoxication. Here, people look to Jolene to help them," Jolene said, tapping her chest to emphasize the point.

As Jolene droned on—she clearly liked hearing herself speak—they played another round. Again, Melinda lost. And again. She resisted the urge to flip the table over. Flashes of the smoldering bodies at Thundering Ridge came back to her, unbidden, the crumpled pinstriped vest, the dead man's hazel eyes staring up at the darkening blue sky through smoke. Instead, she threw her hand down.

"Monster hunter, you say? Hope you're better at that than cards," Jolene laughed. At Melinda's startled look, Dyani smirked and tapped on a small open pipe that came out of the wall near her foot.

"Set of acoustics here, lets us hear everything by the front door," Jolene said. "Bit of ingenious engineering by Dyani here."

"You know I'm trying to stop grems—you know people might be *dying*—and you're wasting time with this silly game?" Melinda stood, her rage boiling. Dyani put a hand on her pistol. "We'll find what we need some other way. Stay here and play your games."

"Wait," Jolene said, almost apologetically. "We get a lot of people saying all kinds of things to get in, can't trust them all. Playing cards gives us a chance to see your intent. And you passed the test."

"I don't care about your test," Melinda nearly spat, and then imagined Lance shooting her a look to mind her temper. She forced a breath and said between gritted teeth. "So, you gonna sell me some of that firepower? Or do you want more people to die?"

Jolene folded her hands.

"Why do you want to kill those little critters anyway?" Jolene said in a way that struck a low warning cord in Melinda, who held still. "They're a path to new opportunities for people like us. Make us a whole lot of money, if we play our cards right, know what I mean?"

"I surely *don't* know what you mean," Melinda said. "They massacre people. They're a plague."

Karla kept the pistol pointed at Melinda's chest and laughed, a high-pitched, forced sound as the pounding started again behind the door.

"You got a grem back there," Melinda realized, going cold. "We gotta kill it, you hear me?"

"Someone caught it, brought it to me as a gift," Jolene beamed. "That's the kind of person I am, you see? People love to give me things. Oooh-wee, it'll make me a pretty penny down in South Bowl. They're offering a lot for people bringing them grems live."

"Keep your little grem and see what happens," Melinda said. "There's a swarm out there that's gonna kill everyone."

"You go around killing critters and that eats up my business, see? I here got a reason to keep em alive. A lucrative reason. You can see how these don't match up." Jolene flashed a fake frown. "Gotta nip this little problem in the bud."

Melinda had slowly been backing up, now just a foot away from the entrance. It opened inwards, so there was no way she could quickly jump out without leaving herself vulnerable. A small window to Jolene's right was too small to squeeze through.

"They gut people, you know that?" Melinda continued. "They're brutal. Lay their eggs inside corpses. You really want to deal with that?"

"You ever heard that saying, break a few eggs to make an omelet?" Jolene said, still with her manic grin, one that came so easily Melinda wondered how unhinged she was.

"A good cook wouldn't waste any eggs," Melinda muttered. "And people ain't eggs. Tell you want, I'll be on my way now. I'll let you be, you let me."

"Ladies, I think it's about time for some excitement down in main street," Jolene stood. "We can't let this one run around interfering."

"Y'all are being fools!" Melinda shouted now. She'd bet her ranch that Lance was hovering nearby and hoped he could hear out the window, so she made sure her voice carried to alert him to be on guard.

Before she could shout again, Dyani grabbed her arms, wrenching them behind her and sending jolts of pain into her shoulders. She had drawn her pistol as well, pressing it into Melinda's back.

Jolene opened the door to the staircase. "Tell Bad Hat to get ready," Jolene said to the attendant, settling a tan hat over her bun and shrugging on a duster the same sandstone color as the Spirals outside. "We'll drop off our little friend right after this."

Jolene stormed through the exit without a second look while Karla hung back to open the back door. Melinda glimpsed a cage as tall as her waist. And in that cage a small white clawed hand gripped the bar as a grem glared out.

Dyani shoved her after Jolene, the pistol still against the small of her back.

Outside, Lance was nowhere to be seen. Good. She hoped he was hiding and scheming. Nox had to be around somewhere, and she had proven herself crafty, and the others were decent with guns. One of them would help her, surely.

"You know what we need?" Jolene asked the half a dozen people milling around. The others around her chuckled knowingly, some grinning. One gave a "whoop!"

As Jolene riled up the crowd, Melinda thought she looked a little deranged, like folks who'd had a lifetime of twists and turns, bad decisions and justifying betrayals and hurts too deep to name. But any sympathy she might've felt disappeared when Jolene said her next words with relish:

"It's time for a hanging."

CHAPTER TWELVE

"You gonna let her hang someone innocent?" Melinda shouted at the people watching as Dyani shoved her down the street. "I didn't do a damn thing!" The dozen or so people outside barely flinched as she yelled. Jolene's gang was clearly the one in charge.

Melinda dug her heels in, slowing herself as much as she could against Dyani's grip as Jolene led the group forward down the main street, the Spirals twisting above them.

"You don't have to do this," Melinda urged Dyani. "I'm trying to help you, not stop you. I've seen the monsters gut people like you wouldn't believe."

Dyani didn't respond.

"So you're dandy with cold-blooded murder?" Melinda asked, her fury getting the better of her.

Dyani's grip tightened. "My family fought off self-righteous newcomers like you and died. If it wasn't for Jolene, I'd have no one," she hissed. "For as long as I live, I will never forget what people like you did."

Melinda gave up; she'd find no help from Dyani. She spotted their final destination at the end of the street. A decrepit building loomed large, its wooden planks poorly nailed with a crooked wooden sign: "HORSE FEED AND BAIT." From the top of the wooden roof extended an iron beam with a massive hook larger than her head. The beam rose three feet out and hung overhead, maybe twenty feet up.

From the beam hung a thick rope.

Deo was up there, his red feathered hat a bright spot against the glaring sky. He stood on the slightly inclined roof, where he finished fussing with the rope.

"Ready, Hank!" Deo shouted down to the ground, where an older man held a well-crafted noose. His long, freckled jowls seemed about ready to drag his whole face down, barely stopped by an impressive mustache.

Just got to keep your cool till Lance comes, Melinda thought, but a primal panic was setting in fast as Hank bound a shorter piece of rope around her hands behind her.

Jolene began to address the small crowd that gathered, while some enterprising soul had taken up shaking a handful of sacks of roasted nuts and a jug, shouting, "Get your redeye juice here!"

Selling concessions at my hanging.

The situation hadn't fully registered yet; everything was happening too fast and Melinda's options were all but nil. She thought to run, but Hank and Dyani were too close. If it was just them she might've had a chance, but not with this many people here, eating up Jolene's every word.

"We've been stuck here in the Spirals!" Jolene yelled. Under her wide-brimmed tan hat, her eyes blazed. "Branded outlaws, expect to sit here till the end of our days. No more!" She pointed at Melinda. "This here troublemaker wants to stop our income. Stop us from getting what we deserve. So, we'll return the favor and hang her up to dry!"

Hank removed Melinda's holster and hat and placed them on a hitching post next to him. Dyani still had her gun trained on Melinda as she listened to Jolene, sweating against the hot air that kicked up, drier than crushed bones.

"I'll be needing that hat back soon," Melinda said as strands of her dark hair whipped free across her face. She hadn't stopped trying to work the rope that burned into her wrists. Hank merely snorted, wiping his sunburnt forehead beneath a brown bowler hat.

"Help me," Melinda said lowly to him. "Those grems are dangerous. I'm trying to stop them. They'll kill you all."

Hank said a line that sounded rehearsed. "Jolene does what she does to protect us."

"Nothing can protect you from the grems," Melinda said. "What in the hell is she promising you?"

"South Bowl wants all the critters they can get. They'll pay us real nice. They're collecting them down there." Hank shrugged. "You know, once you have a reputation like some of us here, fair or not, you can't do too much. Jolene says these little creatures will help us make enough, give us a fresh start."

"It'll be hard to have a fresh start when you're all gutted like cattle!" Melinda said but he didn't answer as he looped the hemp rope over her head. She tucked her chin to give her neck some space, but they were expecting that. Dyani forced her forehead back so the rope went snug.

"You're all pros at hanging people, huh," Melinda spat and coughed as the rope tightened.

Hank tugged the knot to the left side of her neck. "This will help the neck snap faster, so you won't suffer too much," he said with a smack of sympathy.

"You're all gonna die," Melinda said.

"You first," Jolene said to her as the crowd fanned out.

Karla pushed through the crowd, dragging a rope attached to a rickety wooden board on wooden wheels. On the board sat the cage with the grem, two feet tall, hunched over with a metal collar round its stout neck. Melinda couldn't tear her eyes away. For some reason, the grem fixed its red-rimmed gaze specifically on her. Staring. And like the grem that had greeted them at the gorge, this one turned its long lips up in the mockery of a smile.

"Ready for ye," Karla said, brushing the dust from her skirt.

"There's the ticket." Jolene whistled. "Let's get this going."

"Looks good up here, boss," Deo called.

This wasn't happening. She wasn't about to be hung like some common criminal in a lawless land. Melinda kept trying to work her chin down under the rope while squirming against her wrist ties when she heard the voice she was waiting for—but tinged with panic.

"Melinda!" Lance hollered. A fresh red cut bloomed along his shoulder where his sleeve was torn from a recent scuff. He was wrestling with a heavyset tanned man and a pale woman in a button-upped vest with a short dark bob and long scar across her forehead.

Captured.

"Found this one about to set off an explosion," the scarred woman said, pursing her thin lips in what looked like a permanently sour expression.

"Nice work, Clem," Jolene said.

"I forgave him though, since he's such a cutie." Clem slapped Lance's cheek as a few people came forward to stifle his thrashing. "Maybe I'll marry this one."

Jolene glanced back at Melinda with a wicked smirk. "They call her 'Five-Time' Clementine, for the number of husbands she's had."

"All in a bed of dirt now!" Deo hooted from above.

"They deserved it," Clem said primly. She guffawed as she looked at Melinda. "This your girl? She's about as tall and ugly as a scarecrow."

"Let her go!" Lance shouted as they shoved him next to Melinda. He jerked toward her but two of the larger men held tight. She glanced at him with the silent question of what happened to the others – did they escape? His face was distraught but not despairing. They were alive, then, somewhere. But they couldn't rely on anyone else to save them.

"You're next, pretty boy," Jolene said as Dyani and Clem flanked her.

Jolene turned to the crowd. "Y'all get a wild card today! Two hangings!" The others whooped and even Hank next to her was entranced by Jolene's every word. "Let's get this going so I'm not late to South Bowl."

Melinda met Lance's eyes again. They'd work together, *been* together, long enough they could guess what each other was thinking without talking.

He looked purposefully down at her feet.

Free and unencumbered, like his. It would hurt for a second, but it'd give him a chance to get out of it. She gave a little nod as the rope round her neck started to grow more taunt, and started the silent countdown to three that was their go-to.

One…two…three

She leaned forward, grimacing against the tightened noose, and kicked *out*—not Hank, who was nodding at Jolene's words, but the closest assailant, the one to Lance's right. She connected her boot heel to the side of his kneecap, hearing a satisfying whoosh of shocked breath.

She tried to kick the second man but then Hank yanked her back. Nevertheless, it was enough for Lance to gain the advantage. Anticipating the loosened grip to his right, Lance pulled out the gun from the injured man and slammed into his captor on the left, knocking them both clear down.

People shouted and a few onlookers quickly retreated. In the flurry, Lance had spun and trained his gun on Jolene. Dyani started to raise her pistol but Lance fired once above Jolene's head. The grem in its cage a few feet from Jolene hissed at the sound, wrapping its white hands around the bars.

"Untie her," Lance said to Hank. "Or your fearless leader goes down."

Rather than looking annoyed, Jolene started laughing. "Y'all are too much. I love it. You think I'm afraid of a bullet?"

"If it's going through your head," Lance responded. Hank slowly undid Melinda's wrist ties as they talked.

"You're still outnumbered," Jolene said. Dyani and Clem were both tense next to her, ready to draw their weapons in an instant. "And I know you won't risk that. Love's a pain like that, isn't it?"

"They're not outnumbered," a voice rang out. Up on the roof, Brigitta stood tall, her massive belly silhouetted as she pointed her shotgun at Deo, who held his hands up.

"Yeah, skedaddle you cowards. I'll take care of you later," Jolene said as the last onlookers skulked off at the sight of the shotgun. That just left Jolene and five of her gang.

Five they could handle.

"Let Deo go!" Clem shouted.

"Don't move," Brigitta yelled down. "Or your friend with the ugly hat loses his head."

Melinda breathed a sigh of relief to see that Rafi was up there too, quickly untying the rope. He threw it down and the tension against Melinda's neck eased. At the same time Nox came around the side of the building, pointing Rafi's pistol at them. Melinda could tell by the hesitant way Nox held the weapon that she would be all but useless in a shootout. Nevertheless, Hank was distracted by the sight, giving Melinda a chance to finagle the rope off her neck. She grabbed her hat and holster. Six on six now. They had a real winning hand.

Jolene's eyes narrowed. "Damn, how many of you are there? How you doing up there, Deo?" she asked, the carefree note in her voice replaced with sharpness.

"Just dandy boss," he called down. "She's looking to shoot me I think, but it's been a good run."

"Let us go and he'll walk another day," Lance said.

Brigitta gave a grunt and doubled over for a second. Rafi rushed over and Deo started to dart but not before Brigitta straightened, leveling the shotgun at him.

"Looks like your girl up there can hardly stand up," Jolene said.

"*Looks* like…" Lance said it slow. "We got the advantage here."

"Do you, now?" Jolene gave that smile again that made Melinda's jaw clench.

"Lance, watch out—" Melinda began but before she could do anything, Karla opened the grem's cage.

"*Idiots! It'll kill you too!*" Melinda tried to yell but the grem shot out fast as a bullet, directly toward the closest figure in front of it: Lance.

He dove to the side as the grem leapt at him, its claws outstretched. Before Melinda could grab Hank's gun or tell Nox to shoot, Jolene clapped her hands.

The grem fell backwards a few inches short of Lance. Karla, grunting, had a tight grip on a chain that led to the grem's collar. Now Melinda saw how the chain itself was bound up in the cage and had a double-chain mechanism that tightened around the grem's neck when it pulled taunt against its chained leash. Controlling it.

In the hubbub, Jolene's gang had moved efficiently. Clem had disappeared. Dyani, scowling, was back in front of Melinda with her gun and Lance sat frozen, his fate depending on whether Karla loosened the chain. Hank had wrestled the gun from Nox before she could shoot. Melinda tensed, preparing to rush Dyani—she could close the distance in an instant, and knock her gun to the side—when Karla piped up.

"Don't think any of ye wanna be moving now," Karla called. "Or I loosen up this chain so our friend gets a taste of your boyo here."

"Nifty little device, ain't it," Jolene boasted. "Now, no need for us to be barbarians and get blood everywhere, if you all cooperate." She smiled at Lance who still sat, his eyes locked on the grem as its claws strained in the few inches between them.

Above them, Clem had gotten the jump on Rafi and Brigitta, sneaking up to press her knife against Brigitta's neck. Now Deo held the shotgun and Rafi's hands were up in the air.

No, no, no.

They were no match for a band of outlaws, and one with a grem in their control at that.

Hank had tied Nox's hands and then took Lance's gun and tied his wrists too. Karla used the double-chained contraption to coax the growling grem back into its cage.

"We'll be down in a jiffy, boss," Deo yelled.

Jolene adjusted her hat and smirked. Her gaze slid to Melinda's as Hank neared with a fresh piece of rope. Melinda tensed as he started to loop the rope over her wrists, but Dyani waved the gun at her. "Gimme a reason to pump you full of lead," Dyani hissed.

"Bad hand for you, huh?" Jolene said to Melinda in mock sympathy. "Y'all put up a good fight, but Jolene's gang always makes it on top in the end."

Even though everything in her fumed, Melinda didn't let herself react. Something must've showed in her face though, because Jolene grinned, satisfied.

Hank led Melinda, Lance and Nox to sit in a row in front of the bait shop. Melinda glanced at Lance, but he looked back just as hopeless. Now, with a few people pointing guns at them—and them tied and with no weapons—they were out of options.

"She's pregnant!" Rafi bellowed as he and Brigitta came out of the building, Clem and Deo close behind them. "She's about to give birth! Let her go."

"I appreciate that, I'm benevolent, you know?" Jolene said as Rafi and Brigitta were forced to sit down next to the others. Brigitta glared and breathed heavily while Deo tied their wrists.

"Now we got too many headaches to deal with, and I ain't gonna hang a pregnant woman." Jolene snapped her fingers. "Put 'em in the jail cell."

"We don't have a jail cell," Deo reminded her, smoothing his hat feather. At her pause, he went on. "We turned it into storage for moonshine, remember?"

Clem chimed in. "You always said no reason to jail up anyone. Either we shoot 'em or make 'em work for us."

"That's right," Jolene mused. Her eyes lit up in a way that set off an alarm in Melinda. "Change of plans. I'm thinking you all come with me on a little trip. Since you caused such a ruckus, we have a case for retribution."

The others were grinning in a strange way.

"Retribution for what?" Rafi growled, glaring at Hank as he lopped rope over his wrists.

"Broken window, damaged rope, a few other grievances," Jolene ticked them off on her fingers. "Since you can't pay off your debt, we'll have to get our money back at South Bowl."

"And then some!" Deo whooped. The gang looked more excited.

"You're going to sell us? For labor?" Lance said, aghast. "You can't do that."

Jolene touched her hat and smiled. "Can't I, now?"

CHAPTER THIRTEEN

An hour later, Melinda was shoved into the back of a wagon with Nox and Brigitta. Lance and Rafi were put into a second wagon, behind which the gang had hitched the wooden platform holding the grem cage.

Hank settled in the open back of the wagon next to Brigitta and across from Melinda and Nox, keeping his gun up and Melinda's holster next to him. Clem climbed up onto their driver's seat, settling a bowler's hat over her short black bob, waiting as Dyani and Deo got a pair of horses for each wagon.

"You can't take us to South Bowl. Please," Nox's voice had a crack to it that made Melinda turn in surprise. Nox was afraid, *really* afraid, and her eyes were wide beneath wayward strands that had come out of her intricate braid.

Melinda had never been to the South Bowl before and had no desire to go, not even under normal circumstances. Word was their slippery rules tricked people to work for plenty more than what they owed and get stuck into endless debt. Their mentor, Abel, had rarely talked about his time working in forced labor on the railroad, but she had gotten the sobering sense that it was horrific. Horrific enough that Abel and his friend had released a demon just to get out of it, which ultimately caught up with Abel decades later.

"South Bowl gets a bad reputation, but it's got a lot to offer," Hank replied, though he had that same rehearsed tone like he wasn't convinced of what he was saying. The wagons started off at a brisk pace, rumbling over the dust and rocks, and they had to raise their voices over the din to be heard.

"You mean they pay a lot for bodies," Nox shot back, raising her bound wrists for emphasis. "Labor. They find ways to keep you there forever."

"No." Hank looked flustered, mopping his shining forehead with a threadbare handkerchief. "They give everyone a fair shot to work off their debt."

"Don't sound like you mean that," Melinda rasped through her burning throat. Her voice was still scratchy from having a rope around her neck but it was slowly coming back. "You trying not to feel too guilty? Since you're planning to sell us and my things?"

"Quiet now, and I mean it." He waved the gun at her and she slumped back. Next to her, Brigitta's eyes were closed and her face glistened. Her roped wrists rested on her enormous belly over her stained dress. Melinda felt a stab of regret that they hadn't had a chance to get her a change of clothes.

Melinda kept trying to work at the ropes around her wrists as she took stock. No weapons on the wagon except the pistol Hank was holding and her holster that she couldn't reach. Nothing else in the open wagon back that she could see—no loose wooden boards or anything that could be wielded as a blunt object. Hank's calm but guarded hold meant he was a pro. From here, Clem's shoulders were just visible, high up on the rider's seat and out of reach.

"Once we go through the checkpoint at the entrance to South Rim, it'll be all but impossible to escape," Nox whispered to Melinda. "It's a steep valley, one way in and one way out on this side of the bowl. We have got to get out of here."

The wagon went over a bump and a moan escaped Brigitta. Her forehead gleamed with sweat and her groan grew louder as the wagon jerked.

"It's a miracle that baby hasn't popped out yet," Nox observed and Hank's hand went to smooth his thick mustache. A nervous tic, Melinda realized.

Melinda pointed to Brigitta. "Hank, you gotta let her go."

"No can do," he said but sounded less sure, a small fissure breaking through his confidence.

"I'd say birth is imminent, wouldn't you?" Nox said dryly. "I mean look at her. It's a messy business. Certainly not one you want to do in the back of a wagon. You got experience in that area?"

Hank hesitated, his hand going to his mustache again. Outside the wind had started howling as Brigitta's moans grew louder.

"You got kids, Hank?" Melinda pressed. "Grandkids?" At the slight shift in his face, she knew she was right. "Granddaughter? How old?"

"Just born," he said reluctantly. "Haven't had a chance to meet her yet."

"Congratulations to you," Nox said. "Imagine her born in South Bowl. It isn't a place for a baby, you know that."

He looked miserable for a moment. "I can't go against Jolene," he mumbled.

"You don't have to." Melinda held out her wrists. "Get this and I'll take care of the rest."

"Goddamn," Hank sighed.

Brigitta gave an especially pained scream, doubling over. Nox used her bound hands to grab her shoulder as best she could, peering into Brigitta's face.

"Something's not right," Nox said. "She shouldn't be in this much pain, this quick."

Hank's face reflected the same alarm that cut into Melinda. "All right. I'll help you. Just make sure she gets what she's needs, and quick."

He cut the rope from Melinda's hands. Melinda glanced at the driver's seat, but Clem didn't notice anything was going on behind her as she yelled at the horses to keep up with Jolene's wagon.

"Help us take down Clem so we can escape," Melinda said as Brigitta groaned louder, Nox rubbing her shoulder in sympathy with her bound hands.

Hank shook his head. "If I do any more than this, I'm a hung man." He gestured to his face. "If you please."

Melinda gave a quick punch to his left eye, pulling it back a bit so it wouldn't be too painful but would still leave him with a shiner.

"Ooof." Hank held his hand over his face for an instant, wiping at his watery eyes. "That should be good enough."

"One more thing please," Melinda said. "My gun back."

"You only got one bullet left. Promise me you won't shoot Clem and we have a deal."

She nodded and he gave her the holster. The air around them was growing hazy, a whipping wind picking up.

"Best of luck to you," Hank said. He threw himself from the wagon back, landing hard but rolling expertly, just barely missing a sprawling cactus patch. Melinda tipped her hat to him before the winds started up again, sending great billows of dust that blocked her view.

Melinda turned to Nox and Brigitta. "Get the rope off her. We need to get her out of this wagon, now."

"How we gonna get her down?" Nox asked. "Can't very well expect a woman about to give birth to jump from a moving wagon, can we?"

Brigitta stopped moaning, opened her eyes and brushed a braid from her face.

"You were faking?" Melinda looked at her in amazement.

Brigitta frowned, rubbing her belly. "Something is certainly *happening*. I just played it up so he'd leave us alone."

"The sensation will get more intense and faster," Nox said. "I guess you have a few hours to a day or two before the birth."

"Lovely news." Brigitta's lip trembled in worry or grief. She grimaced as the wagon's wheels went over another mound of dirt. "You gonna stop this wagon?"

"I'll take care of it," Melinda said. "Hold on."

She climbed out the back, tying her handkerchief up over her mouth to fend against the gritty wind, and started making her way around the side, using the uneven wooden boards to wedge in her boot toes for a hold against the jerking wagon. Dark strands of her hair flew across her eyes and she used one hand to push them back.

The other wagon with Lance and the others were a hundred yards ahead, with the grem in its cage rumbling in the back. And maybe a hundred yards from *that* wagon, a gate rose in front of a steep drop that led to a massive valley. A few riders and a cart were waiting at the gate, and she could see figures through the grainy wind standing on either side. Patrolling.

Nox was right, Melinda thought and nearly lost her grip as the wagon went over another steep bump. With one guarded gate that led down to the valley, it'd be hard to escape once they were through the South Bowl checkpoint.

She inched around, finally getting better footing, now just a few feet from Clem.

"Damn horses, we're falling behind," Clem muttered to them. "Why y'all so resistant?" She steered alone, a defiant slump to her shoulders beneath her bowler's hat. No gun holster, just a knife sheath. Melinda allowed herself a smile. At least this would be fun.

"Howdy," Melinda said, muffled through her handkerchief but taking satisfaction in seeing a shock of surprise on Clem's otherwise sour face. She slammed her shoulder into Clem's, who gave a startled yelp and nearly fell off her seat.

"You wanna tango with me, scarecrow?" Clem spat. She righted herself and grabbed both of Melinda's hands, digging in her nails to draw blood before Melinda shoved her back. "I've danced with bigger partners than you."

The woman was stronger than Melinda had guessed and must've been made entirely of wiry muscle despite her average build. Clem yanked on the reigns, nearly causing Melinda to fall backwards as the two horses jerked. *Their* horses, Melinda saw. Relief at seeing Pepper and Mud all right was immediately replaced by outrage.

"I'll be taking my horses back now," Melinda snarled as Clem unleashed a knife. It was too small to do a lot of damage until she saw the metallic shine on the blade, likely a coating of poison. Melinda leaned back just as Clem nearly sliced it along her hand.

"You're a crafty one," Melinda said. She could see that, though Clem was tough, she was fighting with an anger and spite that was making her too fast, too careless. Clem lunged forward with the knife again, a move Melinda saw coming a mile away. She timed her dodge and threw a roundhouse punch that caught Clem off balance. An elbow to Clem's stomach sealed the deal, shoving her clean off the rider's seat.

Clem landed hard in the dirt with a scream, possibly a broken arm. She ducked as the giant wagon wheels thundered by within a few inches of her head.

Melinda turned to grab the reins, spotting Lance's wagon arriving at the armed South Bowl checkpoint.

She had to stop them.

She urged the horses to a faster gallop. She thought to untie Pepper and ride solo, but those precious seconds to undo the harness could make all the difference.

"It's too late, they're at the checkpoint already. They got armed guards!" Nox yelled at her from the wagon bed, and she could see it was true. "We should retreat and think of another way."

"I can't leave Lance!" Melinda shouted and pushed the horses to their full speed. It was getting harder to see with every second as the dust storm whipped up.

She strained—she couldn't lose them, not like this.

"They'll capture us!" Nox screeched. "Turn us around!"

Nox was right, Melinda thought grimly. They were poorly outnumbered and with only one bullet to boot. Pepper and Mud slowed as the dust storm descended, making it harder to see.

There was only one thing she could do to disrupt their plan and stop them from going into South Bowl. Melinda squinted through the dust, guessing she had only a few seconds before she lost sight of them entirely. She aimed directly at the grem cage that sat on the back of the wagon.

She never missed.

The shot rang out and the lock flew off. The grem burst out immediately before anyone could grab its chain. Melinda jumped off the wagon and ran toward the checkpoint, watching the other guards scatter and Deo and Karla scramble to grab the chain. Gusts of dust fully obscured Melinda's view, but she heard Jolene shout while shots went off in the chaos.

Melinda skidded to a stop as the grem emerged from the winds.

Beelining right toward her.

Melinda stumbled back. She hadn't predicted this—why would the grem come toward her instead of attacking the nearest human to it, one of the guards?

She tried to shoot, but she was out of bullets. She tensed, ready to slam the creature with the back of her empty gun, kick it away, whatever she had to do.

Instead of continuing to charge, the grem stopped a few feet away. It seemed to heave over the sand, making a hacking sound like a hellcat about to hurl.

What the hell?

Melinda paused, debating if she should attack or not, but then it looked up at her with its gleaming eyes and the sand in front of it shook, turning red. At first, Melinda thought it was a wayward wind from the dust storm but then hundreds of tiny mikrabs emerged from the ground, each with pinchers about the size of grains of rice attached to a red pebble of a body, just barely discernible to the naked eye. Sparks of azure on them almost made it look like a glittering cloud of red and blue rising from the sand.

The tiny crabs swirled up her pants leg with painful pinches followed by spots of numbness before she swept them away. *The grems are controlling them,* Melinda realized. But why didn't the grem use the mikrabs earlier to free itself? Why now?

To stop me, she thought. *But why?*

Before she knew it, hundreds of mikrabs ran under her sleeves and pants, the numbing effect from their pinchers slowing her arms and legs. Voices yelled in the swirls of dust, but she couldn't tell what they were saying.

"Get off of me," she grunted, swiping the crustaceans away fast as she could before her arms fell limply to her sides. Her legs temporarily gave out, sending her falling onto the sand. The grem slowly approached, ready to take advantage of her situation.

She watched its bumpy legs near and struggled to move. She couldn't do anything, maybe this was the end—

"Damn you!" Melinda bellowed, because her voice still worked even if the rest of her didn't. The mikrabs dispersed as quickly as they appeared. Already she felt tiny twitches of her sensation come back as the temporary numbness faded. But the recovery was too slow, the grem was next to her, leaning over, its red-rimmed eyes, each containing a scattering of pupils, drilled into her, too close, *too close—*

Melinda braced as the grem extended its claw, as delicately as a surgeon, to pull her handkerchief down from her mouth and with a hacking wheeze, breathed onto her face.

The rancid air rained down blue sparking prisms. Melinda squeezed her eyes shut and held her breath, but a curious prickling spread into the center of her chest.

The world turned blue for a moment, like a sheet had been thrown over her face.

The blue dust got on Brigitta, and she's been fine, Melinda told herself as she sat up, her limbs becoming more responsive. She wiped her face frantically and her vision cleared. *You're fine. You're fine.*

The grem was gone. Through the dust, she spotted Jolene's gang get the grem back into its cage and the wagon move through the checkpoint.

"C'mon," Nox gasped, appearing out of the dust winds and dragging Melinda backwards. "What happened to you?"

"Mikcrab bites and grem infection," Melinda muttered. "Got the dust on me. We can't leave them." She pulled away to stagger toward the checkpoint, but she couldn't see a damn thing through the wind. Blue washed over her vision again.

Nox somehow got them back into the wagon, climbed onto the driver's seat and hurried them off. Melinda choked back a cry as they fled away from the checkpoint.

And away from Lance.

CHAPTER FOURTEEN

Brigitta groaned in pain as the wagon continued to race along. The sandy terrain gave way to a jolting ride over rocks and dirt, making Melinda's teeth clatter and Brigitta's cries grow louder.

"Hold on back there," Nox shouted as she steered the horses best she could through the brown winds. She held her handkerchief up over her mouth and squinted against the gritty air that pelted them from all sides.

The last of the mikrabs' numbing venom faded, so Melinda could finally move again. Her vision was still tinged blue, no matter how much she tried to blink the color away from her eyes.

As far as she could tell the others hadn't followed them, likely giving up from the worsening dust storm. Her heart twisted at the thought of Lance descending into South Bowl. At least he was with Rafi. She had to hope they would figure a way out.

"We have to stop," Nox yelled, pointing at something. Melinda could just make out a lone ranch on a hill.

"That baby's about to pop out," Nox looked back, taking in Brigitta's moans, real this time. "Let's hope these strangers offer some kindness."

"I'm OK," Brigitta managed but cut off with a quick intake of breath and winced, grabbing her lower belly. "Damn, this hurts."

"Breathe. Your contractions are faster," Nox called over the wind, which seemed to slow momentarily. "That's good. Keep breathing. You all right, Melinda?"

"Just peachy," Melinda tried to say but now her head was pulsing something awful like she had barrel fever. She couldn't tell if the pit in her stomach, swirling like she had eaten days-soured milk, was from abandoning Lance, the grem dust, or both.

They had just reached the small ranch, a modest building made of wood and a slightly crooked roof, when Nox gasped. Melinda looked over the wagon side to see why: a couple, likely the owners, both lay with their faces to the blurred-out sun, eyes open in shock.

Both their chests were cracked open, and no doubt were full of grem eggs beneath the entrails.

"Burn them, quick, before the winds start up again," Melinda said and turned away, but the woman's wispy black hair whipping in the wind and the man's curled hands by his side would stay with her forever. In another circumstance that could've been her and Lance, attacked without warning back home. Home… She had to believe the grems hadn't made it there. That Aunt B and her town were safe.

Nox scrambled off the wagon, uncovering a set of matches from her bag and handing Melinda a cloth. Melinda tried to block the gusts best she could while Nox struggled to light a match in the wind, uncharacteristically cursing to herself as they went through one, two, three matches. Finally, Nox got the corner of the woman's gingham apron to light up, and they watched the flames eagerly spread.

Melinda closed her eyes, trying to will away the swirls of azure that burned into them, like someone shining a relentless light on her. Nothing felt right. It was like her limbs were barely attached, tied onto her torso with fraying string. Whether the strange sensation was from the grem dust or an after-effect of the mikrabs, she couldn't tell. She shook it off and helped Nox unhitch the horses and usher them into the small barn.

"You look terrible," Nox said, muffled through the handkerchief over her mouth.

"Don't fret about me. Tend to Brigitta," Melinda managed, pointing to Brigitta who had unsteadily climbed out of the wagon and now hunched next to it, panting.

"Is this baby going to be alright?" Brigitta asked between breaths.

Nox didn't answer but guided Brigitta to the porch. Melinda wondered if the same thought had occurred to her: that Brigitta or the baby might not make it. Worse yet was the quiet worry no one dared to speak—that Brigitta's exposure to the grem dust might have an effect on the baby. What if she was about to birth a monster?

I'll do what I have to, Melinda vowed to herself even as the decision evoked a heavy, dark dread. *Even if they can't.*

Not that she was in any condition to deal with a grem-baby monster if such a thing were to happen. It was getting harder for her to see through the blue glare and she couldn't shake the sensation of someone pouring sand into her limbs.

"When I said adventure, I didn't quite have this in mind," Nox sighed as they entered the small, kept home. The structure held a modest, neatly made quilted four-poster bed, large wooden bureau and a small stove in the kitchen. "But alas, some of us thrive under duress. You're lucky I'm one of them."

"The pain is getting worse," Brigitta gasped through gritted teeth. "It's so bad... I can't..."

"You can," Nox said firmly, and unearthed a bottle of spirits from the kitchen cabinet. Brigitta took a long swig.

It was hot, too hot. Melinda shrugged off her hat and duster, letting them slide onto the floor, and placed her hands on her knees, willing the dizziness to pass.

"I don't want this baby," Brigitta's eyes were wild. "Get rid of it."

"It's too late for that now," Nox said patiently.

Brigitta covered her face and mumbled, barely audible. "What if it's a grem?"

Nox guided Brigitta's hands to wrap around one of the bed posts. "Hold this. You can stand, squat, whatever feels most comfortable."

Brigitta's body tensed then relaxed and tensed again, her face crumpled in pain. Nox retrieved a bucket and placed it beneath her legs.

"Might be a few hours or a few minutes. You should know I've never done this before, but my boundless curiosity once again proves to be useful," Nox said. "And they say curiosity killed the cat. In any case, we'll make it through." She looked at Melinda. "Could you look for a well, water, sheets, alcohol? And a knife for the umbilical cord. Or, um, if the little one gets stuck."

"I—" Melinda began before she pitched onto the bed. A spear of pain shot through her temple, sending shudders down her spine. A low hissing started along her ears, like someone fast breathing through barely separated teeth.

"What's wrong!" Nox shouted but her voice warped and faded. The Edglings came back full force, eager, it seemed, by the split in her mind from the grem's dust. But now the Edglings were brighter, outlined in a halo of blue as they crouched around the bed, watching her.

"Get away from me," Melinda mumbled but the Edglings inched closer, their mouths stretched in perpetual wails and their eyes like chunks of fool's gold boring into her. This time she didn't have Lance's steady voice to help her snap out of the hallucination.

"Lay down." Nox's command was sharp, piercing through Melinda's vision. She pressed cold fingertips into Melinda's forehead, pushing her back on the small pillow. "Your body must be fighting whatever that grem did to you."

"Losing the fight…" Melinda muttered.

"I'll take a look at you after this baby." Nox cursed quietly and threw another sheet down below Brigitta, whose groans grew into shouts.

A buzzing sound intensified in Melinda's ears, as though her skull was full of insects. Her aching arms and legs shook while the Edglings darted around her. She curled up on the bed, willing the sensations to stop. The Edglings swelled as if resisting, before they disappeared.

Small urgings tweaked in her, like thoughts spanning out that weren't hers. Disconnected sensations, of restlessness, of a need to burrow, of a need to consume. Then—it was like something was digging relentlessly at the back of her brain, loosening herself and shooting her outwards, unspooling into darkness, toward something massive, a mountainous object that she was rushing toward. She screamed and tried to claw away but it was a nightmare folded into a nightmare, making her sink deeper as the bed itself swallowed her whole, squeezing in from all sides.

"Melinda!" Nox yelled and Brigitta's screams slammed her back into the room, along with the stench of sweat and blood. "Hold it together!"

Melinda turned, trying to see. It was like she was looking through a streaked eyepiece to spot Brigitta gripping the bed post in a half squat, and Nox kneeling next to her, hands up under her tied-up skirt. Strands of Nox's sweaty hair matted along her cheek as her brow furrowed in concentration.

"I see the top of the head!" Nox exclaimed. "It's stuck but..." Blood ran down her forearms and Melinda braced for the worse: what might come out if Brigitta had been infected, what would happen if the baby didn't make it, or if Brigitta didn't make it.

Brigitta gave an especially brutal scream. A small head, the size of an apple, appeared between Nox's fingers coated in mucus. The baby slipped fully out, along with so much blood that Melinda blanched.

Melinda struggled to see what was happening. Her chest seized up in panic at the horrible, yawning silence.

"Is it...?" Brigitta asked faintly. She grunted as another dense ball darker than blood fell out into the bucket. The placenta, Melinda guessed. Though she wasn't normally queasy, her head reeled as though she were about to faint.

Nox's hands worked over the small body. Then a sputtering and tiny cry, like a kitten mewling in protest. Melinda breathed again.

"Normal?" Brigitta asked, lowering herself onto the floor with a groan, her eyelids heavy. Her stomach was still ballooning, but nowhere near as big as before. Through her haze, Melinda tried to hear Nox's diagnosis.

"I'd wager so," Nox said finally. "A healthy boy."

Nox bundled the infant in one of the dirty rags and brought it over to them. The baby's smushed, dark face peeked out from the cloth.

"Entirely human by the looks of it," Nox said, pleased. The infant's eyes were closed and swollen below a smattering of matted dark hair streaked with blood. She gently wiped the gunk off its face. "And adorable at that."

Nox gently passed the snoozing infant to Brigitta, who stared at it in a peculiar way—a mix of awe, tenderness and a tinge of worry.

"He's so small," Brigitta said.

The buzzing in Melinda's head receded and she sat up, the bluish tint around her eyes dropping.

"Are you better?" Nox asked.

"Felt like I fought off the worse fever and nightmare at the same time," Melinda said. The unusual feelings were more manageable now. Maybe she had overcome it. Her eyes fell on Brigitta, who still sat among crumpled sheets stained red, cradling the baby.

"So much blood." Melinda stared.

"Everything hurts," Brigitta said.

"That's normal," Nox said. "For now." She helped Brigitta and the baby to settle into the lone rocking chair. "You'll be bleeding for a few weeks."

As they moved away from the bed, the thrumming along Melinda's ears came back, the blue veil fell over her gaze, and the odd shuddering started up through her limbs.

"Wait," Melinda said. The blue faded as Nox and Brigitta turned back to her.

"Something is stopping the grem sickness," Melinda said. The altered vision and sensations receded slightly.

"Hmm," Nox said. "What is it?"

Melinda's eyes fell on the baby and the certainty hit her, sure as a morning sun. "*Him.* Something about him is helping me."

Melinda stood. She let her hand graze the baby's bundle and sighed in relief as the symptoms disappeared. "That's better. But how?"

Nox scrutinized the baby, then Melinda. "Well, if Brigitta did get some of that dust on her like you said, it could be the child had enough exposure in the womb to develop a natural immunity. Was the dust on your skin?"

"I inhaled the dust," Melinda grimaced. "A lot of it."

Nox's eyes lit up. "Now that makes sense. Brigitta, and by proximity, her baby, only had a mild exposure they were able to fight off. But being affected in the womb may have given this child a more potent protection against the grem dust that somehow counteracts your affliction."

"So I just have to stay next to the baby forever to stay cured?" Melinda asked.

"I have an idea," Nox said.

The baby cried suddenly, high-pitched.

"What's wrong with him?" Brigitta asked in a near panic.

"He's hungry, surely," Nox said, helping to position him at Brigitta's chest to nurse.

"Ow! That hurts," Brigitta said. She frowned. "A lot."

"It should get easier with practice. We can also mix up a milk concoction. I had created quite a popular one for mothers who didn't nurse," Nox said, and rummaged through her bag until she had found a small glass vial. "Better news for you, we think he might have some immunity to the grems thanks to your earlier exposure. Would you mind if we take a sample?"

Brigitta nodded and Nox moved the cloth to expose the smallest foot Melinda had ever seen, with toes tinier than rice. She extracted a thin sewing needle and gave the heel a little prick. He cried for a second before going back to suckling.

"What's his name?" Melinda asked as Nox slowly collected the tiny drops of red from his foot.

Brigitta studied the baby with something Melinda hadn't seen in her until now: a deep, heavy sadness that seemed to tug every bit of her face down, ready to swallow her whole.

"Sam, naturally. After his father," Brigitta said shortly. "I will never forgive the grems for what they took away. I can still picture it, how it was supposed to be. Samuel here with me. Holding his…" she broke off and sobbed quietly. Nox and Melinda fell silent, Nox with a hand on Brigitta's shoulder.

"Do what you have to do," Brigitta said, angrily wiping at her cheeks. "Anything to stop the grems."

"All right." Nox straightened with the small vial. "I'll add a swab of his saliva, a little of his skin coating. All the biological materials to be safe."

"I thought you said the grem transferred this muck through breath, not blood," Melinda said.

Nox shrugged. "Infection by contact, likely breathing," she said. "But that can sink into the rest of the body. We know most of our elements within are transmitted through the blood, phlegm and biles, and can come up through the skin or saliva. Clearly there is some force here that transcends matter affecting you and him."

"As long as it works, I don't care too much," Melinda said as Nox finished collecting her samples into the vial. Nox pulled some twine loose from a bundle in the kitchen and used it to attach the vial around Melinda's neck.

"There, see if that helps," Nox said.

Melinda took a slow step back, bracing for the sensation. Nothing yet. She took another, until she was on the other side of the room. "No symptoms," she said.

"Does that mean he's part monster?" Brigitta asked fearfully.

"I don't know," Nox said. "Once I have a microscope again I'd love to take a look at his blood."

As they talked, Melinda's body ached and her head throbbed, but those felt like normal pains. As a deep-boned weariness settled in, she couldn't help but think of Lance and the others, destined for who knew what. She had heard the horror stories: people forced into grueling physical labor for years, tied up in sneaky contracts that made a small debt take a lifetime to work off.

"We can't leave right now." Nox said, watching Melinda's face and guessing at her train of thoughts. "I know you want to charge off and save them. But…" she gestured to Brigitta who sat with a distant look in her eye, ignoring the sleeping baby in her arms.

"How are you feeling?" Nox asked Brigitta. "You must be exhausted. Some parents don't feel a connection to their babies for a while, and that's all right. You've been through a lot."

"I *feel* it," Brigitta said. "I love him. More than I ever expected." She looked down at the infant and sniffed. "He's not just my last link to Samuel; he's so much more. It's a peculiar feeling. To know without hesitation, you'd give your life for someone without question."

"You both stay here," Melinda said. "Take care of the baby. I'll go myself."

"You're *not* going without me." Brigitta started to stand.

"Truth be told," Nox said dryly, "neither of you are in any condition to go marching off right now. And we can't go anywhere with that horrid dust storm raging outside. A day or two is not going to make a difference, Melinda. You know I'm right."

Nox's words echoed Lance's urgings for her to wait and sent a sharp point of pain through Melinda. No matter, she could sneak out at night and go solo. It'd probably be for the best.

What if the vial doesn't work? What if the grem infection comes back?

The thoughts nagged at her, stubborn as horse flies. She'd be useless if that happened—worse than useless. Much as she hated to admit it, her best bet was to stay.

"Let's get cleaned up. Eat. Rest." Nox herself looked uncharacteristically tired and Melinda fully relented, in part because every bit of energy seemed to leave her body at once. She plopped onto a wooden chair on the other side of the bed.

"All right," Melinda said. "And thanks for taking care of things. Helping me when the grem infection took over."

Nox looked surprised, then nodded, smoothing back her matted hair.

"When I hunted a demon last year, it told me there was a darkness in me because of all the monsters I've killed," Melinda said. She didn't know why she was confessing this to Nox right now, but something in her felt compelled. "Do you think that's true?"

Nox smiled wryly. "I doubt that. We all do what we have to. And it sounds like you saved plenty of lives in the meantime. Now rest, please."

"Grems could be coming this way," Melinda mumbled, slumping in her chair.

"Or maybe not," Nox said. "I'll take first watch."

Melinda closed her eyes—*just for a few hours*, she told herself. Her mind drifted to when she and Lance first met, when she had moved to Five Peaks to live with Aunt B after her mother's death. Hardly any time had passed in that small town before she'd met Lance. She'd figured a handsome, charming fella like him wouldn't be interested in a silent, pants-wearing gunslinger like herself. But they had trained together under Abel and Aunt B's tutelage, sneaking swims in the river and kisses between learning all there was about monsters. Their travels across towns, helping to rid communities of monster infestations, had been dirty, dangerous work, but with Lance she felt like they could tackle anything. Maybe this grem infestation was too much for them to handle, a final challenge they couldn't overcome …

She woke up pre-dawn. Still drowsy and before her memory clicked into place, she reached for Lance. Slowly the memories came back to her, each more horrific than the rest. She bolted up, taking in the scene. Brigitta dozed on the bed, the baby on her chest. The house smelled like cinnamon and radishes as Nox boiled something in the kitchen.

You'll rescue him, she told herself fiercely, letting the thought ground her. If one thing was true, it was that. She'd find him, no matter what, no matter how long it took, no matter how many dozens of grems might be standing in the way.

CHAPTER FIFTEEN

"We're what, ten miles from the South Bowl entrance?" Melinda said as they loaded up their wagon under the early-morning sun with a few of the jarred preservatives from the kitchen and some fresh linens. The dust storm had raged for a full two days, blasting the little cabin and their surroundings with screaming winds. Finally, the sun emerged the following morning, climbing a bluebell sky. Dust coated everything, but the air was sharp and clear. They had cleaned up best they could, Nox even ambitious enough to launder her dress.

"What do we need to do to get through—pretend to offer labor?" Melinda continued.

"They would separate us immediately. Easiest way would be to get in as vendors," Nox said. She had retied her dark hair into a simple braid over her shoulder, and her face was tired from helping Brigitta through the nights. Little Sam had woken up, crying and hungry, every two hours. Melinda had slept most of the time, dreamless, but now was rested enough and anxious to go.

"We ain't got a whole lot to sell," Brigitta said, casting a doubtful eye over the wagon back. They had found an embroidered dress from the previous owner that, while a bit big, was a good trade for Brigitta's stained frock. Despite dark circles under her eyes, her brown cheeks and plump lips were bright. Sam was tucked in a sturdy sash across her chest fashioned from one of the sheets. He gave a burp, louder than Melinda thought was possible for a baby, and closed his eyes.

"We'll make a short detour to Devil's End first," Nox said.

"What's there?" Melinda asked. She had scoured the home and shed for weapons, scrouging up a few bullets and a small pistol.

"My contact. He's not the most reputable character but he can help us." Nox frowned. "Last I heard he was taking a break in Devil's End but does the traveling show circuit once in a while. He'd probably have a good idea of how we can get in." She scrutinized Melinda for a moment before climbing onto the wagon's driver's seat. "The vial still working for you?"

Melinda nodded as she sat next to Nox to steer the horses. The vial secured around her neck made her feel almost normal, aside from the occasional disconcerting sensation that her head was floating ten feet over her body. "Peachy as can be for having a monster infection I guess."

They started off, Brigitta in the back of the wagon with little Sam, who squalled for a few minutes until he fell asleep.

"Do you think they're all right? Rafi and Lance?" Nox asked.

Melinda nodded curtly, ignoring the pang of guilt. Who knew what kind of shape Lance would be in when they found him? Even a day might be too much given the horror stories about South Bowl. Worse yet, he could already be in any of the mines or camps across South Bowl's expanse, where it would be impossible to find him amidst thousands of workers.

But she would find him, no matter what. No matter how long it took.

They urged the horses faster under the blazing morning until they reached a handful of buildings on the outskirts of the last town, about half a mile from the checkpoint to South Bowl.

As they entered Devil's End, a stench hit them that was a mix of sweat, dung, burnt meat and something worse: darkbella smoke. Two men in hats talked slow near a few hitching posts, sending out puffs of greenish smoke as they talked. Their dull eyes glanced at Nox's wagon as the horses slowed to a stop.

Brigitta whispered loudly from the back. "Sam's sleeping. Finally."

"Don't think lil' Sam should go in the tavern," Nox said while she and Melinda hitched up the horses. "You stay here. We'll find my contact."

Brigitta nodded in relief, settling back in the wagon and closing her eyes, one hand on Sam.

"She safe alone?" Melinda asked.

Nox dabbed the sweat off her forehead with her handkerchief and nodded. "Most of these folks on darkbellas can barely put together a sentence, let alone rob someone."

Nox led them to the front of a large building with rows of windows, a combination restaurant and saloon. The door was splintered and didn't close fully. No music or jovial chatter floated out, just muttering and the clink of cups.

Nox paused. "This is a bad idea."

"If your contact is our best bet to get into South Bowl, no sense in waiting." Melinda banged into the building. The acidic stench of darkbellas, the highly addictive flower, hit her hard, tickling her nose. A few folks sat, some in a back room thick with the telltale olive green smoke of the plant. These were the people who just got out of their contracts at the South Bowl, or who were resigned to going in for reasons she couldn't guess.

"Stinks." Nox inhaled deeply. "You ever try it?"

"I've seen em in the wild. Darkbellas grow near the Edge and some monster habitats," Melinda said, wrinkling her nose as she thought about the dark, five-petaled purple flowers with green centers that glowed at night. "Hard to believe people harvest what springs up in the footprints of monsters."

"It's the best high you ever felt," Nox said in a way that couldn't hide the bit of nostalgia. "I don't anymore of course," she said quickly.

"Most people can't kick it when they start." Melinda scanned the bar. She froze when she thought she saw Lance, hunched over a table, but it was just a man with the same build and sandy hair, shifting to reveal a much older and gaunt face. Her eyes were still playing tricks on her. She fiddled with the vial, tugging on the twine to make sure it was secure.

"I'm not most people. Ready for this?" Nox made her way up to the bar. "There he is. The magician."

A lanky man sat at the center of the long, nicked wooden board that passed for a table. His dark hair was tucked behind his ears alongside a neatly trimmed beard. But what caught Melinda's eye were how his long nervous fingers absently played with a coin, flipping it between his fingers with the practiced smoothness and quickness of a pickpocket.

"Kenji Shio," Nox greeted. "It's been too long."

"Howdy Nox," he said. The way he stared at Nox reminded Melinda of a man seeing water after a long walk through the desert. "I'm glad opportunity and fate have intermingled to see you once again."

They had history, clearly. Melinda didn't miss how he stiffened imperceptibly, how Nox didn't seem bothered as she slid onto the stool next to him. Like she held some power over him. Hopefully enough power to convince him to help.

"You still do that traveling show?" Nox spoke conversationally like they didn't have somewhere to be.

"I retired in search of something grander," he said, and gave her a meaningful look. "Worked for the circus a bit. Tightrope walker. Not quite as grand as I was hoping." He stared morosely into a mug of something dark.

Melinda cleared her throat and hovered behind him, making sure she was visible at the corner of his periphery.

Kenji gave a start, then turned and craned his neck to look up at her. "Well, that's something. I haven't known you to travel with a posse, Nox."

"That's Melinda," Nox said. "Monster hunter."

"Is he sober enough to be useful?" Melinda asked Nox.

"Coffee is the strongest thing I consume," Kenji replied, looking back into the depths of his mug as though he were deciphering a message.

"He likes to preach the virtue of a clear mind," Nox said.

"Why on earth does he hang out here then?" Melinda took a step closer, half an inch from jostling him.

Kenji shrugged. "Makes me feel better. A reminder of the depths we can all fall to." He made a disinterested gesture to the back room, where a stifled sigh rose up, someone coming off their high. "And staying sober helps to keep my magic sharp."

"Magic," Nox scoffed. "He means tricks."

"That's right. Sleight of hand, a performative art that regales the lands, winning the favor of the fortunate rich and unlucky sloven," he agreed. "Bringing a bit of enchantment to that old grey thing called life."

Nox rolled her eyes. "We need your help."

"Those words always seem to lead me to inevitable, irrefutable trouble." Kenji shook his head and turned back to the coffee. "So, I must surely decline your offer and enticements, whatever they may be. Just going to wallow here and then wait for the unavoidable doom to descend."

Melinda folded her arms. She could spot a grifter from a mile away and suspected he was bluffing, waiting for Nox to make it worth his while. She resisted the urge to shake him into his senses or storm out and head to South Bowl herself. If Nox said he could help, Melinda believed her.

Nox pushed the coffee away from him. "What are you even wallowing about?"

"Well, after you left me–"

"Kenji," Nox all but chided, like someone who'd made the same argument too many times. "I am not interested in marriage or partnerships. We did business together, that's it. You can't still be holding that against me."

"You don't understand. No one is like you. I need someone who's smart. Different," Kenji said. "I could really turn things around with you by my side."

The two seemed to be on the brink of an argument that would certainly derail their passage into South Bowl, so Melinda eased herself in front of Nox.

"You see what's going on out there?" Melinda asked. "Grems are sweeping through like the plague. We don't have time for parlor-room chitchat when people are getting hurt, take my meaning?"

"We need help getting into South Bowl," Nox added. Kenji barked an incredulous laugh.

"Today," Melinda said.

Kenji stood and donned a beaten bowler hat, tipping it grandly at them. "Ladies, I appreciate the consideration of my services, but I must regretfully decline."

If Lance was there, he would've played the nice guy, offering a rolled-up cigarette and they'd do their combo sugar-and-vinegar approach to get what they needed. She'd have to hope the vinegar approach alone would work.

She rose to her considerable height. Kenji, though lanky—nearly gangly—just came to her forehead. He blinked, looking sour as a disdainful cat. Melinda slammed him into the bar. Nox gave a startled squeak but no one else reacted, not even the proprietor, an elderly man slumped in the corner, watching everything with sharp, hooded eyes.

"You're going to help us," Melinda snarled at Kenji. She had to give him credit; Kenji didn't react, maybe had seen his fair share of fights.

"Melinda!" Nox shouted. "Pull in your horns!"

"What do you want, money?" Melinda gave him a shake again before releasing him with a disgusted shove. "It ain't going to mean a damn thing if the grems get us all. But name your price." She was bluffing, somewhat. She only had a few silver coins tucked in the inseam of her boot, but she'd worry about that later.

"Hmm." Kenji brushed off his shirt and adjusted the cords around his neck. "You are thornier than a cactus Miss…Melinda, was it? And a large sum is a good motivator but not enough for that kind of endeavor. Apologies."

"OK." Nox rubbed the bridge of her nose. "How about this? You help us and I'll get you permission to play your show in Sagebrush Junction and Thundering Ridge next year. Assuming society survives this infestation."

A grin cracked Kenji's face and he touched his chest. "Quicker than a bullet to my heart, as always. You've got a deal, my dear."

He rummaged behind the bar for a moment to retrieve a metal-studded, leather scabbard. From it poked a broadsword's metal pommel.

"Tell me you have a proper pistol," Melinda said.

"I prefer this. It takes a certain mastery." Kenji suspended the scabbard from his belt. "I'm good, but you should see my brother. We both trained when we were young."

"We're bringing him for his insights, not his fighting ability," Nox reminded Melinda as they headed out of the bar.

"So, South Bowl." Kenji gave a jaunty smile. "We'll go through the gate. Smooth and simple."

"That's your plan?" Melinda said. "Don't they check papers?"

"They're strict," Nox said. "And prone to arresting people on a whim. Once we go through it's all but impossible to get out."

"I've done it countless times," Kenji said as they reached the back of the wagon. Brigitta poked her head out and yawned, her hand cupped around the baby's dozing head.

"Well, howdy." Kenji bowed deeply at her. "Miss?"

"Kenji, meet Brigitta," Nox introduced. "And Sam."

"An honor to meet you, and the little man as well. All right then, let's take this show on the road," Kenji said.

Nox sat in the back with Brigitta and the baby, while Melinda and Kenji took the driver's seat. Melinda tightened her jaw as they approached the checkpoint half a mile later. The same gate that Lance and the others had disappeared through. Melinda kept her gaze relaxed to catch any movement in her peripheral vision as they approached.

The guard, a slim man with a neat handlebar mustache and more freckles than Melinda could count stood attentively beneath a wooden arch. A rifle was slung behind his shoulder and two six-shooters rested on either hip. Two other guards stood around a barrel a few feet behind the arc, squinting at a game with small wooden pieces. A few feet beyond them stood a corral with a dozing man and what looked like half a dozen empty stalls, and a donkey.

"Business in South Bowl?" The jaunty guard swept a quick eye over them and put a wad of tobacco from his pocket into his mouth. "Everyone out of the wagon, please."

"Best show you've ever seen," Kenji said, spreading his arms, a complete turnaround from the morose fella she had observed in the bar. As they lined up, he squeezed Nox's shoulder and Melinda thought she could detect the suppressed frown from Nox. "A family of magicians we are. And excited to introduce our show to South Bowl."

The guard kept chewing his tobacco and didn't say anything.

"It's true," Nox gave her crooked grin. "We use chemical mixtures and sleight of hand to provide a truly superb show."

"And a baby?" The guard said skeptically. Brigitta ignored him, continuing to stroke Sam's head.

"The little man is the star of the show," Kenji said breezily.

"What does he do?"

"Well, you'll have to attend to see," Kenji said after a beat. "He's famous in the north, and this is his first southern tour. Want to see a magic trick?" With a flourish, Kenji appeared to pull from the guard's ear a ticket, a wrinkled printed thing with no date. He folded it and handed it to the guard. "Free ticket for you and a friend, complimentary, on me."

"Well ain't that something! All right," the guard said with a pleased grin and gestured for another guard to bring him a ledger. "I haven't been to a show in a while."

He jotted something down in the ledger and held it for Kenji to sign. They started to get back onto the wagon when the guard cleared his throat.

"Wait," The guard said. "What about her?" His gaze landed on Melinda. "You don't look like a magician."

Melinda made sure to keep her firing hand relaxed, not drawing attention to it. But she was ready if they decided to draw and take them as labor like the others—

"Why this here is one of the world's finest sharpshooters." Kenji leaned in and lowered his voice. "She can shoot an acorn off a pig's head from 500 yards. Never seen anything like it. Unbelievable really. Legend has it she made a deal with the devil itself to get uncanny powers of perception."

"As the man said, you'll need to see the show to learn more," Nox chimed in. "Opening is tomorrow."

"All right, my day off is tomorrow as it so happens." The guard smiled at Nox before gesturing them through.

"May fate grant you all you wish," Kenji said cheerfully as they settled into the wagon. Stones skidded out from under the horses' hooves as they started down the path.

"About two hours to get down," Kenji said while the horses picked up speed down the narrow, winding decline. He dabbed the sweat along his neck with his checkered handkerchief. "Hot enough to give a toad a sunburn, isn't it?"

"Those tall tales sure came easy to you back there," Melinda said.

"Tales are just words imbued with a bit of magic, bringing some joy to others," Kenji replied and swept an arm out as they turned around a bend, the full view of South Bowl's westmost region sprawling out before them. Melinda had to gape for a moment. The giant valley was full of red-banded rocks with canyons, peaks, and mesas as far as the eye could see. She even spotted a lake, sparkling far off.

"Oh my," Brigitta said from the back. "It's so…grand."

"Truly magnificent," Kenji sighed. "Some 100 miles across, I believe."

A tinge of smoke and coal powder carried on the winds as they descended cautiously. The sounds of birds trilling and the vast views made Melinda's shoulders unknot the slightest bit, until Gold Egg came into view.

CHAPTER SIXTEEN

Gold Egg stretched below them, easily five or ten times the size of towns Melinda was used to seeing. A golden dome shone at the center of dense blocks of buildings.

"A sight," Kenji said. "This is just a corner of South Bowl. It reaches much farther, but this town is one of its crowning achievements."

"It may look pretty on the outside but it's all rotten," Nox said.

Kenji tsked. "Such a provincial mindset, Nox. I'm surprised."

"I didn't know a town could be that big," Brigitta said in wonder. "How are we ever going to find Rafi and Lance?"

"Gold Egg is where the wealthy live," Kenji said. "The laborers would have been carted off to one of the camps for processing. But no need to fret. All is going as planned."

What plan? Melinda thought.

Normally at a main road, the border of a typical town had a watering station with a trough or two, wooden posts to lean on and a tent for shade. Gold Egg had *several* watering stations with rows of tents and troughs and even wooden benches. They parked the wagon and Melinda paid for the horses to get a much-needed rest, wash and feed in one of the barns.

Gold Egg was much more industrial than the frontier towns she was used to, with countless rows of stone streets crammed with jostling carriages and women in big gowns. Everyone seemed to be in a hurry and spoke louder than necessary, like each was trying to outtalk the nearest stranger. Melinda fought to keep her bearings as they navigated along the narrow, zigzagging streets. Soon she was hopelessly lost while they followed a confident Kenji around crowded, smoky corners.

"After we find Lance and Rafi, we need to look for the swarm. For all we know, the grems could be on the brink of invading Gold Egg," Melinda said. She couldn't help but imagine the town overrun, the beautiful gowns torn, the loud chats replaced by screams, blood splattering the cobblestone. She quickly dismissed the vision.

"So what do you think?" Kenji said after they turned into a wider street full of stalls pressed up against each other.

"Loud," Brigitta said, but she didn't look too bothered by it. They threaded through the marketplace, one of the biggest Melinda had ever seen. She overheard some of the prices that were being haggled—a jaw-droppingly high amount if you asked her—as an exuberant band played. One might forget there were roaming monsters while walking along the polished streets amidst the fancy dresses and ties. She fiddled with her vial and tried to shake off a strange feeling, a feeling like she was walking on stilts, like her head had expanded to twice its side and floated over the street.

Nox glanced at her. "You all right?"

"Not used to the commotion is all. And the stench," Melinda said and kept quiet about the strange feelings. They had to focus on finding Lance, not on figuring out what was happening to her.

"That's the smell of progress," Kenji waggled his finger, and Nox rolled her eyes for the umpteenth time.

"I didn't know that people lived like this," Brigitta said as they squeezed past a crowd surrounding a couple harking their patent medicines and panaceas in a variety of glass bottles.

"Like crammed cattle?" Melinda said.

"Seems like you could meet all kinds of folks," Brigitta replied, sounding wistful. "Learn new things."

"A high number of people from various backgrounds can provide reservoirs of culture and knowledge if the conditions are right," Nox said, her gaze lingering on a table crammed with dried herbs. "Though I don't think South Bowl is such a place."

"We're not here for a tour anyhow," Melinda said. "Where are the camps?"

"Southeast of town, further into the Bowl," Kenji replied, continuing deeper into the market. "Miles and miles of camps lay to the east of here. We're not just going to stumble onto your friends. We need information."

Melinda tensed amidst the crowds. She glanced at the others, but no one seemed particularly ill at ease. Brigitta was staring at everything with wide eyes, soaking it in. She didn't even seem to mind the shoulders brushing her as she held Sam close. Nox looked the same, lips pursed in a not quite smirk, passing a discerning eye over the sellers' offerings.

The street spit them out into a circular opening featuring a water fountain nearly as large as Melinda made of painted ceramic tiles. Behind the fountain loomed a statue. Twice the size of a regular man and made of hammered metal, the somber-looking figure was clearly supposed to be an impressive sight. It sat in front of the gold dome they had seen earlier, which rose twenty feet above them, reflecting the sunlight and making them squint.

"All right," Kenji said, refilling his canteen in the water fountain. "We have a few possible ways to find out what we need. We must hire a purveyor of information or two. Now they're not going to be cheap—"

Before he could continue, someone approached them.

A few someones in fact.

Two pairs of men flanked them while a third, older man with an enormous hat and neatly trimmed sideburns stepped forward. Melinda cursed. They were surrounded.

"Please come with us," the older man said beneath a thin mustache. His checkered shirt had a row of small metal pins. Some sort of official, she guessed.

"Certainly," Kenji said, touching his bowler hat in greeting. "Happy to oblige."

"Why should we go with you?" Melinda snapped.

"Need to get your permits sorted and all that," the leader said. His smile came easy. Too easy, Melinda thought. They didn't have time for more detours. Tiredness or desperation made her touch her gun.

"Our business doesn't concern you," Melinda said. Kenji cleared his throat, but she ignored him. She tapped the handle of her gun for emphasis. "We need a permit for just existing?"

One of them men drew his gun.

"Now now, no need for that," the leader said while Kenji nodded in hasty agreement. The leader's eyes seem to linger a second too long on Melinda. Not uncommon; sometimes it took people a second or two to take in her unusual height or her clothes. But he almost looked as though he recognized her. "You're safe here."

"Your approach begs to differ," Nox murmured.

"Pardon my friend here," Kenji said smoothly. "She had a nasty run-in with a few outlaws who tried to strip us of all our worldly belongings just yesterday, so she's wound up tighter than one of those lovely pocket watches you have there. Is this absolutely necessary?"

"PS Rivera is the one who first came up with our barter system," the leader looked reverently up at the statue. "But to ensure the smooth workings of what makes the town as wonderfully thriving as it is, we need to make sure everyone's papers are in working order. And I'm guessing here, by your reaction, that if we take you into our impressive city hall here, that you all don't have the necessary permits. Is that correct?"

Kenji paused. "Sir, you are right. Our papers were unfortunately misplaced in the latest dust storm while we were ambushed by said outlaws. However, we are a well-known traveling act—"

"I'll stop you there, son," the leader lifted a hand. "We'll take you to Carlos to get all this sorted, all right? We'll have you back on your way in a jiffy."

Melinda tensed and Brigitta shifted uneasily while Sam whimpered. Fresh off their last encounter at the Spirals, Melinda didn't trust these strangers one bit. Going with them could be a trap, especially in a place reputed to be as slippery as this one.

"What's to stop you from putting us in one of your infamous labor camps?" Melinda asked bluntly.

The leader looked at Melinda for a moment and then burst out in a wide smile, like he was trying to stifle a laugh. "Well. We got quite a reputation if you think we just round up innocents and do what we will. You hear that, boys?" He chuckled. "We got some work to do on the reputation front if that's the case. So, first time here. Let's give you the proper tour."

Melinda thought his words would have a double meaning, but the leader did indeed give them a tour, his voice swelling with pride as he pointing out the first official building of Gold Egg, a squat and modest former town hall, now a supply store with a variety of horse feeds. Melinda didn't bother to listen. Instead, she tried to get her bearings and figure out an escape. The four other men followed them closely, clearly ready to act should they try to run. Not that they'd be able to make a swift escape in a town they hardly knew.

They trailed the leader toward a row of homes, packed closer together than she personally would prefer, gleaming and tall with fresh white paint over what looked like cedar wood. Somewhere far off trains blared and wagon wheels rattled incessantly.

"If you could relax that trigger finger just a tad," Kenji whispered, sidling next to her, "it will go a long way to helping our situation."

"We don't know what kind of crooked rules they operate by here," Melinda retorted. "I'm not taking any risks. We can't waste any more time."

"I get it. You care deeply about finding your friends," Kenji said. "I too, care deeply about things." His eyes drifted toward Nox ahead, who, along with Brigitta, was listening to the leader rattle off facts about the town's founder. "But I like to think of life as a game of chess. One must have patience and think several steps ahead."

"Life is more like a drunkard with a shotgun," Melinda said. "Things can go sour in a second if you don't watch out."

The group stopped at an especially large home and passed through intricately carved wooden doors. They spilled into an ornate parlor room that stretched larger than Melinda's whole house back at Five Peaks. Marble lined the floor, with small tables twisting up to hold porcelain pots and glass. Though Melinda suspected it was a trap, it felt good to get out of the sun and into the cool shade of the house.

"Wait here," the leader said. "One thing," he added when Melinda passed by him. She tensed, waiting for the inevitable request to turn in their weapons, for "communal safety." She'd rather fight than hand over the meager protection she had.

"Y'all want some grub?" The leader asked and then answered himself. "Course you do. Have a seat while we rustle something up."

He closed the door, leaving them alone.

"I'm hungry enough to eat a fence post," Brigitta said. "They are quite hospitable, aren't they?" She glanced up at the half a dozen paintings on the walls depicting various strangers, with a larger-than-life portrait of PS River centered in the middle of the wall.

"Don't be fooled. Are we locked in?" Melinda asked while she assessed. Plenty of vases and decorative pots they could use as weapons. Two large windows along the far wall that they could break through if needed. Guards likely outside.

"No." Kenji checked, and the doorknob turned easily. "Just run-of-the-mill hospitality."

Nox shot him a skeptical look. "You really believe that? They're all shiny, gold plated here, hiding decay beneath them."

"Are you always suspicious of those who have an appreciation for wealth and progress?" Kenji asked mildly.

"It all looks lovely." Brigitta winced as she sank into a red chair with a comically tall back. She trailed her free hand along the velvet armrest while Sam squirmed against her. "I didn't know people really lived like this."

"Well, you look positively smitten, but all that glitters isn't gold," Nox said, and Melinda had to agree.

"If we're not locked in, let's skedaddle. We need to get to those camps," Melinda said.

"There are dozens upon dozens of mining operations here. For all you know, your friends could be in one a hundred miles away already. The Bowl is enormous." Kenji brightened. "This may be better in fact. If we are to meet the town administrator to handle paperwork, he probably is the keeper of the labor ledgers. He might be able to provide the information we need, especially for the right price."

"We have no idea where the swarm is. Or what kind of state Lance and Rafi are in. We don't have time to dilly dally." Melinda tugged irritably on the vial round her neck, but Kenji was right she supposed. Interrogating the administrator for information here would probably be the fastest way to find the others. She glanced outside the expansive windows to the street, where two children ran by, playing with a stick. She listened for anything unusual that would portend a disaster.

"Want to see a trick while we wait?" Kenji said, taking a seat in one of the polished chairs and leaning his sheathed sword carefully next to him. He pulled out a coin, letting it slip smoothly between his fingers.

"No," Nox said.

The door cracked open and a woman wearing a gray apron with her dark hair in a bun entered. She balanced a silver plate with teacups that looked too delicate to touch, a kettle and a small plate of cakes no bigger than her thumb.

"Excuse me miss, we really need to talk to the administrator," Kenji said. "It's a matter of extreme urgency."

The woman ignored him, and sat the platter down on a squat, wide table in the center of the room. She placed a full cup in Brigitta's free hand, then left without a word. Just as she departed, the door opened again.

A man not much older than Melinda strode in, a pocket watch chain swinging from his checkered suit. His shoulders were relaxed as he swept in with the air of someone used to getting what he wanted.

"Carlos Rivera," he introduced himself, turning his bright blue gaze onto each of them and passing a hand through his curly dark hair. His glance lingered on Melinda a moment too long.

"Always happy to meet visitors. We get a lot through here, but first timers are a special case. Don't mind me saying but you all look tired as worn-out fiddle strings. Sit. Have some tea. Then we'll get you settled up with your paperwork and on your way."

"We appreciate that, truly," Kenji said, bowing his head. He poured a generous amount of tea. Nox stayed standing, picking at one of her bangles while Brigitta slouched even further into the overstuffed chair, sipping her tea.

"It's part of the process, especially with folks clearly coming in for the first time." Carlos gestured at them, flashing a giant gold ring sporting a ruby. His blue eyes reminded Melinda of swirling river water under an especially sharp sun. "We have an orderly society here. No unsavory character outbursts, no wild animals roaming about."

"Orderly…" Nox trailed off. "Lots of people in contracts to do whatever you need, isn't that right?"

He pressed his fingers together with a patient smile. "There's a lot of rumors, I know. What we offer is a rehabilitation program that benefits everyone."

"However you say it, it all sounds the same to me," Nox said, helping herself to a miniature cake.

Carlos turned to Brigitta, his forehead creasing suddenly. Melinda guessed he might chide her for being out with an infant, but instead his words swelled with concern. "How old?"

"A few days," Brigitta said.

He blinked. "My dear miss—please, let us get you a proper fitting for that little one. And perhaps a bath?"

Brigitta tilted her head, too surprised to respond. Carlos gave her an encouraging smile and Brigitta smiled back, charmed, but Melinda didn't buy it one bit.

"That would be very kind," Brigitta said, smoothing her braids. "Thank you."

Melinda opened her mouth to tell her it wasn't a good idea to separate, but the hopeful look in Brigitta's eye was enough to make her relent. She glanced at Nox who shrugged.

"Lucia!" Carlos called. The woman who had brought the tea cracked the door open. "Take her please, for a swaddling and bath."

The woman nodded, leading Brigitta out without a word. Melinda watched with worry as Brigitta departed but focused her attention back to Carlos.

"Is Lucia in one of those contracts you mentioned?" Nox asked.

"Her?" Carlos laughed. "No, that's my sister."

"Could have fooled me," Nox said and Kenji cleared his throat. Melinda had to appreciate Nox's bluntness even if it filled the room with an awkward pause.

Carlos studied Nox for a second. "I can see you have some preconceptions about our town here. I worked hard to get where I am. I've found over time that a lot of people who would criticize are in fact deeply envious. As long as no one's getting hurt, do what makes you happy, I say. Now I'm guessing—and correct me if I'm wrong won't you please—that you're here for something serious and not part of a show."

Melinda tensed at the revelation, but Carlos had spoken just as friendly or relaxed as if he was talking about the weather. She could probably strongarm Carlos if she had to and force him to tell her where Lance was. But undoubtedly the men who had first brought them here were within shouting reach, probably just outside the door.

"What gave it away, if you don't mind," Kenji asked, clearly sensing it was time to give up the ruse. He sipped his tea, looking for all the world like he visited these types of parlors frequently.

"When you're in my line of business you can guess people's professions fairly quickly. No one, save yourself, seems to have the typical showmanship you'd see in the type of traveling group you claim to be," Carlos said, not unkindly. "Now, let's discuss why you're really here and I can see what I can do. Like I always say, there are solutions to any issue. Particularly if you have funds or time to give, we can work out almost anything."

"Now that the game's up, no need to sip tea and pretend anymore." Melinda crossed her arms. "We're hunting monsters. We need to find our friends and stop these grems. You should prepare your city." Her gaze shot to the window. Any minute the swarm could appear, any minute dozens—hundreds—of grems could be burrowing beneath their bustling streets and begin another day of bloodshed. The window grew dark suddenly, as though a cloud were passing overhead.

Not again, she thought, but shadows jumped up as Edglings took form, their movements frantic, chaotic. Bad enough she felt off-kilter from the grem infection; last thing she needed was to hallucinate Edglings again. The visions seemed to come more when she was under duress, but a small part of her had hoped that the grem infection might've warded off the hallucinations for good. Instead, it felt like the sightings had only gotten worse.

Carlos fixed his gaze on her, snapping her out of it. The room brightened. His blue eyes were disarming, his gaze a mix of charm and scrutiny that had probably helped him get a long way in life. She didn't return his smile.

"You don't have to worry about anything hurting us here," Carlos said gently. "We are fortified against any disasters and have many precautions in place to protect our citizens."

"Their friends were mistakenly taken here a few days ago," Kenji chimed in. "They were kidnapped by outlaws."

"Well, that's easy enough to fix," Carlos said. "And I'm so terribly sorry for the mix-up. Let's see if we can get this all straightened out. But first there's something I would request."

Melinda nodded briskly. The catch was coming.

"Let me guess," Nox said. "Promise of our first born? Signature in blood? Lifelong servitude?"

Carlos ignored her comments and gestured for them to follow him out the doors. "A quick carriage ride to where I suspect we'll find your friends. We'll discuss more when we're there."

For an especially large sum no doubt, Melinda guessed ruefully, though relief flooded her. She'd find Lance soon enough, then they could start working on eliminating the grems.

In the glaring afternoon sunlight, she followed Kenji as he approached a four-wheeled, carriage painted a rich black that seemed to be waiting for them. Carlos' righthand man, the leader of the pack who had given them the tour, stood nearby. Carlos himself paused at the carriage, his gaze uncanny in this light.

Melinda stopped abruptly, causing Nox to run into her from behind. Under the dazzling sun, Carlos' eyes were blue. *Too* blue. His irises gleamed a familiar azure hue that made her chest clench.

CHAPTER SEVENTEEN

"Nox," Melinda hissed. As she spoke, she became more certain, watching Carlos say something to Kenji. "Look at his eyes. There's something wrong…"

Nox stiffened, undoubtedly realizing it at the same time. "It's the same shade as—"

"Don't get in the carriage," Melinda shouted, and drew the pistol.

"What is it this time?" Kenji looked exasperated. Carlos stayed relaxed, even as his companion drew his gun.

"He's under the grem's mind control. Like the Edge monsters." Nox pointed. "His face."

Carlos still didn't react, merely smiled. "Control is not quite the right word. More a merge, a connection." He gestured for his companion to lower the gun.

"Where were you going to take us in the carriage?" Melinda demanded. Her heart pounded as questions raced through her mind. How could a human be infected, controlled like the culidae? And how had the grems gotten here already?

"To show you the possibilities," Carlos said. "And how we can reach our next level of societal growth. Of peace."

Nox recoiled. "Your delusion is remarkable. The grems gutted people."

"I admit their method of procreation is unsavory. We've developed a solution. One where no one has to die," Carlos said, looking at Melinda now.

"What solution?" Nox asked.

"It's easier to show you. If you don't want to take part, you can leave," Carlos continued. "But at least see our methodology and come find your friends. I'm certain you will be pleasantly surprised."

Everything in Melinda screamed to not go in the carriage. She made sure to keep her stance relaxed so she wouldn't telegraph her intentions. Carlos himself had a big build and was as tall as Melinda, but even with mass strength on his side, he wouldn't be expecting her punch. His friend examined a hangnail as Carlos talked. She didn't expect Nox or Kenji to be much help in a fight, but she could take on two people.

"Please," Carlos added at their silence. "Take a moment to con—"

Melinda rammed her shoulder into Carlos' at an angle mid-sentence. It was enough for him to stumble, grunting as his head slammed into the top of the carriage door.

Melinda whirled to aim her pistol at Carlos' righthand man but saw that Kenji already had his sword drawn, pointed at the man's throat. She had to admire the grace and ease with which Kenji wielded the weapon, as if it were a natural extension of himself.

"That thing came in handy after all," Melinda said. She gave Carlos' helper a quick punch to the gut that would take the breath out of him for a minute or two at least.

"Let's make a run for it," Melinda said over the man's gasping.

"What about Brigitta?" Nox hesitated, looking up at the house's second-story windows.

"Might I eagerly implore we revisit her later before we get ambushed," Kenji said as heavy footsteps echoed from inside the house, growing faster and louder. "We can come back for her. Follow me!"

They ran, turning into a busy street of sellers and buyers jostling in the long, low pre-dusk sunlight. A hand fell on Melinda's shoulder—a light hand, not one that was aiming to restrain her.

A woman in a blond updo and a smoothed calico dress faced her. "Come with us miss, please." She blinked the same blue eyes as Carlos'.

Melinda shook her off without a word and took off through the crowd, following glimpses of Nox's green dress and Kenji's bowler hat as they wove amidst the crowd.

"Carlos isn't the only one who's possessed," Melinda said when she caught up, trying to suppress her panic as she studied the clusters of people. Most didn't seem to notice her as they sought their last wares before dinner or evening activities. But through the crowd Melinda caught a glimpse of a face here and there, peering intently at her before the crowd shifted.

At the same time, shadows pooled from the cobblestone paths around her and started to creep up, taking the form of the Edglings as the street darkened.

"Dammit, not now," she cursed quietly. Heavy, rapid footsteps behind them—three, four larger men most likely—caught Melinda's attention through the noise, snapping her out of the vision.

"We have to get off the street," Nox said. "Away from all these people. Quick."

They slipped through the crowd again, until Kenji turned down a narrow alley next to a grand building sporting colossal columns at its entrance. Melinda scanned for an escape, something they could climb over or crawl into. She spotted a door at the end of the alley, just barely visible. She ran to it and jiggled the doorknob.

"Locked. Damn." The door didn't feel particularly thick or sturdy, so she stepped back, preparing to kick it in.

"Wait." Kenji held up a hand. "Here." He produced a small pocketknife and slid it into the opening between the door and wall. He managed to jiggle the lock enough to push the door open and they piled into the sudden, cool darkness.

"Quiet so they don't find us," Nox said while they crept forward.

"It's a storage room," Kenji said. Melinda's eyes adjusted to the dim light to see a wardrobe of old-fashioned dresses, scarves and cloaks, and a small wooden structure half-painted with trees.

"Theater by the looks of it," Nox guessed. They approached a door next to a heavy drape. The door was cracked, letting light pour in around the edges along with the muffled sound of people and scuffling.

"This all seems like a losing hand," Kenji said. "You best cut your losses and head out, I'd say. We can find a way out of town. It'll be a hard climb out of South Bowl but we can do it."

"You're not cutting out now." Nox looked at him. "You want the gigs I promised you, you're helping us through this. In fact, it is in your general best interest to stop these grems, otherwise there won't be any towns left."

Kenji raised his hands. "You're right. I am here but to serve."

The voices grew louder through the cracked door. Nox peeked through and immediately stumbled back. "Heavens help us all," she muttered.

"What is it?" Melinda pressed forward to see.

The crack revealed the back of a stage from the left. Beyond the stage, a theater with rows of wooden seats stretched out, about half filled by thirty or so people, staring dutifully ahead. A single stained-glass window showed a complex mosaic of a garden. Dozens of candles sat half melted along the wall.

On stage stood three people, smiling. One shifted his stance, revealing an ornate wooden chair at center stage. And in the chair, rested a man, not much older than Melinda. And on that man sat a grem.

The grem crouched on the man's narrow lap like an albino dog, its three-toed back foot claw digging into the fabric of his cotton pants and shredding it into large pieces. The grem held either side of the man's face with delicate claws. It wasn't crushing or attacking him, but rather hacking into his face. Small motes of blue floated around the man's head.

And the man wasn't straining. He was leaning back, entirely relaxed, his brown eyes clear and his mouth open, eagerly accepting the dust. He coughed and the grem skulked off his lap, leaving small blooms of blood where its claws had scraped his thighs. The man didn't seem to notice. He sat up and coughed once more, before favoring the room with a toothy smile.

The handful of people around him and onstage clapped, their eyes glinting like rippling ponds.

"What in all the hell?" Melinda stepped back, stumbling into Kenji. Through the doorway crack, she could see an elderly woman shuffle up to stage and settle into the empty chair. "Everyone's infected."

"They're doing it willfully." Kenji peeked past her. "We're surrounded by how many of the possessed? These odds aren't good, not at all."

"Shush," Nox hissed. "We don't want them to—"

Behind them, someone's footsteps stopped abruptly at the door that led to the alley.

Melinda drew her pistol. She didn't like shooting people generally but if their attackers were controlled by the grems, there was no telling what they would do. Kenji pulled out his sword. They moved to either side of the door, waiting, while Nox backed up.

"Misses? Sir? You can come out now, we won't hurt you," Carlos' voice rang out. "I mean that. And you have nowhere to go. See, there's a good number of us here."

"What in high heaven is going on!" Brigitta yelled from outside.

"Damn." Melinda's heart sank at hearing Brigitta. "They have her."

A line along Nox's mouth deepened in worry. "And Sam."

"The leverage lies with them it appears." Kenji sheathed his sword. "And us, but hapless rodents in a cage."

"All right, we're coming out," Melinda barked. "Hold your horses."

Melinda strode out into the alley, where Carlos smiled at her from next to Brigitta. Half a dozen of Carlos' guards lingered in the alley and main street.

Brigitta stared at them in bewilderment, hugging Sam in the waning afternoon sun. "Can someone please tell me what is going on?" she demanded.

"Are you all right?" Nox said.

"Did they hurt you?" Melinda asked.

"No." Brigitta looked even more confused. "They've been entirely hospitable. Gentlemen."

"They're possessed by the grems," Melinda said and Brigitta jerked away from Carlos. "Working with them. Helping the grems possess more humans."

"That's not entirely accurate—" Carlos started, sweeping a hand through his hair.

"You can tell by their eyes," Nox told Brigitta. "A slightly heightened luminescence, the same shade as the grem dust."

Brigitta took several rapid steps back from Carlos as she glared. "Figured. Can't trust even the nicest-seeming folks." She spat toward his feet. "You betray your own people."

"Now, please," Carlos said, unruffled. "As I've said, we're not going to hurt you."

"Just hunt us," Melinda retorted.

"M'lady has a point there," Kenji said.

"We have an offer." Carlos said. "We need help."

"Our help?" Nox scoffed.

"No," Carlos replied and said the last thing Melinda expected as his unnaturally bright gaze turned onto her. "*Your* help. We've been looking for you. Well, your demons. We require their assistance."

"My…*what?*" Melinda repeated. Her voice seemed to fade. *The Edglings.* How did he know? And if he knew, then they weren't—

"The flock can sense them," Carlos said kindly. "The demons that have been plaguing you."

Everything froze at his words and her mind swam as the realization hit her.

It hadn't been hallucinations.

I wasn't imagining them after all.

Kenji took a small step back from Melinda as Brigitta gasped.

"Melinda, what is he talking about?" Nox asked sharply.

"One of the side effects of monster hunting," Melinda muttered. "It's not anything."

"Oh, certainly," Nox said, throwing up her hands. "This sounds like a minor inconvenience we can all safely ignore. Did it occur to you that this information might have been entirely useful when I was treating your grem infection?"

"When I was in the Edge fighting a demon, I encountered the Edglings," Melinda said numbly. "But I didn't realize they had followed me out…that my hallucinations were real…"

"They are," Carlos nodded solemnly. "Or at least, some remnants tied to you. In any case, we need their help. Help us and we help you."

"Or I just shoot you all and we'll find our friends on our own," Melinda replied.

"Now, now." Carlos gave her a patient smile. "I'm sure you're terribly skilled but you won't get very far if all of us and the flock decide to stop you, now will you?"

"Let's not do that," Kenji said nervously. "Melinda, can't we just do as he says?"

Melinda fell silent. She had been literally haunted by the Edglings for a while now. Whether that was better—since she wasn't losing her mind like she had feared—or worse, she wasn't sure.

Carlos hadn't broken his gaze from Melinda. "Help us and we can help you. Free you."

"What are you saying, exactly?" Melinda snarled.

"We can get rid of your demons," Carlos said. "Forever."

"How?" In the darkening alleyway, the Edglings now hovered on her periphery, wobbly shadows that didn't quite fit correctly along the walls.

"I'll show you. We have the carriage ready to go." Carlos waved his hand to the street behind them. "Why don't you take a moment to discuss. I think you'll find it's a win-win. Let the flock remove the demons that have been plaguing you and we'll find your friends in the meantime."

"Our fates seem decided," Kenji said quietly as Carlos and his friend murmured to themselves, waiting. "Clearly, they're not going to let us walk away, even though they pretend as much. Perhaps we can make another run for it. There is a path that leads out of town."

"We aren't leaving Rafi," Brigitta said briskly.

Melinda chewed her lip to think. Usually something like this is where she'd consult with Lance. She couldn't rely on the others to make the best call. Kenji's tall tales came too easily–she didn't trust him as far as she could throw him, though he seemed a decent fighter at least. Brigitta was set on destroying grems, so she wasn't thinking with a clear head. Melinda looked at Nox, who so far had proven to be the most reliable in lieu of Lance.

"What do you think?" she asked Nox.

"We'll feel awfully foolish for walking directly into their trap," Nox said. "What's to stop them from feeding us to a herd of those monsters? Might be best to cut our losses, and–I hate to say this–consider the others are gone. Dead, I mean."

Melinda shook her head. Her mind raced over the possibilities: they could strong-arm their way into the nearest camp, but they'd risk it being the wrong one… For a moment she felt like she was plummeting off a cliff or being crushed in a darkness with no idea which way to go.

Lance, you must save Lance. The thought snapped her back, helped her instinctively pick the best option.

"Even if they do mean to put us in harm's way, going with them will put us closer to the others," Melinda said. "And if they really do have a way to work with the grems—truly—we need to know. Maybe we can use it to our advantage. And we won't get far if we try to run."

Nox sighed and gestured toward Carlos. "I mean, they're under mind control. They're probably herding hapless victims to feed to the grems."

Melinda shook her head. "I've seen Edge monsters push their mind control on humans before. It usually looks different. More painful, more violent. This…" Even as she hated to admit it, she said it: "seems to be mutual, or they seem to have some of their wits about them."

"So, you trust them?" Brigitta asked skeptically.

"Not one bit," Melinda replied. "But maybe they can give us more insight into the grems." If there was one thing Melinda did know, it was that humans always had a weakness. She didn't want to say anything yet, but she had a hunch that maybe they could use Carlos's understanding of the grems to their advantage.

Carlos cleared his throat nearby and they stepped back, opening their circle.

"Well then?" Carlos asked. "Have you decided?"

"Not much of a decision, really. We'll go," Melinda said.

"Thank you kindly for the offer," Kenji chimed in. "We're eager to see this new development of which you speak."

Everything in her sinking, Melinda entered the carriage with the others and hoped it wasn't a fatal mistake.

CHAPTER EIGHTEEN

A short carriage ride later and they had exited the east side of Gold Egg, the thick block of buildings behind them, and up the steep rocky path. Melinda felt ill at ease and tense, ready to fight. But they rode quietly in the large carriage, Carlos' driver whistling to himself up front. Carlos perched next to Kenji, while Melinda, Nox and Brigitta crammed in the seat across from them. Brigitta nodded off almost immediately and Sam snored in his sling at her chest.

"What does the 'connection,' as you call it, to the grems feel like?" Nox asked, curious despite herself. She spoke softly so as to not wake up Brigitta or Sam.

"Unusual," Carlos admitted. "But utterly worth it. Before my connection, I was in a cave, blindfolded and with cotton in my ears. Now the light floods forth, now the cotton and cloth have fallen away." His uncanny gaze settled on Melinda, dropping down to the vial around her neck. "I understand one from our flock tried to entice you to join already, but you resisted. You cannot connect with them if you resist." He stared at Melinda intensely. "You have a different mind than most. I can appreciate that."

She didn't answer but shifted so the vial moved beneath her duster lapel, out of sight. What if the grems were already influencing her thoughts, her decisions? But surely Nox would've noticed a new glint to her eyes, if Melinda had been infected. She tightened her fists and thought of Lance. She had to stay attentive.

"Power, traditionally, is about the ability to make and execute decisions without needing a majority consensus or support," Carlos went on. "It usually requires manipulating or wrestling dominance from other groups. But grems show us the power of consensus. You'll see what we can achieve together."

"Sounds like brainwashed talk," Nox dismissed. Through the open windows of the carriage, the terrain dipped and rose as the rocky road curled upwards.

Carlos gave her a pitying look. "Aren't you tired of always having to fight for your place in the world? Of having to demand to be taken seriously? Of…" He swept his hand out toward the open window. "Of all the bickering out there. The bloodshed. The fighting."

"And what happens to those who don't accept the grems as our grand savior?" Nox asked dryly.

Carlos smiled and gestured upwards. "'The moon!' one child says, pointing to the sky. Immediately all the children around him point as well. 'The moon, the moon!' they cry. We all copy each other from a young age. That's because we are meant to think together as a group. This is to help us to survive: if one person sees a predator, others will quickly be aware of it."

"Surely we can do that without letting monsters into our minds," Melinda muttered. "I've had demons in my head before. Trust me, it's not a good idea."

"The connection makes it possible for us to achieve true freedom. It makes us understand each other fundamentally." Carlos ran a hand through his hair. "Failed communications, overwrought emotions, these are—" he snapped his fingers, "*kernels* that can blossom and explode into problems. By using the flock's enhanced communications, strife is resolved easily."

The carriage turned and the flapping flags of an outpost came into view.

"Do you dig for gold here?" Kenji guessed, straightening an inch.

"Gold, ha!" Carlos said. "Previously we used to mine for minerals. And yes, I had sought gold with a singular focus. But now, with our flock's guidance, we dig for something else."

Looking at the flags, Melinda's vision blurred. Shadows looming at the sides of her vision, materializing into too-long fingers that stretched into the carriage window eagerly toward her face. She turned away, sweat beading her forehead. *The Edglings are real*, Melinda reminded herself. Whether it was that realization or something else, the Edglings looked nearly substantial now, their silent open mouths bringing back a memory of last year's battle with a demon she had barely defeated. Melinda focused on Carlos' words, willing the shadow creatures outside of her window to disappear.

"The flock started great work but hit a barrier, one of the supernatural kind," Carlos was saying. "Not uncommon around these parts, unfortunately. Even though the Edge is miles and miles north, the monsters seemed to like it down here. Do you know how many perfectly good mines we've had to close up due to this or that monster infestation? Still, we'll persevere. Especially with the help of our friends, all working in unison."

"How did you get the grems docile? To work for you?" Melinda asked, her teeth chattering all of a sudden despite the heat.

"They want to," Carlos said and pointed out the other side of the carriage. "We merely provide them with the flesh they need." For a second, she had a horrific vision of humans in the barn offered as sacrifices, but then saw it was a field of cows, their bodies completely gutted, visible for a few seconds before the carriage turned.

"The flock likes warm mammal blood to breed. Humans are the perfect size and temperature. But they'll use cows if they must," Carlos explained as the carriage stopped. Peaks within the massive valley rose north to their left. A closer peak loomed to the right, blocking the view to the south. "Through our connection, humans are off limits." He watched Melinda's face, and his smile broadened. "You see? It is a better way."

"You sound like you've been working with them for a while," Melinda said while they clamored out of the carriage into the unforgiving late afternoon sun. "But the swarm wasn't too far from Thundering Ridge when we were there. That was just a few days ago."

Carlos nodded. "The final wave. We've been waiting for them. Their siblings have been here a few weeks." He led them toward a guard keeping watch at a wooden gate beneath the two yellow flags.

Something didn't add up. Before Melinda could ask how the grem groups had gotten separated, Nox piped up.

"You keep saying the flock," Nox said with a shiver. "How many are you talking about?"

"See for yourself."

An unsettling sensation buzzed at Melinda as they stopped at the guard's post, as though something stirred below the earth, like an imminent earthquake. She shook off the feeling, but Edgling shadows pooled at her vision again.

Not now, she told them fiercely.

The group peered down a short, sharp incline next to the guard's post to a clearing some 100-feet across, enclosed from the north, east and south sides by sharp rocky peaks. The camp contained rows of tents and mining shacks: neat piles of timber, boxes of explosives, a row of worn pickaxes and hammers, coils of rope and other mining equipment. At the far end of the camp rested a defunct mineshaft. Dozens of people worked around holes in the clearing. Next to the people were grems. Not bound, not chained.

Melinda stiffened, hand flying to her gun.

But the grems weren't attacking. They were digging rapidly, sending up sprays of rocks. The humans stood in a wide circle around them, frantically loading up the rocks into wheelbarrows and moving them away as fast as the grems could dig. A handful of grems stood, calm as trained dogs, near fire cattle, albino bovines from the Edge with too-wide mouths like sharks, exceptional strength and tempers, and an ability to exhale fire. The fire cattle were oddly docile, hitched to two wagons full of debris that they moved.

"Quite a feat," Kenji said. Brigitta's face next to him darkened, and she held Sam closer as she looked down on the scene.

"How?" Nox gaped.

"Like I said," Carlos beamed. "Symbiotic. We are helping the flock find their home, but a supernatural barrier confounds us. We tried everything. Digging, exploding powder, even the flock's claws–nothing can surpass it." He looked to Melinda again. "They sensed your demons' unusual abilities and believe they can help us get through the barrier."

Melinda thought of the grem that Jolene had brought here on the promise of payment. The grems *wanted* to be here. That's why it hadn't used Edge monsters, like the mikrabs, on her posse. Instead, the grem *let* Jolene usher it here.

"Seems to me that if you hit a supernatural barrier, best to let it be," Nox observed but Carlos waved her concern off.

"She's got a point. What's down there that you need so bad?" Melinda asked.

"The flock lost something long ago," Carlos said and spread his hands. "That's all I know."

"That doesn't sound ominous at all," Nox said.

"Where are our friends?" Melinda said. Her throat closed up in knots as she neared the viewing glass mounted on a wooden railing next to the guard. The guard stepped back and smiled welcomingly at them, his eyes under bushy black eyebrows giving off the same bright glimmer as Carlos'.

"Take a look," Carlos said. "Half of the workers have joined the flock. The other half, well, they need some time still." Melinda swept the scene below with the viewing glass, taking in the dozens of dirty, dusty faces. Some of the workers looked serene, while others seemed oddly blank, though whether it was from fatigue or shock she couldn't tell.

Lance is fine, Melinda told herself as she scanned. He was a fighter, like her. She spotted his tousled sandy hair amidst the line of people and moved the viewing scope back.

He wasn't fine.

His face was gaunt even though it had only been a few days. A fresh slice across his forehead made her stifle a gasp. But the detail that really made her lungs clench was the vacant look in his eyes, one she'd never seen before.

"Lance!" She shouted. She lunged at Carlos and grabbed the velvet lapels of his vest. "What did you do to him?"

Carlos stumbled back in surprise, then straightened as the guard pushed Melinda off him.

The Edglings came back faster than a migraine now. Two shadows leapt toward Melinda in blobs of darkness against the bright afternoon light. She fought to not wildly swing at them as Carlos brushed off his vest.

"He is fine," Carlos said. "If the workers refuse to join the flock, we give them a concoction to help them relax and ease the transition into labor."

"You drug them," Nox said in disgust.

"Unfortunately, the flock cannot force anyone to join," Carlos replied.

"It sure felt forceful when one infected me," Melinda said.

He cast a sympathetic look at her. "I'm sure it was unpleasant. But we can't have our workers down for the count if they are resisting the flock. The drug helps us to ensure everyone is operating to the best of their abilities."

"What about Rafi?" Brigitta pushed her eye to the scope. "Let me see him!"

Carlos' eyes glimmered and he looked distant for a minute. "Ah, yes. I've spotted him through one of our workers. The one called Rafi was especially uncooperative. He had to receive a double dose of the calming concoction."

"Crooked half-wits!" Brigitta cursed at Carlos and the guard. "He'd better be all right."

"We will take you to see him right after this," Carlos promised. "But first…"

An Edgling face neared Melinda as Carlos talked, its mouth gaping wider than a scream, as if it were trying to tell her something, and she couldn't help but flinch. Two more Edglings seemed to be made of flowing ink suspended in space. They darted as if they were readying to attack her, leaving an icy breeze in their wake.

"Melinda?" Nox asked. "What is it?"

She shook her head even though something was wrong. Her sightings of the Edglings were too strong. Melinda clenched her jaw and did her best to pretend the growing shadows weren't there, but it was getting harder and harder to ignore the glare of their gold eyes, the too-long fingers snatching at the air by her face.

Good thing I'll be rid of them soon.

"So how do we do this?" she asked between gritted teeth.

"Join the flock," Carlos said. "Temporarily if you wish. You have become a sort of vessel for the demons. The flock can siphon them off you. You've already had exposure to their dust, but we'll need more for a full connection."

Something moved quickly in the corner of her eye. An Edgling—no, a grem. The monster had run up the steep path to leap next to them. It jumped onto the wooden railing near the telescope a foot or two from Carlos.

Nox and Kenji stepped back with gasps, and Melinda moved instinctively in front of Brigitta and Sam.

"Relax," Carlos said. "No harm is meant here."

"No harm," Brigitta said bitterly. "Right. We oughta shoot them all right now."

"Let's not aggravate anything here, please," Kenji said, though his hand had flown to rest on his sword's hilt.

"This will be quick," Carlos said. "I think you know how it goes."

It took everything in Melinda not to pull her gun. The grem stayed perched on the wooden rail, its chest heaving in and out as it watched her.

"Melinda, remember what happened when the dust got on you last time," Nox warned. "And you don't know if you can really get rid of the grem influence, despite what he says. It's looking more and more like a bad idea, all around, if you ask me."

"Have I given you any reason to consider I'm not a man of my word?" Carlos looked annoyed for an instant, the first time Melinda had seen him drop his polite, jovial air. "She will have the choice."

"Nox is right, it didn't go well the first time," Melinda said, trying to stem her chattering teeth against the sight of the grem's slack mouth, its silver teeth, its red-and-white eyes with multiple pupils that watched her. "What makes you think this will work?"

"You—and your demons—resisted joining the flock's connection previously," Carlos says. "But the choice is entirely up to you. You have the power here. But first…" He looked pointedly at her neck.

Down below, one of the grems snarled as a worker tripped. Her eyesight was sharp, but she couldn't tell what happened exactly. There seemed to be a scuffle before a grem jumped toward the figure. The figure fell back in line, as if shepherded. She forgot about the Edglings as a vision of Lance's chest gutted by a grem came to her unbidden.

"You get them out of there, now," Melinda said over the pounding of her heart. "While we do this."

"Of course," Carlos said.

Melinda gripped the vial with Sam's bit of blood sloshing in it, her hand trembling the slightest bit. She removed the vial from her neck without looking at the grem a few feet from her.

The blue light crept into her vision as a roaring filled her ears. It was like the grem sickness she had felt at the farmhouse all over again: her bones grinding like they were shattering, her insides turned to broken glass smashed and shoved together. She moaned and pitched forward. Nox grabbed her arm while Kenji and Brigitta watched in horror.

"You're resisting," Carlos said gently. "Remember, sometimes change is difficult, but worth it. Resistance makes it worse, like a sickness. Now, if you accept them, it don't feel so bad. Feels pretty peachy in fact."

"This isn't looking promising!" Nox said, still gripping Melinda's arm.

"Stay back," Melinda managed, pushing Nox off. "So you don't get the dust on you."

Melinda tried to unclench her muscles. Carlos was closer to her suddenly, his face filling up her vision and outlined in blue like a painting. He held Melinda's arm to keep her upright. "Relax," he said. "You're still in control, Melinda. Let us finish what we started."

His warm hand enveloped hers to remove the vial. The grem opened its mouth and gave a violent hack, sending out a swirl of glittering blue. As the others scrambled backwards, Melinda instinctively jerked to follow them, but Carlos' grip held fast.

"It's all right," he murmured. "Breathe in. Now."

She held her breath, then released it. The next whoosh of air into her mouth tingled and spread a prickling cold through her chest. The blue swam into her eyes, blurred and then sharpened, cleared like she was looking through eyes, but they weren't her eyes.

She let the grems in.

CHAPTER NINETEEN

"Melinda, are you alright?" Nox's voice floated to Melinda, but her words were drowned out as other thoughts ran parallel to her own.

She could sense—clear as day—the twenty or so humans in the camp that had bound to the flock. The psychic connection to them buzzed pleasantly alongside of her thoughts. And farther than that, she could feel dozens more in Gold Egg who had also joined the connection. Some fifty in total she could feel, seeing what they see, sensing their intentions.

And they were all welcoming.

Melinda absorbed the feeling of being at a bustling party where everyone was a close friend. That sense of peace wasn't artificial like after too much whiskey. Somehow, it was authentic, a deep breath of relief that moved through every inch of her. It was as though Abel was still alive, as though he and Aunt B and Lance were all around the dinner table with her. Like her momma was there too, emerging from another room to join them.

"Are you still yourself?" Kenji asked. "Though if you were truly possessed, I assume you'd answer yes anyhow."

"I am," Melinda said, and it was true.

"What does it feel like?" Nox asked her lowly.

"Hard to explain." Melinda squinted, but it wasn't her actual eyes that had changed. "Like I have a new sense." Her words couldn't convey it. The blue tinge remained in her normal vision but gave her a sense of another space, a layer of the other connected people's sensations on top of hers. It was like flat paper dolls shifted into complex and intricate machines with layers upon layers of intent and interests.

She could see it all.

Her worry for Lance was still there, but now it was a self-contained ball of distress, separate from her. She could feel it if she wanted to, but there was no need. Those working in the camp sensed her worry and a few glanced up. She didn't observe any malice in them, mostly just peace in doing their duty and following Carlos' lead with a steadfast pride. It reminded her of Hank's loyalty to Jolene.

Carlos grinned broadly at her. *Carlos—*

His proximity to her made the psychic connection more potent. Observing him went well beyond her normal way of trying to tell a person's intentions by the cock of their head or their stride. Her perception was enhanced: instead of a dozen cues, she had thousands more. And not just smell, sight or sound. Her intuition was ratcheted up to 100 percent. She could see she had been mistaken about Carlos; he wasn't the money-grubbing opportunist she had written him off as. She couldn't hear his thoughts, like she half expected. Rather, his ambition sparked like a rotating prism and felt as if it were her own, along with other attributes. His earnestness. His intelligence. His passion for striving for something bigger, better, was a tangible light that pulsed, nearly hypnotic. He saw a new way for humanity—and he had the confidence to guide it.

"You understand now," Carlos said. His words were more than words; the sounds contained velvety undertones, his conviction emanating warm waves she could practically see like a gently lapping tide. "Amazing, isn't it? And that's just the start. A new type of society. Can you imagine it?"

"Do you sense the grems?" Nox asked, her forehead creasing in concern. "What do they want? Why are they so set on procreating? Where did they come from?"

Melinda held up a hand to tide Nox's questions. "I don't know."

Her eyes fell on the creature still sitting on the wooden railing next to her.

At first, she didn't recognize it.

The creature looked more humanoid. The shock of white muscular limbs dusted with blue that she remembered was muted—now the creature was a calm gray. Its eyes above a slack mouth drew her in. Intelligent and colorless, watchful and calm, those eyes seemed to envelop her. The humans felt amicable, even devotion toward it. And the fear and rage she was so used to was absent, a curious sensation.

This isn't right, Melinda thought. *That's not what they really looked like.* She rubbed her eyes and shook her head, trying to remember. *Maybe they aren't so bad after all,* a part of her wanted to believe, but a deeper part resisted, screaming at her to remember.

Carlos' words came back to her as a rallying cry: *Change is difficult, but worth it.*

And now, new words from him, spoken aloud: "Use your new vision, Melinda. See what is really there."

The creature next to her radiated raw power along with its nearby siblings. She could feel them, though not as vividly as the humans. Boiling low and beneath the creatures' watchful patience was a bloodlust—*no, not bloodlust, just intensity,* something in her corrected. A barrier, like a mental wall, blocked her from fully feeling the creatures. But she saw what Carlos undoubtedly knew: the flock's strength. Their intelligence. Their potential.

And past the minds of the flock, she could faintly sense the other Edge monsters they had swayed and brought into their psychic link—the culidaes, the mikrabs, the fire cattle—like a web spiraling out. But there was something else bigger… Her eyes fell on the mine shaft. Something beneath the ground, beneath all the new sensations, that she couldn't quite place.

The flock's desperation flared, making Melinda's eyes prickle. They yearned with the intensity of children to get themselves deep into the Earth. They shared a memory of landing into the small ditch in Fallows that started it all, and a memory of a past time when another like them had fallen… The memory dissipated quickly, leaving only the forlorn sense of being far, far from home.

Had she really been afraid of these small creatures whose chasms of deep craving for a home, for comfort, struck similar chords in herself?

"We don't need to be scared of them," Melinda told Nox, whose worried crease along her mouth deepened. Brigitta and Kenji both gaped at her.

"You're turning more cult-like by the second," Nox said and Brigitta nodded in agreement.

"No." Melinda heard how flustered she sounded. "I'm not brainwashed. It's hard to explain."

"Are the demons off her yet?" Brigitta asked testily. "So she can snap out of defending these bloodthirsty monsters?"

At the thought of the Edglings, a hunger bubbled up from the flock, an insistence that lapped at Melinda like hungry dogs. The shadow beings that plagued her manifested like a curse made visible thanks to the new vision the flock's connection bestowed on her. Three, four—no, *six*—Edglings clung to her like misbehaving shadows, tethered by inky threads that contracted and retracted like a heartbeat. She hadn't seen them this clearly since she had been in the Edge itself, but now their stick-like, pointy limbs sharpened against the background. Humanoid but not as tall, their mouths opened in perpetual silent wails. Their fingers twice the length of human ones, sharpened to shadowy points, flailed. Their eyes the only color of sickly yellow gold.

The Edglings strained around Melinda, lunging toward Brigitta, Kenji, Nox, but then pulling back. Something in their movements was wrong. They weren't just tethered, she realized, they were trapped: stuck in some temporal place between her physical reality and the demon world they had come from through the Edge. They had fed on fear in the Edge, and served the demon entity she fought last year, the one that killed Abel. Now, she saw, they seized on her moments of weakness, worry, fatigue. She had had no idea they had continued to feed on *her*, like *parasites*—

Her rage swelled, and the humans connected to her watched solemnly through her vision.

"Take the Edglings off me," Melinda said. "Now."

The flock's presence moved forward, a force like a knife coming into a slow precision cut, waiting for her to release the Edglings to them.

Do it, she thought. *Take them.*

The flock's psychic force rushed forward along her consciousness to slice the tethers of the Edglings. The Edglings screamed as the black umbilical cords that bound them to her were cut. There was no pain, rather the sense of something sticky being removed, a blast of waterfall spraying off all the dirt and grime and everything else that had clung to her for so long that she had stopped noticing.

The grem on the railing breathed out, creating a cloud of sapphires suspended in the last of the sunlight as it tried to bond the Edglings to itself. But the dust rained past the Edglings, dissipating harmlessly.

"Why isn't it working?" Melinda asked. Before Carlos could answer, inky threads flicked out from the Edglings and back onto Melinda. "No!" She stepped backwards, shooing at the cords, but it was too late. The familiar heaviness of distress from the Edglings settled back over her.

"What's happening?" Nox asked.

"They couldn't do it," Melinda muttered, trying not to sound as angry as she felt.

Carlos' eyes flared as he appeared to be listening intently to a silent message from the grem. "Interesting. Your fledgling demons require a human host it seems. They are immune to joining the flock's full connection because of their incorporeal nature."

"So they'll stay stuck on me forever?" Melinda had the sudden, absurd urge to laugh. She instead looked toward the camp, where the flock had stopped their work and watched them, excited, presumably, by the promise of the Edglings' help.

The grem on the railing next to them hadn't moved, just cocked its head a fraction, its bulging eyes intent on Carlos.

"Hmm." Carlos appeared to be listening to wordless instructions from the grem. "Yes, I think you're right. We need a vessel."

"Are you offering yourself?" Melinda said.

"I sense the extreme duress you face when the demons are possessing your space," Carlos said. "Of course, I will make the necessary sacrifice and let them latch onto me once we are ready. For now, this should contain them."

Before Melinda could react, Carlos uncorked the vial he held of Sam's blood, tapping it empty before she could stop him. Nox sighed loudly. He wiped the outside of the vial with his handkerchief, held it up and the creature breathed into it in a short, loud hiss, filling the glass with a deep, thick blue.

"This concentrated amount of breath should be enough for the flock to hold a psychic cage until I can get down to the barrier," said Carlos. "Now, if you please, try to remove the demons again."

Leave me, Melinda thought to the Edglings and the grems. She braced at the sensation of her skin being tugged off her body as the flock again used Melinda's mind to slice the Edglings' cords. The Edglings fully sloughed off her and fragmented with silent screams, dissolving into tiny swirls of gray that seemed to flow over and dissipated into the vial.

"They're trapped," Melinda gasped and reeled at the sudden release, like a heavy sack had but cut from her shoulders. The grem next to them leapt down, dashing back toward the hole in the camp faster than a bobcat.

"You look happier," Nox observed.

"She's still possessed. She's *smiling* for goodness' sake," Brigitta said. "Can we get Rafi now?"

"Thank you." Carlos looked ecstatic as he capped the vial, where the grem powder swirled like crushed sapphire in a curious way, as though it was suspended in a thick liquid. Melinda couldn't see the Edglings anymore, but a sense of them remained as they faintly struggled against the concentrated dust that held them in place.

Carlos strung the vial of Edglings around his neck and Melinda breathed a sigh of relief.

"That certainly caught the attention of your friends." Kenji pointed. The flock had stopped digging below to raise their heads up at the sky, as if a pack of dogs had caught a whiff of something irresistible in the air or a clap of thunder rumbled overhead that only they could hear. The humans connected to them, including Carlos, all froze for a moment before resuming.

Melinda paused for a different reason; the sensation of not being weighed down by her thoughts was startling. It was a lightness she hadn't experienced in years, since before her mother died. She had forgotten that feeling. It was a type of peace that came in flits and dashes, mostly when she was in a quiet place among the trees and all she could hear was the rustling of the leaves. She hadn't felt it in a long time. And never like this.

"You did it." Carlos stepped almost protectively toward her, the vial swinging from his neck. He gently clasped her shoulder in gratitude, while turning the vial to watch the blue swirl like ink without gravity. "Thank you. I will take this down to the barrier after we get your friends."

They trudged down the short path to the camp below. There, the humans and flock kept to their tasks and barely acknowledged them, even though they were only a few feet away. Now that they were standing in the camp, the stink of sweat and something else made Melinda's nose wrinkle and took a minute to place. The monsters' particular odor, like rotting animals left in the sun and cattle gutted and left to dry, permeated the place.

"I've seen mining operations and I've seen railroad operations." Kenji whistled. "But I've never seen anything like this."

They stopped by piles of coiled rope and boxes of explosives next to the largest hole to observe the groups at work. Three towering piles of rocks surrounded the 20-foot-wide hole. The human workers feverishly worked to remove the debris but every time a human carted off rocks, the grems' frenzied digging dredged up more. All 50-some of the grems had moved to work on this hole, galvanized, it seemed, by the vial of Edglings that Carlos wore.

"I recognize him now, your partner and your friend." Carlos said as his eyes flared. Melinda sensed him looking through another connected human's eyes. "I am truly sorry to have caused you this trouble."

Now that Lance would be rescued—and those damn Edglings banished from her—Melinda could breathe easily. Her shoulders lifted to the dusky sky above and her attention drifted to her new vision and the bustle of the flock. She closed her eyes and tried to trace a mental path back through the flock, following a faint feeling that wanted to make itself heard.

A rustle next to them snapped her out of it as the guard approached.

"Lance!" His name died on her lips as he and Rafi staggered forward, stripped down to pants and undergarments stained with dirt. Her heart jolted at seeing the slump in Lance's shoulders, the blankness in his face. In a blink, she was at his side as the guard handed over the men's clothes and belongings. "We're here. Lance, it's me."

Brigitta embraced Rafi who didn't seem to notice her. His normally sharp brown eyes were glazed over, as though he were looking at pictures in his head. Nox snapped her fingers in front of his face, to no avail.

Lance's eyes fixed on Melinda, and a dim spark of recognition made his face crack out into a wide smile. "Mellie," he slurred and then pointed up at the sky before his eyes went unfocused again. "Aunt B'll be waiting for us," he said.

Rafi, meanwhile, was mumbling incomprehensibly as Nox peered into his eyes.

"They're acting drunker than a skunk who found the barrel," Kenji said.

"The concoction is quite a marvel," Carlos said. "Dulls the mind but not the body."

"Quite horrible, I'd say," Brigitta snapped.

Melinda touched Lance's face, his neck, his shoulders, patting him briskly to snap him out of it.

"How long till it wears off?" she snarled. She thought to threaten Carlos but her connection with him—with all of them— softened her rage, gave her the sense she was talking to a brother or someone she had known for a long time. She knew they didn't intend malice or ill will.

"It'll fade soon," the guard offered.

"It better." Melinda gave Lance a gentle shake, watching his eyes slowly come into focus.

Lance's sluggish gaze turned to Melinda again. "You look different."

"Got the equivalent of a curse lifted off me," Melinda explained. A small crease of confusion appeared under the dirt on his forehead, and she shook her head. "I'll tell you more later."

Rafi looked worse off than Lance, but he seemed to finally register Brigitta, his face brightening. "You…you…" he said.

"This is Sam," Brigitta showed him the blinking infant, her voice trembling the tiniest bit. Rafi's confused glance dropped down to the bundled infant across her chest before a beaming smile split his face.

"Sam…" Rafi repeated.

Kenji cleared his throat. "Something is happening with your monsters, there."

Melinda turned to see the flock digging swiftly in the large hole next to them. To the others it probably looked frenetic, like the flock was burrowing angrily. With her new vision, she could see that they actually moved in harmony, the vibrations from the ground and their motions synchronizing to maximize the force they put into upheaving the rocks. It reminded her of birds in flight or a school of fish turning in unison. She stepped closer to the pit, the excitement of the flock a magnetic draw.

"It really is quite magnificent," Carlos said before Rafi gave a moan and nearly stumbled. Kenji quickly righted him.

Nox tsked. "I'm sure I have something to counter the drug. Or at least help the substance flush through their blood and bile faster." Nox led Lance and Rafi to sit on one of the crates as she rummaged in her bag. Brigitta and Kenji trailed them. Melinda started to follow but paused when a grem caught her eye.

Leading the digging effort was a grem twice the size of the others and coated in a darker blue dust. It reminded her of the grem she had blasted in Thundering Ridge. It wasn't the leader in the typical sense, Melinda knew intuitively, but more like one of several lieutenants. Now that she was connected, she understood that a handful of grems grew larger and more dominant, directing the individual swarms and acting as central points in their psychic webs.

She neared the hole to watch, and Carlos joined her. All the grems were energetic, eager for Carlos to bring down the vial of Edglings to soften the barrier. She didn't fully understand how, but the flock seemed convinced that the Edglings' presence could disintegrate the supernatural barrier and help them push through it.

Push through to what? Melinda wondered but part of her didn't want to look at what they eagerly sought, in a cavern full of rot and strangeness—

Melinda jumped back at the menace that waited, fuming, ready to explode. Her breath shot out of her.

"Melinda, what is it?" Carlos asked in alarm. He reached for her, and she jerked back.

"Don't touch me." She pressed her hands into her eyes, the looming danger of what she had just sensed made her feel like she was teetering at the edge of a precipice. She couldn't place it, let alone name it, but the sensation of a potent weapon lying deep underground was unmistakable.

What have I done?

CHAPTER TWENTY

"You have to stop digging," Melinda said, trying to get some air back in her lungs. She glanced back at Lance and the others talking by the lumber, two dozen feet away and just out of earshot. "There's something bad under there. The Edglings are going to help them unleash it. Tell the flock to stop."

"I'm afraid we can't." Carlos ran a hand through his hair. "The flock needs a home."

"You lied," Melinda growled. "They're not looking for a home—they're trying to open it up, to get to some sort of weapon—"

Carlos gripped her hand. The sudden intimacy of it shocked her as a buzz of warmth ran from his fingers to hers, as their mutual touch was enhanced through the connection.

"We know each other now," Carlos said. "You *know* I wouldn't mislead you. There is no weapon. They are searching for their home. What did you see?"

"I don't know exactly, but whatever it is, it's not good," Melinda said, but the vision was fleeting already, a nightmare that dissolved upon waking except for a few tendrils of unease. "A weapon is the best way I can describe it. And the flock is keeping it from you. And I want out of this connection. Now." The look of surprise intermingled with sadness that flashed across Carlos' face gave her pause.

"Like I said from the beginning." Carlos frowned. "You can choose to cut off the connection at any time. If that's what you really want."

As soon as he said the words, Melinda felt exactly how to do it. It was simple as a thought to sever the chains that moved from her to Carlos and the rest. She hesitated, not wanting to lose the feeling of kinship and closeness.

You know who you are, she reminded herself and shook her head as if to disperse a swarm of flies. She glanced back at Lance on the crate, gripping his head and wincing as Nox and Brigitta hovered over him and Rafi.

She was a monster fighter. Lance's partner. Aunt B and Abel's student.

And not one who would ever mistake evil for good.

With a thought, she broke the connection, forcing it away from her. The flock and humans protested, but Carlos had been correct; the flock's psychic influence was not strong enough to force her to stay.

A jolt of loneliness slammed into her, cracking a pit of grief open in her chest. The worry for the others returned but heightened: not just her friends but for the dozens of people connected to the flock, and for Carlos. She still felt a kinship toward them, though not as intense.

The grems digging in the hole didn't look like intelligent, patient humanoids anymore. It was as though she ripped off paper glasses and now fully saw them again in their true form—their sickish blue tinge, their rageful eyes, their relentless bloodlust.

"Your little mind connection jumbled me all up, but I know this," Melinda said forcefully. "Whoever is helping the grems is in the wrong." She spoke a little kinder at seeing Carlos' crestfallen face. "I know you think those monsters are the way to a better world. But they're poisoning your mind, even if you don't know it. And whatever weapon they're trying to unleash will kill everyone."

Carlos shook his head, dark curls gleaming in the light that was nearly diminished, as if the last rays of sun were eager to flee whatever came next.

"I thought you understood. You're better than this. Smarter," he chided, and Melinda actually felt a rush of shame. "Society cannot continue as it has been. This connection offers us a new way to thrive."

She looked back at Lance, who was rubbing his temples as he handed Nox back a tube of powder she had given him. But his eyes were clear again and met hers. She glanced at the explosives box next to him and then at the massive hole where the grems dug, relieved to see him nod in understanding.

Her partner was back. And this was their chance to stop the grems.

"You have to stop all this," Melinda said. "Or I will."

"You won't," Carlos said, stroking the vial around his neck. "They don't mean us harm; you saw that yourself!"

Melinda didn't answer but instead unholstered her gun. Two of the grems paused in their digging, looking over at them from the hole as they sensed Carlos' concern.

"Um." Kenji neared Melinda, his voice bordering on panic. "What's going on?"

Lance stayed by the lumber with the others, now with a large dynamite stick in his hand.

Carlos shook his head, looking distraught. "Melinda, I want to protect you all. *Help* you."

Out of the corner of her eye, she saw more grems nearing them and she calculated. So far, her line of sight was clear from Lance to the large pit but that would change momentarily.

"This is for the best, Carlos," Melinda said. His mouth opened in protest as Lance tossed a dynamite stick in a perfect arc over their heads.

"Don't!" Carlos shouted, but Melinda fired her gun just as the stick fell toward the base of one of the rock piles next to the hole.

She never missed.

The pile of rocks exploded, blasting out shards of stone. She and the others ducked and clamped their ears as debris spilled into the hole, rapidly filling it. One of the human workers screamed as a fist-sized rock hit him in the shoulder. The grems' howls pierced through her ringing eardrums before the rocks piled in, muffling them and trapping them in the hole.

"No!" Carlos bellowed.

"Nice shot," Brigitta shouted as she, Rafi, Nox and Lance hurried over to Melinda. She had her hands clamped over Sam's ears, but he had started to wail.

"Are they dead?" Kenji asked, helping to steady Rafi who still had a glazed look and wavered on his feet.

"Not yet," Melinda said. "The grems can dig out of there. We need to set off a few more explosives, get more of those rocks piled on them." She turned to the dozens of humans who stood in shock. "We need your help. We've got to pile more weight to crush them before they get out." Some of the workers hesitated.

"We protect the flock," the guard yelled. A few others nodded in agreement along with Carlos.

"Idiots," Brigitta snarled.

"You won't change their minds," Nox said.

"The grems are monsters," Melinda said to the guard and Carlos. "They aren't going to help you or protect you. They've murdered dozens at least. And more, if they unlock whatever weapon is down there."

The workers looked unconvinced. The fact that they weren't fully brainwashed but still willing to defend brutal killers made her angrier than before.

"You are lashing out," Carlos said tightly to Melinda. "You haven't been able to get past your hatred of creatures different than you, have you? I felt it when we were connected. You let your fear cloud your mind, your actions."

Lance scoffed at that, lifting a handful of dynamite. "Way we see it, you're the one looking to help gut-bustin' monsters," he said.

"Not everyone is equipped to see a brighter future," Carlos responded, stepping back to join the loose ring of humans that had lined up. They stood in front of the caved-in hole, blocking it from Melinda and the others. All of them flashed blue eyes.

Lance called out to the nearest worker. "What about you? You want to stay here like this? Working to your bone, heeding to the whims of monsters?"

The woman smiled gently. "The flock is going to help us all be free, better. *Stronger.* We help them, they help us."

"That's what they want you to think," Nox said.

"It's hard enough fighting monsters when people want the help," Lance murmured to Melinda as they backed up. "Now it's a losing hand."

"People are sheep," Nox said.

"People are horrible," Brigitta added.

"You all want to be controlled!" Melinda shouted at the nearing crowd in frustration. "I know the connection feels good, but you all can't be that thick-headed." Despite the explosion, she could see the stones over the caved-in hole shake and rumble as the grems started to dig upwards. "We've got to hurry!"

Lance handed her a dynamite. There were two more 10-foot-tall piles of debris around the former hole they could blast to pile onto the buried grems. But the workers had grouped to stand directly in front of each pile.

"Out of the way, or you're dead too," Melinda said to the workers, but their glowing eyes stayed resolute.

"Hold steady," Carlos instructed them. "I know her mind. She won't hurt you."

Melinda lifted the dynamite to toss it. "I will do it, Carlos, to save everyone."

It was a bluff, and he knew it, giving her a small, sad smile.

Remember how many more will be saved if you destroy the grems for good, Melinda thought but couldn't bring herself to throw the explosive at the line of people.

She lowered the dynamite and Lance did the same.

"Damn," he muttered and glanced at her. "What are we—"

The first grem burst out of the hole, and everyone ducked as stones flew outwards. Grems poured out of the small opening in the dusk.

Melinda and the others retreated, backs to the defunct mine, while the line of humans and grems blocked them from the one entry point that led back to the road. Brigitta and Nox quickly moved to hover in the entrance of the mine for cover, while Rafi, his eyes clearer by the second, stood in front of them.

"Leave us alone!" Brigitta hollered from behind Rafi. "I wish I had that shotgun still!"

Two of the grems broke into a run toward them, but Melinda slowed the left one with a quick shot, and Lance took down the right one. Kenji unsheathed his sword next to them.

"No more deaths!" Carlos yelled. The humans filed in line between the grems and Melinda and Lance.

Protecting the grems.

Melinda scowled. "Move out of the way!"

From their vantage point behind the humans, the grems began hurling rocks overhead. Melinda ducked as the stones rained down and even the humans started pelting them with rocks.

"Carlos, stop this!" she yelled and cursed as one rock caught her in the ankle.

Carlos just looked at her sadly as the line of humans slowly advanced. He was ready to let her and the others die to preserve his vision, Melinda realized bitterly.

"What do we do?" Nox screeched from the mine's entrance.

Kenji held his sword with two hands so it pointed forward and at an upward angle, ready to attack. "They're getting closer!"

"I have an idea. Lance, the dynamite there." Melinda pointed to the wooden entrance of the mine above Brigitta and Nox's heads.

Lance hesitated for an instant, doubt flickering across his face. "You sure?"

"Do it!"

Lance stuffed the two explosives in the wooden entrance. "Ready."

"All of you, in. Set it off once we're inside!"

"Melinda, don't," Carlos said. The rocks stopped flying as he neared her.

Nox and Brigitta had moved deeper into the mine, while Lance, Rafi, Kenji and Melinda stood at its entrance. Lance passed Rafi one of his pistols as they prepared to defend. Two grems slinked out with hisses, shadows she could barely see in the dark twilight.

"You have done a lot of harm," Rafi said to Carlos with a glare that would've made most squirm. "Your set-up here turns people into animals. And now, you work with these grems, for what? Further gain?" Rafi pointed his pistol toward Carlos, fury making his hands shake.

"Wait," Melinda said, keeping her gaze on the pair of grems that flanked Carlos now, like pet dogs. Kenji inched into the mine, his sword still poised.

"Please don't go in there," Carlos said, stopping a foot away, ignoring Rafi and Lance entirely. "That mine is old and unsafe. That's a death sentence certainly. It doesn't have to be this way. Let's discuss an agreement."

"Don't listen to him, Melinda!" Brigitta yelled from behind her.

"Snake salesman selling his snake oil." Lance's eyes narrowed but Melinda gestured at him to hold his position.

"This is for you," Melinda said. "For all of humanity. You'll see, in the end." She felt a twist of regret, as if she were betraying a longtime lover, as she darted forward to wrench the vial from Carlos' neck. She barely registered Carlos' look of shock and rage as he lunged to snatch it back while the two grems leapt forward. At the same time, gunshots rang out: one from Lance's, taking down a grem mid-air. But the second shot from Rafi wasn't directed at the grem.

He had shot Carlos in the chest, ignoring entirely the monster leaping toward him.

"Rafi!" Brigitta shrieked.

"Blow the mine now!" Melinda screamed, yanking Rafi backwards as the grem landed on him. Lance shot the explosives, a painful blast ripping through her ears while rocks fell and the last of the light was blotted out.

CHAPTER TWENTY-ONE

In the darkness within the collapsed mine entrance, Nox fumbled next to Melinda until a match flared up.

Melinda rubbed her sharply aching side and elbow and sat up. Rafi—

His hulking form was next to hers, limp. And then he stirred.

"My foot," Rafi grunted. She turned to see his ankle disappearing into the pile of fresh rocks. Next to it extended a grem hand, coiled and still, the rest of the grem crushed beneath the pile.

Rafi grimaced in pain as Melinda tried to nudge the rock from his foot. "It doesn't feel broken," he said in relief. "Just stuck."

"Wedged under at least a ton of rock," Lance said. "It'll take hours to get you out. That's if we have the right tools."

"Melinda," Nox said, waving the flame beneath her dust-streaked face. Around them the limestone walls reflected pale yellow with dark streaks. "Why are we trapped in a mine?"

"Sure, we're safe from the flying rocks, but this doesn't seem a whole lot better," Kenji agreed as Sam wailed. "We'll die of suffocation, starvation, dehydration…"

"It does feel hard to breath," Brigitta said, gripping Rafi's hand as he sat up.

"We need to get Rafi freed. Then we're going to find the grems' weapon and stop them for good." Melinda said. She tried not to think of the last glimpse of Carlos' face. She hadn't seen where Rafi shot him, but at that close range she doubted he could've survived. *You don't even know him,* she reminded herself but still had to push away a sharp pang of regret. She hadn't wanted him to die.

"What about these?" Nox opened her bag to reveal four sticks of dynamites. "I took these and some rope while you all were talking by the hole."

"Can't you use one of those dynamites to blast the rocks off him?" Brigitta asked.

Lance shook his head. "Could make things much worse."

Candles lined the floor of the wall, which Nox bent down to light. Shadows from the propped-up timber and a sheet of canvas over more lumber made bizarre shapes against the walls of the cave as Nox lit the candles. Behind them, illuminated by the new candlelight, the mine stretched about 40 feet deep, with a crooked wooden track leading the way to a large, dented cart.

"Listen." Brigitta paused. By the entrance of the mine, the faintest scratching could be heard.

"It's the grems. They're trying to dig through," Nox said in dismay. "To get to us."

"To get to this," Melinda said and opened her hand to show them the vial. Though she couldn't properly see the Edglings anymore, she could very nearly feel them. "The grems contained the Edglings with the blue dust. Don't know how long it'll hold, but let's hope long enough."

Lance stared at her. "The Edglings?"

"They're real." As soon as she said it Lance's face looked stricken. "Haunting me since I came back from the Edge," she explained. "The grems need their help to get through a supernatural barrier to some sort of weapon."

"I thought all this time, they were in your head…" Lance broke off.

Brigitta cleared her throat and Kenji looked on with interest.

"I didn't know they were real either," Melinda said. "But they won't bother me anymore." She tapped the vial's cork as the blue whirled like a miniature storm cloud.

"So, what's the plan?" Kenji said.

"Uncork the vial, get rid of the Edglings?" Nox offered. "Then the grems stop chasing us. And they can't get to whatever weapon you speak of, right?"

"I have a better idea," Melinda said. "We're going to use the Edglings to set a trap. You have the dynamite. We find this weapon and destroy both it and all the grems, once and for all."

The others stayed silent until Lance nodded slowly. "Risky but it's the best way to wipe out the grems," he agreed. "We might not have a chance to get them all together again at once. And given how fast they breed, we'll be hunting them forever if we can't take them out in one shot."

"What about Rafi?" Brigitta said.

"There's another problem," Nox said. "How are we going to find said weapon to set a trap?"

Melinda's gaze drifted down the tunnel along the lit candles and to the large cart resting next to a pile of supplies. "The grems' hole was what, 20 feet from the mine entrance?"

Lance touched the cave wall. "Before they drugged me, I overheard the guard talking about some cave system. Maybe we can find our way closer to where they were digging."

"We can't leave Rafi here," Brigitta said stubbornly.

"You can," Rafi said, his face solemn in the candlelight. He had gotten himself into a sitting position best he could with his trapped foot. "If the monsters make it through, I'll slow them down for you."

"Maybe it won't come to that," Melinda said, gnawing on her lip. "They can sense the Edglings. They'll follow us."

"So we lead them away," Lance said. "It might work. But it might not, if this is the easiest path for them."

"In any case, you must go," Rafi said. "Destroy the grems."

Melinda nodded and grabbed one of the candles before heading for the cart. "This way!"

"You heard her," Lance said to the others as he picked up a candle. "Let's get."

Brigitta stayed where she was, one hand holding Rafi's and the other rubbing Sam's back.

"You must," Rafi said softly. "I will be all right."

"You've stayed by my side this whole time. I won't leave yours," Brigitta replied. "I'll help defend you against the grems."

"With what weapon?" Nox interjected. "Staying here is probably a death sentence. Going may also be a death sentence, but the odds are likely better."

"You and Sam will be safer with them," Rafi squeezed Brigitta's hand before letting go.

"You don't know that!" Brigitta cried. She stood, torn.

"For little Sam," Rafi said softly. "Please. I will be all right."

"Here." Melinda spotted his fallen pistol and handed it to Rafi. "You have a few shots left. Make em count."

Brigitta wiped angrily at her eyes but let Nox lead her away.

"We'll come back for you," Lance promised. "As soon as we can."

As they squeezed into the cart, Melinda cast one last look at Rafi. He watched them intently and nodded to her when he met her gaze. *Good luck*, Melinda thought.

"Works out to have the big guy stay behind, since we can barely fit six in this thing," Kenji said and clamped his mouth shut at Nox's glare. He pushed the cart forward and hopped in.

The cart gained steam, hurtling at a considerable decline some 50 feet before reaching a steeper drop than Melinda expected. She stifled a gasp and focused on the rush of air, refreshing in the stuffiness. They rode for a full five minutes until the cart levelled out and screeched noisily to a stop.

"Well, we're away from the grems but it's a dead end," Kenji said after Nox relit the candles. They climbed out to a small circular space where the tracks ended. Melinda flinched as a few spiders the size of her hand darted past on the wall next to them.

"Not exactly," Nox said, lifting her candle. At the wooden tracks' end, a thick knotted rope dropped into a hole about six feet wide. Kenji kicked a rock down. They all listened for the drop an instant later.

"Twenty or so feet, maybe," Lance guessed.

"Is that even the right way to the grems' weapon?" Brigitta asked.

The matter seemed to swirl faster in the vial and Melinda could feel the Edglings resisting. There was something there, something they didn't want to see…

"Yes." Melinda settled the vial around her neck again and tried not to look into the darkness below as she set herself at the edge of the hole.

"Fortune help us," Kenji sighed.

A shadow the size of a large centipede skittered along the ground a few feet away and Melinda gritted teeth as she tried not to imagine how far down it might actually be. What if the rope disappeared before she expected it, what if Kenji's pebble had not hit the true bottom but a ledge…

"I'm right behind you," Lance said.

"Here goes," she muttered and started to shimmy down. The rope swung slightly as she descended, faster than she could control. She reached the bottom a moment later with a thud, the rope ending a foot above the ground.

"It's all right!" Melinda called up.

"Feeling not so peachy," Kenji said after they came down, looking pale in the candlelight that Nox relit once more. "Patch of bad air maybe."

Lance raised the candle to see two splitting intersections, where the manmade part of the mine clearly stopped, opening up to natural limestone caverns. "If my sense of direction's holding up, this way would put us under the hole the grems made."

Brigitta rubbed her temples. "It does feel peculiar down here. Like someone beating my head in."

"I *know* this feeling," Melinda said as the eerily familiar sensation of walking upside down, of a dizziness deep in her skull, grew. "This feels like…"

It couldn't be. The vial buzzed like a bee, and she fought off a moment of vertigo.

"Lance, you have that map?" she asked.

He fumbled at his pockets. "Here."

She hoped she was wrong, though she knew she wasn't. She smoothed out Lance's map, on which he had doodled sketches of monsters in the margins.

Melinda pointed to the top right of the page, where the Edge was marked in jagged mountain lines above South Bowl. "Here's the Edge." She tapped the mountain range. "Where the Earth split apart a century ago and unleashed hell at the Monster Massacre of Double Moon." She traced her finger straight down to South Bowl on the bottom right.

"We thought the Edge was only in the Northern Ridge Mountain range. But it didn't stop there. It goes underground," Melinda whispered. "It extends to here, to where we are." She continued, even as the words didn't make sense: "It's not bad air or claustrophobia. We're getting close to the Edge. That's why we feel off."

Total silence filled the stuffy tunnel.

Lance's face, barely lit by the flickering candle, stared at her. "It's not possible. Monster origins were only ever traced to those mountains…"

"The Edge extends underground, south of the mountains," Melinda said, the words ringing true in her bones. "A region no one suspected. When I went through the Edge, I found a doorway to another world. But that was only part of the Edge."

Lance looked thoughtful. "But we've seen records of disturbances and emergence of monsters all traced back to within a mile of Northern Ridge, establishing the Edge boundaries."

"That's right, the chasm where the monsters emerged was well defined," Nox piped up.

"But no one considered that the chasm—the Edge—ran underground too," Melinda said.

"That's why they hit a supernatural barrier down here," Lance said slowly. "But that means, if the Edge is this large, there's more entryways into monster worlds."

"And I don't think it's a coincidence that the grems' weapon is here," Melinda said grimly.

The rest of them paused and Nox sighed. "Well, good thing we have that," she pointed to the vial, "and that we're getting there first, right?"

Her forced optimism didn't entirely rub off; Kenji was looking more unhappy by the minute, Brigitta was scowling, and Lance's forehead furrowed.

"I'm no expert, but from what I've heard no one returns from the Edge," Kenji said, his gaze shooting to Melinda. "Present company excluded. Tell me again why we don't just break this vial, let the demons escape so the grems can't use them?"

Brigitta piped up, patting Sam's head. "I like that idea."

"They'll find a way." Melinda recalled the feeling of their single-minded drive and shuddered. "They will do anything to get their weapon. If they don't get the Edglings, they'll figure it out eventually. They'll never stop."

"We stick with the plan," Lance said. "We set our trap, destroy them all in one swoop. And the weapon too while we're at it."

"This way," Melinda said and felt the tingle at the back of her head grow along with the vertigo. "I'm sure of it."

They continued through the narrowing tunnel, stepping over broken geodes and making decisive turns at each junction. She followed her intuition now, pressing forward even as the tunnel shrunk, forcing them to walk single file.

"I don't know," Nox said behind her. "It's getting awfully narrow."

"The weapon's close, I feel it," Melinda said. The rocky passage narrowed enough that she had to back up to undo her holster and hat before squeezing through. "We have to keep going."

"I hear them," Britta said suddenly from the back of the line. Melinda strained and she heard it too, a steady scratching coming from somewhere above and to the left.

"Let's keep moving," Lance said. "If they catch us in this narrow tunnel, we're goners."

"Getting a tad tight in here, wouldn't you say?" Kenji said a moment later and Nox's breath grew more labored.

"You all right?" Lance called back to Nox. A too-long pause before she affirmed. "We don't know how much good air is down here," he said. "Try to control your breathing."

"Just a little farther," Melinda added, but the first niggle of doubt came into her as the rock walls seemed to press in from all sides. What if she got stuck? She banished the thought and held her breath to squeeze through the tightening space.

"Mellie," Lance said with a trace of worry. "Don't get st—"

Melinda pushed through and pitched out into a yawning space.

"Keep going!" she called to the others. The words echoed around her, jarring. She rose her candle to see a 100-foot-high cavern. The far wall, some 50 feet away, pulsing a faint mauve luminescence. She recognized that sickly violet color: it was the same hue she had seen when she entered the Edge. Stalactites hung from the chamber between stone columns. The air stank of rot and spoiled eggs.

The others squeezed through the rock tunnel with gasps and grunts.

"What is all of that?" Brigitta asked faintly. Melinda followed her gaze to the ground. The stone ground was coated in dark blue powder like an unnatural snow.

"Face coverings up," Lance barked, and they all tied their handkerchiefs over their noses and mouths.

"I wonder if this dust will have a psychic effect on its own." Nox bent down to examine the powder, scooping some into one of her glass tubes.

Kenji perked up. "That would be something."

"This isn't a natural history expedition," Melinda said.

"Is that it?" Brigitta asked. She had put a loose blanket over Sam to shield him from the dust. She pointed to the violet wall, which Melinda could see was in fact partially transparent. The group crept toward it, picking their way past jagged stalagmites that sliced upwards like a giant's mismatched teeth.

"Can't shake the sensation of walking underwater," Lance remarked, and Melinda had to agree. It was as though her limbs were weighted down with molasses. The Edglings in the vial, in the meanwhile, seemed even more frenetic, the cerulean motes crashing against the glass and giving off a chaotic vibration that made her teeth grind. Maybe they were excited about being close to the Edge again but whether it was that, or agitation, or something else, she couldn't tell.

As they neared, they could see the cavern stretched on even farther past the purple wall.

"The supernatural barrier," Kenji said, his voice laced with wonder. "Now that is truly uncanny."

"It looks like a thick substance is filling that entire side of the cavern," Nox said as they closed the last few feet. "Almost like jam. And there's something in it."

Melinda squinted through the otherworldly material to see what weapon was trapped on the other side, as Nox and Lance stifled gasps next to her.

Beyond the Edge barrier, a pale mass towered above them over 20 feet high. The mass was dimpled and bumpy, like the cold flesh of a stretched chicken leg. Coiled tufts along the mass poked up here and there, coated with thick cobalt dust.

Melinda's mind struggled to catch up, as she put together what she had sensed but couldn't fathom until now.

The true Gremlin Queen.

CHAPTER TWENTY-TWO

The Grem Queen loomed, the back of her head the size of a horse, nearly ten feet wide. Melinda had never seen a monster that big, a *grem* that big—

"Oh no," Kenji moaned. "No, no, no."

"It doesn't see us." Nox's whisper held the slightest tremble. "And clearly can't get through the barrier. I think we're safe for now. At least until the swarm gets here and pries that vial off you."

Melinda nodded, unable to tear her eyes from the Grem Queen. Her eyes fell to claws as long as human arms motionless against the limestone. The Queen hadn't moved; she looked frozen as if in gelatinous ice.

"How is it possible?" Brigitta demanded.

"The Queen must've gotten stuck down here," Melinda said. Thoughts shifted and lodged in her mind, small subconscious pieces she had gleaned from being connected to the grems. "Long ago. Maybe she was trying to come out of the Edge and got stuck under here. And the grems have been trying to find her ever since…"

No, that wasn't right, she knew instinctively. She thought back to Fallows and the first appearance of the grems. She was missing something but couldn't place it now.

Nox used a small rock from the ground to gently push against the purplish Edge barrier, testing it. "Firm," she said. "Whatever supernatural material this is, the Queen is most certainly trapped."

The persistent sound of digging grew louder above them, and they all paused.

"Let's set up the dynamite, quick," Lance said, snapping them out of it. He kept his eyes on the Grem Queen as they all backed up. "Before the rest of the grems get here." He scanned the cave ceiling and pointed to two particularly large rock formations. "Put the sticks there and there. Should be enough to cave in and bury the grems for good."

Kenji and Lance set to rigging up pairs of dynamite and connecting their fuses, while Nox fussed about with more rock samples and Brigitta lifted her blanket to check on Sam. Melinda stared at the back of the still Grem Queen, scanning for any sign of movement.

"All right, we have these two to light." Lance pointed to the fuses as Kenji finished. "Then we'll see a nice boom. It'll kill everything in here and bury all access to her."

"We wait in the tunnel, then blow it," Melinda said.

"What if the grems come through the tunnel?" Nox asked. "We'll be surrounded."

They had all moved to the opposite end of the cavern from the Queen. The scratching grew louder.

"I only hear them from above," Lance said. "I think we're safe."

"Let's hope," Nox said.

"A lot of things could go wrong, but it's our best bet," Melinda said, wiping sweat off her forehead and glancing at Lance. She pictured the tide of grems, burrowing relentlessly into the cavern, dozens of them poised to surround them in a second. If Melinda and the others couldn't make it through the tunnel in time, they wouldn't have a chance.

"We can pull this off," Lance said firmly. "With timing. And luck."

The smoke was spinning frantically in Melinda's vial now, making her vertigo worse. And she couldn't stop looking back at the slumbering Queen.

She's trapped, Melinda reminded herself.

"I hear you."

The garbled, booming words made them all flinch. Melinda realized in an instant, even as Nox cupped her ears, that the sound came from within their heads.

"She's—it's—" Kenji stuttered but he didn't have to point it out. Even though they were on the other side of the cavern, the frozen Queen was talking to them.

The blue dust on the ground—darker and more potent-looking than the dust that had seen from other grems—swirled up as if caught in a sudden breeze. They coughed despite their face coverings.

"Come closer," the Queen said, remaining motionless. Her words whipped through Melinda's head like a slither that moved from one ear to the other and then to the base of her neck, sending a shiver down her spine. Melinda saw suddenly that she had, without thinking, obeyed the Queen and closed the distance to the barrier. Now Melinda stood just a few feet from the Edge barrier, looking up at the Queen. Melinda's vision blurred again but she ground her heels in.

"Hey!" She shouted to the Kenji, Lance and Nox, who had similarly neared the Queen, their eyes rimmed with the slightest hint of blue.

Lance snapped out of it first, swiping at his ears. The others blinked and hastily backed up.

"How is she doing this?" Kenji asked.

"All this dust gives her a psychic influence even through the damned barrier." Melinda gripped the vial in her hand, but the Edglings seemed safe for now.

Brigitta had trailed after them, staring in confusion. "What is happening?" She asked as she cupped Sam's ears. His wide brown eyes, open for once, looked up at her. "I can hear the monster, but why the hell are you all so close to the wall?"

Nox glanced at her. "Your proximity to Sam may be shielding you somewhat from the Queen's infl—"

"Open helpers. Release me." The Queen's words were somehow directed at Melinda, though the others winced at the forceful sound. Now that they were closer, Melinda could see shards of a large, thin white shell sticking up from the ground near the Queen.

You are not going to open the vial, Melinda told herself through the haze. Her shaking hand gripped the container tightly. The Queen's urgings bombarded her but weren't quite strong enough to take over completely. Melinda dropped the vial, letting it settle back against her neck. She stepped backwards with difficulty, like quicksand was clinging to her boots.

"What do we do?" Kenji yelped, sweat pouring down his face. Somewhere above them, the rumbling of digging grew more frenzied.

"I'd wager most things can be stopped with a bullet," Lance said. He fired at the Queen and cursed as the bullet sank into the barrier harmlessly.

"*Help me.*" A plea, even as the Queen didn't move. Images and sensations bubbled up in Melinda's mind: the sight of her releasing the Edglings and of the barrier dissolving, followed by a feeling of kindship. The Queen finding her children, a feeling of home, of reuniting. Carlos had been right and so had she: the Grem Queen was both a weapon and a home. The flock's home.

"Where did you come from?" Nox asked. Everyone's eyes glowed the slightest blue as the Queen imparted her psychic vision to them. "Why are your grems killing humans? How did you get stuck?"

Too many questions, Melinda wanted to say but the images came quickly from the Queen.

A feeling of hurtling through darkness and cold in a protective egg-like shell. Through the deep mountain or endless sea… No, that wasn't right, Melinda realized as she saw the sun burning bright, its size and shape all wrong. The sensation of moving faster, of blue and brown differentiating into mountains and seas, clouds whipping by as the Queen crashed into the mountains.

The grems weren't from the Edge.

Melinda physically recoiled as the thought hit her, hard and true. Judging by Lance's quick intake of breath next to her, the others had seen it as well.

"That's why they're so much different, smarter than the Edge monsters," Lance murmured to her.

Melinda saw through the Queen's eyes how the Edge had called to her, irresistible. The grems were from somewhere far beyond the sky and had been drawn to the Edge, like a bright beacon in the darkness.

But when the Queen crashed, she had gotten stuck, half between this world and the Edge. Waiting for help as she stayed in a stasis, feeling like no time had passed at all. And the grems hadn't been able to find her for over a hundred years until the Edge flared again, which happened not that long ago…

As the Queen unfurled the thoughts to them Melinda squeezed her eyes shut. She didn't want to know, she didn't—

"She was drawn to the Edge when it first formed and released a supernatural energy so powerful that she felt it through space," Nox said, narrating even as they all saw it. "And her grems saw a second signal from the Edge when something disturbed it again…" She trailed off, her eyes bluish as she watched what the Queen showed them.

"She's been stuck, waiting for her brethren to find her. Grems traveled here. Crashed at Fallows and South Bowl," Kenji recited as if he had memorized the words. "There was a surge of power at the Edge last year that caught their attention."

Last year.

Everyone's eyes slid to Melinda and Lance.

"When I entered the Edge," Melinda said numbly. "I opened and closed a doorway there to another world. To try to save my friend." *Failed to save,* something in her corrected, and she trailed off, remembering the earthquake in the demonic world as she had raced to escape after defeating the demon that cost Abel's life.

"The change must've let off supernatural ripples that her grems were waiting for, that helped them to find her," Nox concluded.

"So, all this is your fault," Brigitta said bluntly and then bit her lip when she saw Melinda's face. "Not that you knew," she added hastily.

Brigitta was right. Melinda had brought the grems here. She had caused all this to some degree. The knowledge twisted and broke off something inside her. She tried to brush it off despite a coldness washing over her. *No time for guilt now.*

Kenji moved uncertainly forward. "If the Queen is freed and reunited with the grems, maybe they'll leave."

"She hasn't shown us why she came here in the first place, what she wanted from the Edge," Nox pointed out.

"Or maybe she's lying about it all," Lance said.

"She's not lying. She can't," Melinda said and at Lance's quizzical look she explained. "I know it, from when I was connected. Something about the psychic link. We would sense a lie." Her words came quickly from knowledge that the Queen shared with them. "They procreate so fast. They need more homes. They need more space. She thought the Edge might be their next home. But now…"

"Now, she sees that her grems are thriving on the surface," Nox added quietly. "They've already found their new home."

"*Help or pain.*" The Queen's annoyance and anger rippled out like a wave.

She was tired of waiting.

"What do you mean, pain—" Lance started to ask.

The voice boomed again, a piercing growl that made Melinda grab her head and shout.

Kenji and Nox fell to their knees, gasping in anguish.

"Stop this!" Lance bellowed and doubled over.

The ongoing growl twisted Melinda's gut, made her feel like her limbs were being cut off and restitched. She dropped to the ground like the others, curling up instinctively into a ball as the pain morphed and grew, turning into a fire that raced through her blood.

"*Stop when you help,*" the Queen said.

Somehow the pain increased, and Melinda couldn't think over the flames exploding in every inch of her. She glanced up to see Brigitta looking at them terrified, but not nearly in the same amount of pain. Melinda's eyes fell on Sam bundled on her chest, who wasn't crying.

"Will Sam's blood block the Queen's influence?" Melinda moaned to Nox.

"The psychic pull is too strong. I don't know—" Nox's eyes fluttered, and she doubled over again with a muffled shriek, holding onto a stone outcropping.

Melinda pulled out her small pocketknife and hesitated. *How much blood, how to best do it*—but her thoughts were quickly mashed by the ripples of agony through her limbs. She squinted through her haze of pain, focusing on the bundle at Brigitta's chest, the top of the little tuft of black hair. Melinda staggered forward and raised the knife.

"Melinda, don't!" Brigitta screamed.

Brigitta's panic-laced voice twanged through Melinda's pain, giving her pause. *Proximity*, Nox had said. Melinda lowered the knife, coming forward instead, feeling the pain ebb but not disappear entirely.

"Everyone, get close to Sam," Melinda gasped as she grabbed Brigitta's arm. She pulled her and Sam to the others. After a second, they all breathed easier and slowly stood.

"Sympathy didn't work. Pain didn't work," Melinda spat at the Queen as a handful of rocks tumbled down. "Your flock is coming soon, and you'll all be destroyed. Face it, you've lost."

"Release helpers. Free me. Be master. Others will serve."

"Serve?" Brigitta said.

Melinda saw an image of humans lining up, of one human—like the Queen—ruling them over.

"She's gonna control everyone with her psychic power," Lance said, his voice low with horror. "That's her plan."

Nox paled. "Once she's out she can likely exert enormous influence. A hold over how many people, who knows. All of us. All humans."

Blue dust began to lift, as if the Queen's will was enough to move matter. The azure cloud swept around Melinda's boots and enveloped her, giving the Queen's words more sharpness. Something twinged in her periphery—that hovering feeling of closeness, of warmth—the psychic connection the Queen was offering. *If* Melinda would bond with her and help guide the Edglings to the barrier.

"Release helpers. Be my benefactor. Your wish complete." The Queen's words slipped to Melinda's mind, then grew quieter, more insistent, a whisper: *"Legions at your command. Protect those you love. Eternal protection. Save everyone. No fighting."*

Vivid images hit her, so real that Melinda thought she had transported for a moment. She was back at Five Peaks, at Aunt B's dinner table, happy, laughing. The land was devoid of creatures, as grems reigned in the Edge monsters. She glanced at the others faces, realizing they were hearing different things.

"She's trying to get into our minds!" Nox said, twisting her hands together. "Offering us temptations."

Melinda quickly stood close to Sam again, but his nearness didn't stop the Queen's insidious words from trickling into her consciousness.

Your plan will fail. My flock will free the helpers. You cannot stop the new world. Help me now. Rule. Have my thanks.

"No!" Melinda said and the blue cloud dropped from her and swirled to Lance.

Anything you wish, the Queen said to Lance as the dust covered him. He gritted his teeth and shook his head though the action seemed to pain him.

The cloud of dust flowed to Brigitta next. *Revenge on my children that took your mate. Your friend's safety. Eternal protection for your kin.*

Brigitta yelped as the blue enveloped her and Sam. The way she held still and listened intently made Melinda think she was considering the Queen's offer, until her scowl deepened.

For you, everyone will listen, the Queen said to Nox, whose face remained unchanged as the blue cloud enveloped her next. *Eternal respect.*

And for you. The dust spun around Kenji. *Eternal love.* The dust dropped abruptly. *You have my offers.*

Kenji moved first, slightly squaring his body toward Melinda. And the vial.

"Don't you dare," Nox said to him.

"You're the smartest person I know, so you must see it too." Kenji spread his hands wide and snapped his fingers. "Our odds are terrible. She'll make good on her deal, and we can survive before the grem swarm comes in. If I become her human leader, I can make sure you're all OK. You said yourself she can't lie to us."

"You'll take the Edglings over my dead body," Melinda said, and Lance moved next to her.

"Want to see a trick?" Kenji murmured and her hand flew to her neck. The twine was still there but—

Melinda cursed as the untied twine slipped between her fingers. She looked up to see Kenji holding the vial.

CHAPTER TWENTY-THREE

"You don't understand." Kenji's eyes glimmered the hue of the dust, a stark cerulean against his dirt-coated face. As Melinda and Lance started to draw their guns, Kenji's sword appeared less than an inch from Lance's throat.

Lance gave him a hard stare. "You gonna murder us for the monster? Get your head on straight, partner."

Melinda held perfectly still next to Lance, quickly going through her options. A damned broadsword was not a weapon she typically faced, and she couldn't see a good way to close the distance or to get her gun out without him noticing. Any sudden movement and Lance and Melinda would both be taken out with one lateral swipe.

"I hope you're not thinking what I think you are." Nox glared at Kenji. "Really. That's below you."

"No one had ever understood me like you," Kenji said. "I've had nothing since you left. You don't know what it's been like." His voice caught as his left hand gently turned the vial between his fingers, his thumb ready to push off the cork. "Minds like ours start to eat themselves, *consume* themselves, if they don't have anyone who understands. I know you're lonely too, Nox, you've just convinced yourself that's the best way to live. It is our fate to be together, I see that clearer than anything."

More rocks tumbled down and Brigitta looked up anxiously, covering Sam's head. "We better do something, quick," she warned.

"You're not opening that vial," Lance said to Kenji, despite the tip of the sword hovering half an inch from Lance's throat. Melinda tensed, but still didn't see a clear option to stop Kenji.

"Even under mind control, I will never have feelings for you!" Nox threw up her hands. "Look at me. *Hear* me."

Kenji hesitated, his thumb pressing against the wooden cork.

"She will not have a choice," the Queen hissed. *"Will be at your mercy."*

"No!" Nox shrieked as Kenji slowly slid up the cork. He paused before pushing the top back on and letting the vial slip to the rock by his feet, his hands shaking. Melinda winced but the vial didn't break. Instead, it rolled a few inches to rest against a stone.

"Not like this," Kenji muttered to himself, passing a hand over his face and lowering his sword. "She wouldn't be my Nox. Not truly." He seemed to brighten. "I'll win you over, I'll show—"

Nox started to interrupt him before a fresh cascade of fist-sized rocks rained down, nearly hitting them as they ducked and scattered.

"The grems are coming. Get ready to set off the dynamite!" Lance said. A stalactite smashed down next to him, partially obscuring the tunnel entrance. Above them, a crack appeared, widening and running along the cavern's ceiling.

"If the rocks block the tunnel, we're never getting out of here," Nox said.

Melinda went to scoop the vial, but it had vanished from the floor. "Where is—"

She looked up to see it in Brigitta's hand.

"I'll guard it," Melinda said, holding out her palm.

"Kenji's right." Brigitta's hand closed around the vial. "The grems are here. I can't lose Sam." Her voice cracked. "Not him."

"Our plan will work!" Lance said as more rocks tumbled down.

"Stay back," Brigitta told them, one finger pushing up the cork. "I'll open it right now if any of you move." She shot a steely look at the Queen. "You'll keep us safe. Sam safe. And destroy your monsters that killed my husband. Deal?"

"I sever the ones that hurt you. They die. You live. Your brethren live," the Queen said.

"It's a trick! You have to see that," Nox pleaded.

"Like Kenji said, if I make this deal, I can protect us all," Brigitta retorted, cradling Sam's head with one hand. He had started to whimper. "I'll avenge Samuel's memory and make sure my child survives."

"Don't do it," Melinda said. Her heart sank as she spotted the pain in Brigitta's eyes, bright and glaring. She had been through too much.

Brigitta opened the vial.

The Edglings exploded outwards with an invisible force that made Brigitta trip. Melinda stepped back against the sudden rush of unabating wind.

The Queen howled again, this time in triumph. Edglings swirled around Brigitta. The lapis dust outlined the jumping shadows in glowing blue as Brigitta screamed and Sam screeched.

"What's happening to her?" Nox cried. She darted forward to snatch Sam away. Brigitta, still shrieking, covered her eyes.

"The Edglings are trying to latch to Brigitta!" Melinda shouted. "The grems couldn't control them directly so they need a human to be their in-between."

Brigitta convulsed and muttered, like a puppet whose strings were being jerked as the Edglings haunted her. Nox had retreated to stand in the tunnel entrance with Sam, watching apprehensively.

"I help you. You help the helpers," the Queen commanded. *"We work together. For your wish."*

In an instant, every mote of blue dust in the cavern gathered in front of the Queen's barrier. The dust moved as though it were a living thing, a miniscule swarm onto itself. It compacted into a condensed ball that floated in front of the Queen.

"What is that?" Kenji cried in alarm.

"A concentration of her psychic power. She's going to offer Brigitta a connection," Melinda said. "Then use her to control the Edglings."

The hovering, glowing ball of dust pointed toward Brigitta.

"You must let me in," the Queen said, and the orb shot forward.

"No!" Melinda jumped, ignoring Lance's protest as she threw herself in front of Brigitta.

The dense cloud of blue was liquid fire, nearly choking her and freezing her chest. Melinda fell to her knees, trying to suck in a breath.

"Mellie, what did you do?" Lance said and helped her up. His face filled up her vision.

"I'm fine," she managed. The psychic link from the impact of the Queen's power was immediate and much more amplified than the last time she had joined the grems' connection under Carlos' instruction. Even from down here, she could feel the connected humans on the surface, their frantic work. She sensed the flock of grems just above them, digging through the last of the rock—

"Your eyes!" Lance said. "They're glowing."

"Brighter than the moon," Kenji said, holding Brigitta from collapsing.

Melinda could see, with the new vision, the six Edglings in relentless detail. Their stick-like figures with yellow-dotted eyes rippled closer, drawn to Melinda. Their nearness evoking a familiar sense of despair that sank into the base of her spine.

Once the Edglings latched onto her, she could feel their excitement at being close to Edge matter again. And it wasn't just the Queen's barrier—more of the Edge lie below them, pulsing like lava beneath the cavern floor.

The Queen was excited too. From the glowing orb that hovered around Melinda's chest, the Queen extended tendrils of dust to tighten around each of the six Edglings.

Melinda had become the human conduit to the Edglings for the Queen.

Brigitta gave a shuddery sigh, wiping the tears from her eyes as she pushed Kenji away. "What the hell, Melinda!" She cried.

"I saved you," Melinda said.

"I didn't ask you to," Brigitta snapped. "I could've handled it— should've handled it—" She pressed her hands into her face and fell silent, Kenji patting her awkwardly. Lance was saying something, but Melinda ignored everyone as the Queen spoke to her:

"Bring them to me."

With Melinda's renewed link to the grems' connection, the Queen's voice was sharper than needles in her temples. The Queen's command collided and spiraled through Melinda's mind in a dizzying echo that never ended.

The Queen coaxed the dust tendrils from Melinda's chest to pull the Edglings toward the barrier.

Home, home, home, the Edglings screamed to Melinda, their voices like cracks racing through broken ice. She had never heard the Edglings communicate directly before, but then again, she had never been part of a psychic link like this one.

She tapped into that psychic link now to mentally yank the Edglings away from the Queen.

"Mellie!" Lance's voice broke through her focus. She could sense the dozens of grems gathered just above the cavern.

"The flock is a few seconds from breaking through," Melinda said through clenched teeth. "All of them are above us. The trap will work."

"In the tunnel, now!" Lance shouted to the others. "Get ready to light the dynamite!"

Melinda dropped to her knees while she fought to hold onto the Edglings, but the Queen's pull was too strong. Her tendrils of dust physically dragged Melinda closer to the barrier. Lance yelled and grabbed her, but the tendrils were forceful enough that he skidded forward too.

"I can't—" Melinda grunted as one of the six Edglings ripped off from her entirely. The Queen's dust tendril lifted the Edgling and slammed it into the supernatural barrier. As soon as the Edgling's jagged shoulders hit the Edge material, it was like a hot cattle prod melting snow. The purplish goop of the barrier began to soften and drop.

The Edglings could alter the Edge matter, Melinda saw. When the Edgling absorbed into the wall, part of the barrier fell in piles of lavender sludge.

The massive Queen turned slowly in the loosening substance to reveal two white-and-red rings, larger than wagon wheels.

Those are eyes, Melinda thought faintly.

The Queen blinked, the white bumpy lids sliding over those terrible eyes before the red circles came back like burnt-out suns. The gargantuan mouth opened to show gleaming teeth the length and width of human arms, with strands of thin blue saliva stretching from her jaw.

Melinda ducked as rocks rained down.

"The wall's coming down! You've got to stop her, Melinda!" Kenji cried from the tunnel's entrance.

Lance gripped Melinda's shoulder. "You can do this!"

Melinda willed the remaining five Edglings to stay with her, but a second one flew off her and hit the Edge wall. Its black body expanded like ink on wet paper, disintegrating more of the Edge material that had held the Queen frozen for so long.

"No, no," Melinda cried. Doubt overwhelmed her. What if she couldn't save them? What good was she? She had failed in the past, absolutely. But not like this. Never like this.

Lance was shouting something at her urgently. He believed in her, Melinda reminded herself. He believed that she could do it.

She refocused and held on with all her might to the four remaining Edglings. But her efforts were futile—the Queen faced them, her mouth stretched wider than a sea creature preparing to devour its catch. Her claws scraped limestone. The two Edglings had been enough: the Queen was free.

CHAPTER TWENTY-FOUR

"Melinda, let's go!" Lance yelled and fired twice at the Queen through the Edge matter that continued to drip and disappear. As the bullets hit, a cobalt light sparked, the Queen's psychic power acting as a shield. "We can still blow the place down and take them out!" he said.

"It won't be enough to stop her!" Melinda's mind raced. "We have to get the barrier back up somehow. It's the only way."

The Edge barrier was still falling away in clumps, letting the Queen squirm out, fully free. Her bulging eyes—a gelatinous texture like a jellyfish—peered at them as she emerged. Within her red-rimmed eyes, clusters of dark pupils were striated with bands of blue and brown like a river stone, like Melinda was looking at a bouquet of her mother's dying flowers through blurred teardrops.

Melinda froze utterly, everything in her body pausing at the sensation of an ancient predator coldly evaluating its potential prey. It was, Melinda imaged, probably how a smaller animal felt when encountering the quick gaze of an alligator or shark: the most precious of instants where its life could go either way, ending or continuing. Melinda–the prey–waited as her own primal calculations clicked into place of whether fleeing or fighting gave her a higher survival rate.

"Get out of here!" Lance shouted to the others, who hovered by the tunnel entrance, watching them. Brigitta looked recovered, cradling Sam again, giving them one last torn look before she disappeared through the tunnel.

Nox motioned frantically. "Watch o—" she started to scream.

Melinda felt them before she saw them; the final crack above widened and the grem flock began to jump down, two, three, four at a time, their white bodies luminescent and hued in blue as they landed in the cavern. In an instant, the crowd of grems were blocking Melinda and Lance from the others—and from their escape into the tunnel.

"Go!" Lance hollered. Between the grem bodies, Melinda could just make out Nox and Kenji, hesitating at the tunnel. Kenji's sword was drawn but there were too many monsters—too many to shoot, too many to slice. And with Lance and Melinda stuck, there was no way to blow the dynamite without them getting caught in the blast. Kenji sheathed his blade before he scrambled into the tunnel.

Lance cursed and reloaded his gun as the last of the grems dropped around them, but Melinda put a hand on his arm.

"Wait," she said. An emotion bubbled up through the grems' psychic connection so powerful it nearly took her breath away: joy.

The grems were ignoring Melinda and Lance as they fixated on their Queen, who had emerged fully through the barrier, violet Edge material sliding off her in massive chunks. The grems bounded to her, some climbing up her body as they reunited. The swarm opened their mouths to hack over the Queen until every inch of her flesh was coated in blue dust.

"C'mon," Melinda whispered to Lance as they slowly walked the twenty feet back to the tunnel. The grems flowed past, ignoring the humans in their eagerness to get to the Queen.

"That was a close one," Lance said once they were at the tunnel entrance. He looked back at the dynamite. "Ready?"

"It's not enough," Melinda said, watching the grems continue to jump around the Queen, radiating warm feelings of homecoming, of family. *They're monsters,* she reminded herself and forced a memory of the bodies at Fallows and Thundering Ridge to sharpen in her mind. "She's too strong, even our bullets don't bother her."

"Let's at least get rid of this swarm with the blast."

"The Queen will survive. She'll dig out and make more grems."

"So, what do we do?"

"Edglings affect the Edge material. Maybe they can create a new barrier," Melinda said slowly, an inkling of an idea forming. "Another trap to hold all the grems here forever."

"If you think they can do it, try it quick!"

You want to return to the Edge, Melinda mentally told the four Edglings still bound to her. She felt them listening so she commanded them forcefully, hoping it would work. *You sense the Edge below us. Reach it, expose it!*

The Edglings obeyed, flicking down and around the cavern while remaining linked to Melinda. The grems meanwhile stayed fixated on their Queen.

The Edglings danced over the rocks, trying and failing to pierce the cavern floor.

"Damn," Melinda said. "They aren't strong enough."

"Let's worry about the Queen later. We'll find a way, we always do," Lance said, crouching into the tunnel. "Shoot at the fuse to take out this swarm at least. Even if the Queen survives, at least her brood will be slowed down. I know you can make the shot. Ready?"

Melinda hesitated at the entrance of the tunnel. Edglings fed off fear and anxieties. If she gave them more, it might strengthen them enough to do what she wanted. A cold certainty washed over her. She had brought the grems here in part, she had started this, unknowingly. But she would fix it.

"Lance, I can do it," she said. "I can make the Edglings strong enough to create a new Edge barrier. But I have to stay as their anchor. I can't protect you."

At the same time, she spoke to the Edglings: *Take what you need from me.*

"I'm not leaving without you," Lance said. His face fell at seeing her expression.

"I love you," she told him, and moisture pricked her eyes, but she had to do it.

She would stop the grems, whatever it took.

She opened her mind and emotions entirely to the Edglings, feeling the full force of every failure, of Abel's death that rested squarely on her shoulders, and her mother's infection that she hadn't been able to stop. Worse yet—she had been the one that had led the swarm of grems here when she inadvertently disturbed the Edge last year, creating a supernatural beacon. She had been responsible for all of those gutted by the monsters…

Guilt drummed through her, threatening to wrench her apart. The Edglings fed off the hopelessness and doubled in size as she gave them full rein. Their long fingers stabbed eagerly into the cavern floor, drilling into the stone.

Lance's face crumbled in a look she'd never forget, one of confusion and shock as she shoved him back. The purple shimmer of new Edge material—like a dense fog—bubbled up throughout the cavern floor, closing off the tunnel and separating her from Lance.

The Queen screeched and lashed out, sending rocks crashing down. Snarling grems reached for Melinda with their claws outstretched, but their bodies moved slowly, stifled. The Edge matter flowed around her and them, solidifying like molasses in the cave.

Got you, Melinda thought with grim satisfaction.

The Queen hissed and tried to psychically stop the Edglings, but they were too strong, fueled on the distress Melinda had let them feed on. Their long, branch-like arms plunged into the rocks below them, breaking stone and summoning more spurts of Edge matter.

The Queen was at their mercy now.

"Do not hurt us," the Queen pleaded to Melinda. She poured images into Melinda's mind, revealing the grems' truth, their fundamental nature. At first Melinda couldn't place it, because it was a nothingness, a blankness. It took her a moment to understand the Queen had landed here, not as a bloodthirsty creature with its brood, but a blank slate, looking for a new beginning, with a psychic ability to absorb the feelings and essence of whatever she neared.

When she landed, the Queen had absorbed the horrors of the Edge and the land's history of mass slaughters, of senseless killings of innocents, of children. Melinda reeled with the dizzying horror of the revelation. The Queen had soaked up the fear, hate and injustice of war, followed by the pain and brutality of the South Bowl's forced labor camps that came shortly after.

The Grem Queen had drawn in all the hatred for humanity, with none of the good.

"Let us go." All the grems echoed the Queen's request at the same time, as if they were all together in a cavern infinite larger than this one, their request echoing and ricocheting for all time.

Melinda almost felt bad for them.

Almost.

"You're monsters," Melinda told the Queen. "Killing humans. I can't let you live."

Before Melinda could command the Edglings to finish the job and encase all the grems in Edge matter, the Queen hacked out a giant ball of blue. It was like the orb of dust that had hit Melinda earlier, but this was one made of blinding colored light. A pulsing sapphire heart that connected the Queen to each of the grems.

The heart slammed into Melinda and she screamed as the full force of the Queen's psychic abilities fused into her.

"Tend to my brethren." The Queen said. She made the ultimate sacrifice, Melinda realized—giving up her connection and transposing it on Melinda. One last desperate ploy to save the grems and her legacy.

The pulsing blue core of the Queen's power lit up Melinda's chest, an alien matter that wasn't *right*, was too potent, too strong, turning her whole body aglow like the hottest star.

Melinda was the Grem Queen, connected to the grems at their most fundamental level. Controlling them. Feeling *them*. Feeling the ghosts of the past, the rage of South Bowl where greed and evil led to unspeakable acts. The cavern spun around her, and the full horrors the Queen had absorbed started to peel her skin, break and extend her bones, sprout pewter claws from her fingers as she yearned to destroy all of the humans that had caused this, to raze everything to the ground and start fresh with her grem flock.

She could see it then, a future sprawled out of her own making. A future where the grems help her destroy all the monsters that had ever caused harm, and the humans that enabled it. Remaining humans would heed her every command once they were in the psychic network, letting her create a safe world where no one would be hurt again.

This isn't me. This isn't right, Melinda thought and tried to remember why. She had to separate her thoughts from the grems but their consciousnesses were mushing together, as though she were all of them and they were her: one mind, fusing. The grems were attentive to her, their new leader, ready to please.

Even the Queen waited, crouching, submitting to Melinda. All the monsters drawn to her like she was a flame to a moth, even as they slaughtered humans, and she just wanted them to leave her alone—

Focus on the good, Lance had always urged when she got into a dark mood.

Focus on the good.

The memory of his words formed a beacon in the darkness. Melinda strained to remind herself of more. Brigitta's bravery. Nox's curiosity. Aunt B's kindness. Rafi's devotion. Abel's care.

Lance's love.

She forced back the irresistible urge to *unleash,* to *destroy,* to let the grems carry out her every whim. She thought of Brigitta's rage and pain, of Kenji's desperation and loneliness, the memories crystalizing a thought for her:

No one should be able to remake the world to their liking. It's too much power.

"I don't want it," Melinda gasped and hesitated for a second. The glowing orb in her chest floated in front of her, and she rejected it, snuffing it out with a thought.

As the blue light faded, the source of connection to all the grems were severed, neat as a knife cut, destroying their link to the source that gave them life.

The dozens of grems were instantly silent, their minds turned off and void, their bodies empty, nothing more than shells. The Queen's ferocious howl echoed alone, growing until it nearly shattered Melinda's skull.

We need more Edge material to hold the Queen, Melinda told the Edglings. *Keep going!*

The four Edglings expanded and contracted, rippling around Melinda and the empty grem bodies. They sank into the rocks, breaking apart the ground. Cracks in the rock by Melinda's boots appeared in the shape of lightning bolts. The cracks glowed amethyst, as if she stood above a bedrock of lit crystal.

She looked up to see the Queen trying to charge forward in fury, but the seeping Edge matter slowed her down. The ground lurched violently, and it felt as though the rock ruptured for hundreds of miles, the earth itself splitting in two. A chasm halved the cavern's floor, revealing molten fissures of harsh purple light that repulsed Melinda at a fundamental level, everything about the color *wrong*.

That pit contained the Edge, on the other side of which was the origin of the monsters that had plagued her most of her life. During her brief time in the Edge last year, she had glimpsed a demonic world. She had no idea what world or worlds this part of the Edge might transport her to and had no intention of finding out.

Stop, it's too much! Melinda called to the Edglings, but in their frenzy they didn't heed her.

More of the ground was falling away and the tunnel was completely caved in. She only had a few feet of solid ground left, and even that was crumbling beneath her toes as she strained to move backwards. She crouched on a small outcropping of rocks against the cavern wall.

This is the end, she thought, her body wracked with trembles that were miniscule compared to the shaking of the cavern.

The Queen howled and tried to jump, but the floor of the cavern fell away beneath her as glowing Edge matter surged. She plummeted in slow motion through the rapidly widening gap, her outstretched claws reaching for nothing.

"*Stop!*" Melinda screamed but the Edglings weren't listening to her anymore. They flew into the expanding purple after the Queen, returning to their home in the Edge, leaving Melinda alone as wave after wave of Edge matter swelled up like a volcanic eruption. The material filled the cavern and muted all sound, light, movement.

Then:

Peace, darkness.

Silence.

CHAPTER TWENTY-FIVE

The darkness was complete and all consuming.

The Grem Queen and grems and Edglings all had vanished. What had been a potent psychic connection was replaced by an abyss, a darkness that seemed to stretch on and on.

Melinda was alone.

She was trapped in the limbo between the Edge and her world. No sense of time, of space. Just her, alone. Stuck, as the Queen had been, within a new prison of Edge matter.

It was fitting, she supposed, that she should die like this. A deep shudder, worse than any earthquake, rocked her at the enormity of her situation. She was buried alive. Not just alive but frozen. Forever, perhaps. Immortal, here, in this dank, silent place.

She didn't know how much time had passed in her cage. Shadows danced and writhed against the darkness. She watched, their erratic movements lulling her to a peaceful half sleep, half wakefulness. She didn't let herself think. If she thought, she'd panic, and if she panicked here, well, she'd lose her mind.

So, she watched the shadows play. She suspected they were entirely in her mind, something to occupy herself in this nothingness. The shadows brushed against her, curious, questioning, angry—a tirade of little emotions peppering her that she mentally swatted away.

What happened? What's happening? Where am I? Where is Lance?

The questions came and went, passing through her drowsy state.

Sometimes she remembered her last glimpse of Lance's face right before she had unleashed the Edglings. His expression had been one of worry, shock, and confusion. The memory threatened to wrench her heart in two before a heavy daze settled over her again, numbing her anguish and sucking any emotions into the void.

At times, something rumbled in the distance. Maybe it was the Queen, coming back for her revenge. But the faint booms were next to her or above, not below.

Rocks fell in her mind, haunting her with visions of an endless cascade of stones that separated her from Lance, her from everything she knew.

Eventually she stirred out of her half sleep. No... *something* stirred her.

A tiny star, blooming above her. She wondered if she was in space, hurtling down some cold and distant path. The spark of brightness widened into a lone star, trembling but brave despite the darkness. Melinda tried to move toward it. It was growing, or maybe she was getting closer.

And a sound. A sound that was a name.

"Melinda!"

Groggy memories came back to her as if she were waking from a deep sleep where the dreams felt realer than life. An image of a vial, emptied. A baby crying. Nox shouting. And the monsters, the *Grem Queen*—

Melinda touched her hands in a panic, expecting pewter claws. But it was her fingers, she saw in the growing light. They were cracked and bloodied, covered in purple goop that was condensing and falling off her. She quickly wiped off the Edge matter that was dropping away from her like melting snow.

They were her hands, at least. That thought made her feel better.

"Melinda!"

She could move again. She shook off more of the dripping Edge material and floundered through the darkness, toward the light.

CHAPTER TWENTY-SIX

"Melinda!"

It was Lance, Melinda realized as she forced her way toward the bright pinpoint. But he sounded different. Wrong.

The light expanded at the end of the tunnel, and she found a hole to squirm through. She reached out her arms, knowing he would help her up, as he always did.

But this time, the helping hand didn't come.

"Lance," she croaked. Her voice was a rusted tool, slowly warming up. She pushed into the too-bright light and used the inside of her duster to get the dirt out of her watering eyes. "Can't see a damn th–"

She blinked, her vision adjusting to see Lance silhouetted against a sharp blue sky and yellow light. He stared at her open-mouthed, like she was a ghost. He had changed, wearing a wool vest she didn't recognize.

"What's the matter?" Melinda glanced behind her to see she had emerged from a small hole in the side of the hill. It was oddly cold, the air with a sharp bite to it as though it were winter. She wrinkled her nose. Something didn't smell right either. Under the stench of burnt gunpowder lingered a hint of rotten animal. Not the bitter smell of grems, but more like a barn of horses that had never been washed.

"Was I buried alive?" She shivered, her memories slowly clicking into place. "The Grem Queen, we got her at least."

"You were…" Lance's gaping loss for words made Melinda instinctively touch her face, wondering if her dream of becoming the Grem Queen had been true. But her cheeks felt normal, her teeth not sharp. She scrutinized Lance, and noticed how skinny he was, how a scraggly two-inch beard had grown along his chin. And any hint of a smile or his dimple were gone. Instead, his chin had a new stubborn jut to it, his eyes had a hard shine she didn't understand.

"Lance." The worry made Melinda's voice shake. "Tell me what the hell is going on. What happened to South Bowl?" She turned to get oriented, but Carlos' mining camp had disappeared. Instead, the landscape had unfamiliar peaks and dips to it, and the ground was churned as though it had been through an earthquake.

About thirty feet behind him down a small hill, Melinda spotted Brigitta in pants and a linen blouse, her hands to her mouth as she watched them. Melinda barely recognized the woman—she was slimmed down and lean, with a leather vest over her clothes and a rifle slung across her back. A three-foot-high child with curly dark hair ran circles around her legs, giggling to himself.

The child…

"How?" Lance swallowed, his eyes wide as saucers. "You haven't changed." He rushed forward and squeezed her hard enough she thought her ribs might crack. She hugged back, her nostrils catching a whiff of something on him, something bitter she couldn't place.

Changed?

"What happened?" she asked, feeling small under the arching blue. She wondered why Brigitta stayed back and didn't come any closer. "How long was I trapped?"

Lance pulled back, still staring at her with that wide-eyed look that just wasn't right. "Almost three years," he said.

She stared at him. "Three…*three?*"

"We suspected you were in an Edge hibernation, like the Grem Queen. Nox figured it out. She and Kenji took some of that Edge barrier sludge and grem dust back, turned out it was useful for all kinds of stuff. Their experiment ended up giving them both some unusual properties," Lance said with a humorless laugh. "Ended up as real magicians after all. She was able to fix up something to help me with the excavation."

"Rafi? Is he?" Melinda pressed her hands to her palms and tried to breathe. *Three years.*

"Rafi made it out. The grems had burrowed beneath him, a shortcut to us and the Queen. He was stuck until we were able to get to him. After we…after you…" He cleared his throat. "He was lucky."

Melinda looked back toward Brigitta, who was walking briskly away from them, the child toddling along next to her. "Sam is older." Though it was obvious, she said it aloud to help convince herself this was real. "And Brigitta looks different." She shivered again as a frosty blast of wind shot past them.

She had been stuck for three years.

"Something about the exposure to the grems before Sam was born did something." Lance's eyes flicked in worry. "Monsters seem especially drawn to him. So Brigitta had to train to fight, like we trained. Aunt B taught her everything she could. Then she came out here to help me with the excavation."

"Excavation?" Melinda rubbed her eyes, taking in the dozens of blown-out holes in the hills, stretching as far as she could see. It would've cost loads of dynamite, supplies, labor… "How did you do this? Afford this?" she asked, her mind spinning.

"I've been searching in this region for a long time. The ground quakes moved everything around, so we had a wide area to cover." He paused as a sound like a deep, long horn blast billowed through the air. She jumped at the odd noise, but he didn't explain it.

"Spent every last cent we had," Lance continued as he gestured for her to follow him up one of the many hills. "Sold the ranch. Worked odd jobs exterminating. Never stopped looking, even when people told me it was time." Lance's head hung a moment, and he looked so worn, more worn than she had ever seen him. And harder, like he was a statue of himself, cut from crude marble and brought to life.

"The horses?"

He half-smiled at that. "Still kicking. Pepper will be mighty glad to see you."

"Happier than you." It slipped out of her mouth before she meant it, but she pressed on anyway. "Can't help but notice you seem lukewarm to see me."

A long pause before he nodded shortly, as if resolving to tell her. "After all this time, I can't believe I finally found you. I never stopped looking. But I can't seem to get over the fact that you picked a monster over me." A chill in his voice was like an icicle sliding down her back.

"I didn't." Melinda's head whirled and she stopped abruptly. How could he not see that? "Of course I picked you. I chose to *save* you."

Lance shook his head and her heart sank.

"I did it for you. For everyone," Melinda said. An ember of anger flared up. "You think I wanted to be buried alive down there?"

"You did it for yourself. Because you hate monsters so much," he replied. "Let's forget it. It don't matter now."

The wind picked up and she sniffed, finally able to place the oddly familiar smell emanating from him as the other details moved into focus: his prickly words, the careless glint in his eye that didn't ease up.

"Damn fool!" Melinda cried. "What the hell did you do? You got yourself hooked on darkbellas?"

"You were gone!" Lance bellowed back and Melinda recoiled. He had never yelled like that before. His eyes shone for a second with the full brunt of his despair, making something in her crunch up like it would never be undone. "I thought you were dead," he said quieter.

"But darkbellas?" Melinda replied. Now she recognized the distracted look she had seen in other poor souls who ended up needing the intoxicating plant so intensely they pushed everything else out of their life. "How could you turn to that?"

"You were gone," Lance said again. "You remember in South Bowl, when they detained us?"

"Of course I remember, it was yesterd—" Melinda started and stopped at his pained look.

"Whatever they gave us in the labor camp to dull us up put an itch in me. That along with you being gone…well, let's just say that things could've been way worse than using a bit of bella now and then."

It's a dream, Melinda thought, her tired mind trying to find an explanation that made more sense. It had to be. It just wasn't possible that she had been stuck in the mountain for three years, that he …

A darkness covered them for an instant as something passed in front of the sun. Melinda ducked instinctively. "What is that?"

"That," Lance said flatly as shadows shifted overhead beyond the clouds in a shape larger than a ship. "That is a behemoth."

"No…" She closed her eyes as all her senses seemed to be shutting down. "Behemoths can't exist. They're extinct. Stories from ages ago."

"That's right." A sharpness to his voice rang almost cruel while teeming with a muted despair. "When you destroyed the Grem Queen, a new Edge opening formed. It was—what did Nox call it—a reaction that set off another reaction. Like an avalanche. While you were trapped, a slew of new monsters came through. Giant ones."

"How many?" Melinda asked faintly.

"See for yourself." He walked briskly up the next, larger hill and it didn't escape Melinda how he didn't wait or walk alongside her. She hurried up the steep rocky path to look over its drop.

The view took her breath away even as she tried to comprehend the geography. A giant chasm split the Earth in what had been another South Bowl camp. More camps sprawled out, ruined and deserted. What looked like a herd of elephants moved in the distance. But these creatures were the hue of amber, and with four tusks and two swinging trunks. Far-off smoke curdled the sky in large billows. Through the smoke soared three enormous behemoths—she glimpsed a flipper, a long flicking tail. One emitted that strange, horn-like bellow and Melinda winced at the sound.

"More monsters than we can count." Lance gave the ghost of a smile, reminiscent of his old self, as he lit a rolled cigarette. He took a deep puff and let it out.

"If you're ready, we've got work to do."

ACKNOWLEDGEMENTS

I am deeply grateful to Steve and Heather at Brigids Gate Press for being wonderful partners in publishing and supporting the Monster Gunslinger series. Their passion for horror, fantasy and fiction is inspiring, as is their dedication to their authors.

I'm fortunate to have had Luke Spooner at Carrion House once again create my cover. His artistic eye and distinct style perfectly capture this weird west world. I'm beyond thrilled to include an eye-catching map in this book as a result of Becky Appleyard's creative approach to mapmaking. Additionally, a big thanks goes to Stephanie Ellis for the layout and chapter headings.

Another heartfelt thanks goes to my beta readers, in particular David Orange for his eagle eye and passion for the weird west and Shane Hawk for his thoughtful and informative sensitivity read. I am grateful to those who enthusiastically support the *Monster Gunslinger* universe and my work overall: Tasha Reynolds, Greg Mollin, Timaeus Bloom, Jeremy Billingsley, Trevor Williamson, Care Dipping, Jonathan Caraker, and many others. There are several giants in the genre whose work I admire and draw inspiration from, including Jonathan Maberry, Joe Lansdale and Victor LaValle.

The camaraderie of the local San Diego and SoCal writers, especially the members of the San Diego HWA chapter (and the larger HWA community in general) is a constant source of support.

Special thanks to Dennis K. Crosby and Sarah Faxon for being partners in crime, as well as to Jonathan and Henry Herz for hosting the Writers Coffeehouse and fostering a robust community of authors.

A big kudos goes to the SoCal indie bookstores that do a phenomenal job promoting genre books, including Mysterious Galaxy, Verbatim Books, Artifact Books, Space Cowboy Books, and others. (Note: You can place online orders to have books shipped directly to you!)

I'd like to also give a shoutout to my local Breakfast Republic, where I spent many an early weekend morning dreaming up monsters and ghouls over bottomless cafe de ollas and fluffy buttermilk pancakes.

Finally, as always, my deepest thanks goes to the fam: Jason for taking care of our wildlings when I run off to write; the wildlings themselves for showing me how to slow down and see the world in new ways; my dad for the many edits and for helping to plan out the map; and my mom for the endless love and encouragement.

Last but not least, one of my biggest thanks goes to my sister, Vivian, for reading my stories more times than any one person should have to, and for your fierce, inspiring support.

ABOUT THE AUTHOR

KC Grifant is an award-winning Southern Californian author who writes horror, fantasy, science fiction and weird west stories published in podcasts, Stoker-nominated anthologies and magazines.

She is author of the supernatural western series *Monster Gunslingers* (Brigids Gate Press) and of *Shrouded Horror: Tales of the Uncanny* (Dragon's Roost Press, 2024). She is editor of *Women of the Weird West* (Brigids Gate Press, 2026) and co-editor of *Dread Coast: SoCal Horror Tales* (No Bad Books Press, 2025) and *Of Terrors and Tombstones* (Stars and Sabers, 2027).

Her stories have appeared in *PseudoPod*, *Andromeda Spaceways Magazine*, *Unnerving Magazine*, *Cosmic Horror Monthly*, *Dark Matter Magazine*, *Sley House Presents*, *Fission Magazine*, *Tales to Terrify*, the *Lovecraft eZine*; *Shadowplays*; *Musings of the Muse*; *Dancing in the Shadows—A Tribute to Anne Rice*; the Stoker-nominated *Chromophobia*; the Stoker-nominated *Fright Mare: Women Write Horror*, and many others.

She teaches genre and short story workshops and has been a moderator, panelist and speaker at dozens of conferences and events. She is co-founder and co-chair of the San Diego HWA chapter, a member of the Science Fiction & Fantasy Writers Association, and a SFWA mentor. Learn more on her website, www.KCGrifant.com.

Links:

www.tiktok.com/@kcgrifant

www.facebook.com/kcgrifant

www.instagram.com/kcgrifant/

https://www.goodreads.com/author/show/8288519.K_C_
Grifant

www.threads.com/@kcgrifant

MORE FROM BRIGIDS GATE PRESS

MELINDA WEST: MONSTER GUNSLINGER

KC GRIFANT

KC Grifant comes out guns blazing with Melinda West: Monster Gunslinger—a devious action-packed adventure set in a very weird version of the Old West. Fast, furious, and a hell of a lot of fun!"—Jonathan Maberry, NY Times bestselling author of Son of the Poison Rose and Relentless

In an Old West overrun by monsters, a stoic gunslinger must embark on a dangerous quest to save her friends and stop a supernatural war.

Sharpshooter Melinda West, 29, has encountered more than her share of supernatural creatures after a monster infection killed her mother. Now, Melinda and her charismatic partner, Lance, offer their exterminating services to desperate towns, fighting everything from giant flying scorpions to psychic bugs. But when they accidentally release a demon, they must track a dangerous outlaw across treacherous lands and battle a menagerie of creatures—all before an army of soul-devouring monsters descend on Earth.

Supernatural meets *Bonnie and Clyde* in a re-imagined Old West full of diverse characters, desolate landscapes, and fast-paced adventure.

NOOSE

BRENNAN LAFARO

It's been 15 years since Noose Holcomb perpetrated the Buzzard's Edge Train Robbery of 1872, leaving Rory Daggett an orphan. Settled in with a new family and a second chance at life, Rory never quite sheds the thirst for revenge.

When one of the gang members returns to Buzzard's Edge, Rory's life is violently upended once more. Capturing the rogue spurs on a furious chain of events that pits Rory against each member of Noose's gang, every one more twisted and terrifying than the last, in order to work his way to their leader.

With the help of a fellow orphan whose life Noose turned upside down and the town's sheriff, Rory will stop at nothing to be the man who ends Noose's reign of terror, but can he do it without becoming the man he seeks to kill?

BLOOD IN THE SOIL, TERROR ON THE WIND

ED. KENNETH W. CAIN

Whether in an old weathered mine shaft, somewhere off the beaten path, out in the woods, or right here in the middle of this ghost town, danger awaits. We're going to take you way back, drop you right smack dab in the middle of the Old West at its finest. But we're not just going to give you shootouts and bullet wounds and blood splatter. Yes, those things are prominently featured, but there's so much more to this anthology of western horror.

Maybe it's a well-known creature popping in for a visit, or some new creepy crawly monster sucking out your soul, we're going to turn the Old West inside-out and explore its guts to the fullest. There are new adventures to be had, monsters both familiar and unfamiliar to be thwarted… And we're not always going to be the victors. Life in the Old West is hard, trying at its best, and it can wear you down quick.

So, prepare yourself to be transported back in time. Get yourself up on that rickety stagecoach, draw your guns, and let's get going. There's vast territory to cover here, and your journey begins now.

221

THEY HIDE

FRANCESCA MARIA

Who are we if not for the monsters that we keep?

They Hide: Short Stories to Tell in the Dark collects thirteen chilling tales that weave through the shadows, exploring the nature of fear, powerlessness, and control.

- A series of murders in a New England colony

- An untamed beast in pre-revolutionary France

- A mysterious stranger who invades 18th-century Ireland

- A traveling circus that takes more than the price of admission

- A gathering of the Dark, telling tales on the longest night of the year, and more.

Come play with vampires, werewolves, ghosts, zombies, ghouls and the devil himself. Make sure you check under the bed and don't turn out the light.

223

Visit our website at: www.brigidsgatepress.com